B

C000098836

ELIZABETH ENGSTR(
suburb where she li
of Salt Lake City, where she lived with her mother). After graduating
from high school in Illinois, she ventured west in a serious search for
acceptable weather, eventually settling in Honolulu. She attended
college and worked as an advertising copywriter.

After eight years on Oahu, she moved to Maui, found a business
partner, and opened an advertising agency. One husband, two
children, and five years later, she sold the agency to her partner and
had enough seed money to try her hand at full-time fiction writing,
her lifelong dream. With the help of her mentor, science fiction great
Theodore Sturgeon, *When Darkness Loves Us* was published. Since
then, she has written fifteen additional books and taught the art of
fiction in Oregon colleges and at writers' conferences and conventions
around the world.

Engstrom moved to Oregon in 1986, where she lives with her
husband Al Cratty, the legendary muskie fisherman. An introvert
at heart, she still emerges into public occasionally to teach a class in
novel or short story writing, or to speak at a writers' convention or
conference. Learn more at www.elizabethengstrom.com

GRADY HENDRIX is a novelist and screenwriter whose books include
Horrorstör, *My Best Friend's Exorcism*, and *We Sold Our Souls*. His
history of the paperback horror boom of the Seventies and Eighties,
Paperbacks from Hell, won the Stoker Award. You can stalk him at www.
gradyhendrix.com.

Cover: The cover painting by Bob Eggleton originally appeared on
the cover of the 1988 Tor paperback edition. Bob Eggleton is a multi-
award-winning artist in the fields of science fiction, fantasy and horror.
He has done book covers since 1984 and was recently honored with the
L. Ron Hubbard Lifetime Achievement Award for the Arts.

ELIZABETH ENGSTROM

With a new introduction by
GRADY HENDRIX

VALANCOURT BOOKS

Black Ambrosia by Elizabeth Engstrom
Originally published by Tor in 1988

Published by Valancourt Books, Richmond, Virginia
http://www.valancourtbooks.com

ISBN 978-1-948405-50-8 (*paperback*)

Also available as an electronic book.

All Valancourt Books publications are printed on acid free paper
that meets all ANSI standards for archival quality paper.

Cover text design by M. S. Corley
Set in Dante MT

INTRODUCTION

THIS is a book about a vampire.

Angelina, the main character, is assaulted by two men while hitchhiking around the country, which awakens her vampiric nature. She kills one of them and hits the road, sucking blood to survive, mesmerizing men with her eyes, sleeping in a coffin, and turning into fog when necessary.

This is not a book about a vampire.

Angelina's vampirism isn't the result of a curse, she wasn't bitten by a master vampire, it's not something lurking in her DNA. She becomes a vampire because she wills it. Throughout the novel's pages, what's really happening is that she's going insane.

"Do you remember the Slenderman incident?" author Elizabeth Engstrom asks, referring to the 2014 case in which two 12-year-old girls lured their friend into the woods and stabbed her 19 times in an attempt to impress the non-existent urban legend known as Slenderman. "Teenage girls between 13 and 15 get caught up in stuff. They're searching and they want to figure out what they are. Boys do it when they're a little older—that's how the military grabs them— but girls do it earlier. They're not fully formed, they're experimenting.

"It's exactly like those girls who stabbed their classmate over Slenderman. They thought about it, they became excited by it, they decided to identify with it, and then they went and tried to murder their friend. Angelina decided she would be this thing, and she became this thing."

Written in the first person, the more Angelina rejects reality and embraces the delusion that she's a vampire, the more straightforward *Black Ambrosia*'s narrative becomes, and the more comfortable the book becomes for the reader. Which is the problem with writing a book from an insane person's point of view.

"It's the only first person book I've ever written," Engstrom says. "And I'll never write another."

To solve the problem of how to tether the book to reality, each chapter ends with an italicized recap of its events told from another character's point of view, keeping the reader at least a little bit aware of what's happening in the real world as Angelina sinks deeper and deeper into her vampire fantasy.

So *Black Ambrosia* is a book like *We Have Always Lived in the Castle* about a strong-willed teenager trading the real world, with all its humiliations and discomforts, for a gothic fantasy, no matter how much damage that causes to herself and the people around her. But you wouldn't be holding it in your hands right now if it wasn't also a vampire book.

"As I remember, we were working on the paperbacks of *When Darkness Loves Us* and I reached out to Elizabeth because that's what you do," remembers Melissa Singer, then 25 and an editor at Tor. "You make sure you have any corrections, make sure the author's bio is right, and I naturally asked if she was working on anything else."

Engstrom did have another book, already completed, but she wasn't about to let Singer see it. When she'd finished *Darkness* she was on a high. *Darkness* had done well, sold overseas, and become a book club selection. She sent *Black Ambrosia* off to her agent with high hopes, already planning the next stage of her literary career. Then she received a letter from her agent.

"If this is your idea of fiction," it read. "We are not suited to each other."

Crushed, Engstrom wrote "Bad Book" on the manuscript box and stuck it on a shelf, picked up the pieces of her broken heart, and moved on to her next book.

When Singer called and asked what she had, Engstrom

mentioned the "Bad Book" but said she didn't want anyone to read it. Singer seduced it off her shelf however, and a few weeks later called and said, "To whom do I make an offer? You or your agent?"

"When I found out she had a novel, that was the first good thing," Singer says. "But when I found out that it was a vampire novel, that was the second good thing."

Because vampire books obey different rules than horror novels.

"A lot of people who don't read horror will read vampires," Singer says. "They don't think of vampires as horror. Vampire fiction is a perpetual motion machine."

Everyone knows the vampire backstory (ancient Greek *lamia*, John Polidori's *The Vampyre*, penny dreadful *Varney the Vampire*, Bram Stoker's *Dracula*, *Nosferatu*, etc. etc. and so on) but modern vampire revival heated up in the swinging Seventies. In 1975, Fred Saberhagen published *The Dracula Tape* and in May 1976, Anne Rice published *Interview with the Vampire*, which just seemed to keep selling. In October 1977 a stage version of *Dracula* starring studly Frank Langella opened on Broadway with sets and costumes by Edward Gorey, and ran for 925 performances, before closing in 1980. In 1978 Chelsea Quinn Yarbro published the first in her long-running gothic vampire series, *Hotel Transylvania* (now at around 30 books).

By the time Suzy McKee Charnas's *Vampire Tapestry* became a finalist for the Nebulas in 1982, vampire fiction was a big thing, and it only got bigger in 1985 when Rice published her blockbuster sequel to *Interview*, *The Vampire Lestat*.

"Vampires are their own subcategory," Singer says. "And readers have a lot of variety to choose from. Sometimes it's more pop, sometimes less, sometimes people want stories that play with the tropes—vampires who can walk in daylight—sometimes they want traditional. It's very a robust genre that never seems to die."

But while *Black Ambrosia* saw publication because vampire books sold like blood-cicles at a vampire carnival, Engstrom hadn't even read *Interview with the Vampire*.

"I certainly read *Interview with the Vampire* afterwards," she says. "If I had read it first I never would have written *Black Ambrosia*. It was so brilliant."

Engstrom created Angelina because she wanted to write about a teenager with a strong will, a teenager who's looking for something to be, a teenager who winds up choosing to become a monster.

"Being a vampire is her thing," Engstrom says. "She believes it and so she becomes it. When I was a teenager my thing was drinking alcohol. I wanted to be known for that. I kept beer in my locker at school. I was proud that I could drink more than anyone else. So I know that mindset. You have to be careful what you identify with because that's often who you become."

Engstrom had Angelina pick vampires because they're a little bit sexy and a little bit cartoony, which was how she saw Angelina. And as Angelina invests herself more and more of herself in becoming a monster, she finds herself falling into the left-behind spaces of Reagan-era America.

"When I was drinking, I used to hang with the underbelly of society," says Engstrom, who got sober and started writing in 1980. "And the worse they were, the better I felt. They lived in the shadows."

As Angelina drifts through the humdrum lives of people on the bottom rungs of the economic ladder, she preys on the drifters and hustlers, johns and hitchhikers, creeping through the blue collar underbelly of the Eighties. As she walks from one nowhere town to another along the trash-choked shoulders of empty highways you can feel the hard-packed frozen dirt beneath her heels, you can feel how cold Reagan's Morning in America felt to the people standing outside the walls of his city on a hill.

"Horror always does better when times are tough,"

8

Singer says. "The Eighties were the era of Reagan and there was a lot of tension in this country, a lot of divisiveness. You had serious conversations about banning gay people from schools and workplaces because of AIDS, then you had gay friends and family who were literally fighting for their lives. You had more women in the workforce, and Phyllis Schlafly telling women to go back to the kitchen. It was a tough time economically—the cost of living went up but salaries did not, and people had to squeeze to make their money go further. Horror has always done better when people feel nervous about what comes next."

Black Ambrosia may have captured the Eighties, but it was out of step with Eighties horror fiction which didn't do women or monsters as main characters, and Angelina was both. Clive Barker's *Books of Blood* with their seductive monsters had just started hitting American shelves, but in most mid-Eighties horror novels a book's main character was its hero, the good person who was going to slay the monster. Angelina *was* the monster.

And, as Singer notes, "I could probably name a bunch of women writing horror, but at the time it felt like the genre was dominated by men. So this book was very different because it had a female author *and* protagonist."

At the time, Tor was just dipping its toe into horror and didn't have a lot of data about its readers. (To be honest, neither did anyone else.) As a result, they hadn't yet clued into the fact that horror readers were primarily female, and so female main characters were rare. Which made the cover a challenge. Usually, if a woman was on the cover of a horror paperback she was presented in a highly sexualized manner and was a secondary character promoted to a place on the cover in an attempt to appeal to male readers. Putting a monstrous main character who was also a woman on the cover felt risky, so Tor went with Bob Eggleton's "object cover" showing Angelina's cane. It was a classy solution to a marketplace problem.

When *Black Ambrosia* came out, it didn't do as well as *Darkness* but it got optioned for a movie and helped Engstrom find her current agent. It also garnered a lot of fan mail from high school students. But to this day, Engstrom has mixed feelings about the book.

"My feelings were so hurt after it was rejected by my agent that I had a bad taste in my mouth," she remembers. "I didn't want anyone to see it. I guess I just didn't have any love in my heart for it anymore. I was heartbroken. But it didn't stop me from writing."

The will to keep writing, even in the face of rejection, is like the will to keep living even when the world rejects who you are. When the world has no room for you because you're gay, or you're a woman, or you're poor, you can either give up, or dream a new world into existence. You can double down on your identity, or you can invent a new one. And sometimes that new identity has fangs that tear apart everyone who ever hurt you, and everyone who tries to get too close.

Angelina becomes a monster and that identity becomes her coffin, the lid nailed down tight, trapping her real self inside. But somewhere in this brutal, beautiful book that real self turns into mist and drifts away, and all that's left of her is the monster.

GRADY HENDRIX
September 2019

Acknowledgments

I am fortunate indeed. My support structure is comprised of willing, talented, and dedicated friends.

Those in my writer's group—Maggie Doran, Marie Johnson, Geri Kaeo and Madge Walls—were indispensable to the construction of this book. Dot Bergstrom, Carol Bearman, Ross Nodem, and those at the Banana Farm Writer's Retreat helped me with life's perspective. Tonia, Steve, Susan, Nancy, Mike, Peggy, Polly, Jeannie, and Pam helped me with eternal perspective. Bob Gutzmer, Pauline Merner, and Clarice Cox continued to believe in me; Susan Bredesen picked me up off the floor every time I started to scream and beat my fists, and Melissa Ann Singer gently urged this tender manuscript off the shelf and helped me make it strong.

Most of all, this writer needs the ongoing stability, love, and laughter (along with a few tense moments) generously supplied by an astonishing assortment of relatives—blood, step, and in-law, but especially from Evan, Eron, and Nikki.

I

I certainly never intended to become a vampire. The thought had crossed my mind, of course, as I immersed myself in literature of all types, but I dwelt on it maybe only a little more than I dealt with the fantasy of growing up to be an heiress, or a queen. Few people, I believe, set their minds on a lifetime path when they are young. I'm sure there are those who are like that; I was not. My dreams were of power over others, of that there is no doubt. I had no power when I was a child.

But my youthful dreams were impotent; I had little self-esteem. I was the odd duck, the misfit, and I always struggled with life, argued against it, all the while knowing I was at its mercy. The best I could hope for was an innocuous lifetime assignment, with a few plump moments of pleasure. Life would ultimately do with me as it wished, I thought. I was powerless.

Today, of course, I know differently.

I was born Angelina Watson to John and Alice Watson when John was sixty and Alice was forty-three. The reasons for their childlessness up to that point are matters only for speculation since both are now dead, but I was a surprise to them, to say the least. Mother said I was a gift from the angels. Hence, my name.

My father passed away when I was eight. I remember little of him but his big, warm hands, his thin gray hair, and his extraordinary booming laugh. He'd been a newspaper-man all his life, and because of this, the whole town knew Mother and me, and greeted us on the street, whether we knew them personally or not.

Mother and I got along on what he'd left us, supplemented by what she earned as a file clerk, and what she made working for a janitorial service three nights a week. We didn't have a lot, but we seemed to have enough. I was never chided because of hand-me-down clothes, like some of the other children. I was never chided at all, in fact. I was left alone. I was always alone.

When I was twelve, Alice fell in love with a man fifteen years her junior. They married, and he moved in with us. Rolf was his name, and he had a huge moustache and big, bushy eyebrows. He was a very nice man, good to Mother and me. He treated us well, bought us nice things, and eventually moved us to an improved neighborhood, to a new house on the nicer side of Wilton.

I remember the first night they were home after their weekend honeymoon. I was in my bed and they tucked me in and kissed me good night, then went to their room across the hall and shut the door. I heard the bedsprings creak as two people settled down on them; then they began to creak rhythmically, and I knew what they were doing in there. I'd heard at school, but I never really believed that Mother would do something like that, especially with Rolf and his eyebrows. I crept out of bed and sat next to their door and listened.

I remember pulling my knees to my chest, working my toes in the hallway runner. My bum got cold as I sat on the wooden floor, listening to them talk and moan and bounce on the bed. I began to rock back and forth until my flannel nightie got too hot for me, and I wanted to take it off, but that seemed entirely improper, so I huddled up against the wall instead, rubbing my thighs together and chewing on the heel of my hand.

Just as I heard Rolf give a mighty gasp and groan, I bit through the skin of my palm.

The springs settled. I heard Mother talking softly, and I could imagine her smoothing the sweaty hair from his forehead as he lay collapsed atop her.

Then the springs creaked again as Rolf rolled over, and I sucked the warm, salty blood from my hand.

Soon I heard snoring, and in the dim light from the street-light out in front, I could see the pattern on the wallpaper and the dark little drops that oozed from my palm. I licked them away, one by one as they appeared, and wiped the last one on the wallpaper next to the bedroom door.

"I remember my father saying to me, 'Boyd, someday you're going to hunt something that's just a little too smart to be hunted, or a little too warm and pretty to be killed. And when that happens, you'll hang up your shotgun.' He never could understand my passion for hunting, and I could never understand how he could just one day give it up. My brother, too. They just sort of stopped going out, but I kept on. There was a challenge to it, there was timing, and knowledge and fresh air and beauty. But it was never enough. There was never enough challenge, never enough beauty, never a big enough thrill. The kill always came too soon; it was always too easy; it was never just quite right. I guess that's why I kept on—I kept looking for the right chase. I knew it was out there, I just had to find it."

2

Alice died when I was fifteen, and Rolf and I mourned together for a short while. Then, being realistic, I decided it would be best if we went our separate ways. Mother had been the common thread that ran through our lives, and now there was nothing to bind us.

I stayed with him until he sold the house. I sold what little things Mother and I had that were of any value and gave away the rest. The light-headedness of being free from the burdens of ownership was an extraordinary feeling. I was now responsible only for myself and my small collection of carefully chosen belongings, which I folded and packed into a small cloth backpack I'd bought with the money from the sale of Mother's jewelry.

On our last night in the house, Rolf took me out for a pleasant dinner and as his sad brown eyes filled with tears, he told me how much he'd adored my mother and how he hoped we'd always keep in touch. I reassured him as best I could, which wasn't very well as I was anxious to be free of burdens and commitments; I wished to divest myself of every obligation. He patted my hand and said, "Angelina, Angelina, Angelina," and he wiped his eyes, then pulled an envelope from his jacket pocket and leaned it against the rose vase. His soulful eyes encouraged me to look inside. It was a check for a substantial amount of money. From the sale of the house, he said.

I didn't want the burden of it, but I took it.

Sometime during the middle of that night, I awoke with the sound of my bedroom door opening. I wasn't afraid, because already the night was my friend—it was the daytime that held the horrors of society. I lay very still and wrapped the familiar cloak of the darkness about my shoulders and watched the bedroom door open very slowly. I knew it was Rolf; he'd been downstairs drinking. I assumed he would be drunk, and that meant he was in my room for one of two things: to rape me or to cry. I was old enough to understand either one of those.

He came to my bedside, and though I could smell the liquor on his breath, I don't believe he was drunk. I could barely see his glistening eyes in the dimness of the room as I looked up at him towering over me. He stood there for a long time before he spoke.

"You're awake," he said.

"Yes."

He fell to his knees next to my bed. "Angelina—Angelina—will you . . ." He choked a bit. "Will you pray with me?"

While it was not what I had been expecting, I wasn't

taken totally by surprise. His grief was far more enormous than I would ever have imagined.

"Of course, Rolf," I said.

He knelt next to my bed, wearing his striped pajamas, and he steepled his hands just as children do when they pray, and he began. He prayed for Mother and me and himself and for the forgiveness of all our sins. Then he started on the world, praying for peace and an end to disease, and I began to fidget with the more maudlin of his recitations. So I inched over in my twin bed and held the covers up and he choked out a premature "amen" and got in. He turned his back to me and his sobbing shook the bed.

I placed my hand gently on his side, my cool cheek against his warm back. Even in the farthest nether regions of my experience, I could imagine nothing that would cause me to behave as Rolf was now behaving, and that made me feel quite odd. I knew nothing of this grief, this devastation, these *feelings* he owned.

I pondered this for a while as exhaustion tempered his sobbing. Surrounded by an aura of peacefulness and finality, soon we were both asleep.

In the morning I brushed my teeth and my hair, packed my nightie, and said good-bye to Rolf. He hugged me fiercely, squishing the breath out of me as he whispered in my ear, asking me if I was absolutely sure that I had to go away. I nodded against his chest and he released me, the tension of the question still trembling on the edge of his ample lower lip. I laced up my walking boots, shrugged into my backpack, and stepped out the door. I needed to visit the bank to deposit Rolf's check and draw out my personal savings, and that would be the last of my responsibilities.

I would never become enmeshed again.

ROLF BREZINSKI: *"Angelina Watson, you say? Angelina. After all these years. Yes, I knew her. Of course. Married her mother. Beautiful woman, Alice was. Never found one better. How she got* saddled with a child like Angelina must have been one of God's little jokes.

"Angelina. Like steel, she was. So hard she glinted. And it all showed in her eyes. Her eyes were—I don't know. Mesmerizing, almost. Like no other eyes I've ever seen. You know how sometimes you can look into someone's eyes and see love and softness? Alice had eyes like that. Well, when you looked into Angelina's eyes, you knew right off that someone was in there, lurking about. No God-fearin' mortal's got any right to eyes like that.

"When Alice died, Angelina hung around until the house sold. Alice willed half of the house to her, of course. Then Angelina sold all her mother's things—even her grandmother's jewelry—and packed up and took off. She was just a young'un, but I was glad to be rid of her. And I haven't heard of her since. Until now, that is.

"Angelina. God damn. Back like a bad penny.

"Must be bad trouble. Bad trouble, I can tell. I knew it then. That last night—I spent almost all night downstairs, thinking about her, about her ways, thinking about her loose with all that money, and I knew there would be trouble. I'd just come to decide that if I was a real man, I'd do something about her. So I went up to her room, ready to ... ready to kill her, I guess it's time I confessed to it—I was just going to push a pillow on her face and keep it there ... But when I got up there, all I could see was Alice's soft brown eyes, and how she loved that strange child ...

"I could never really do something like that. I could never sin like that. Never. A couple a brandies give me false courage, I guess.

"Are you here to tell me I was wrong, that I should have gone through with it?"

3

I left Rolf in Wilton, Pennsylvania, and began my tour of life. A matron in a cream-colored sedan stopped for me, and when I got into the front seat, she asked my destination. I thought for a moment and realized I had no answer. After

18

a hesitation, I asked where she was going, and she said she was off to Columbus, Ohio, to visit her sister, and I was welcome to travel the distance with her. She seemed nice and smelled clean, so I agreed.

We rode together for five hours. At first I was loath to talk of myself, but as she shared of herself and her family, of their difficulties and their joys, I came to understand some of her feelings. She had been widowed the year before, and she felt an anger about the desertion that we discussed in depth. I was no stranger to desertion by death.

We parted in the early afternoon on the outskirts of Columbus. She suggested I might enjoy traveling in the South, so she left me at the freeway interchange, where I could get a ride going down through Tennessee.

I'm sure more than two hours passed before my next ride stopped for me, and in that time I thought much about families, desertion, death, and this journey of mine. I had been on the road for less than a day and my joyous exuberance had already turned to introspection. This adventure was a learning experience, and I would pay close attention. I wanted to see the whole range of life during this time, from normalcy to lunacy, from safety to trouble, and everything in between. And I did.

Trouble remained elusive, in fact, for an entire year— until that terrible new-moon night when a demon named Earl Foster, fueled by the wildfire of alcohol, tried to damage me. In retrospect, I'm sure I could have avoided the entire situation, had I taken time to think for a moment before acting. But I didn't, so perhaps the whole experience was inevitable. That was after a year of ceaseless roaming, however, ceaseless, priceless learning.

For over a year, I lived as a transient. While I tried to do nothing illegal, I exercised some very naive judgment. I learned about bulls in farm pastures and the perils of climbing fruit trees. Naive indeed. Young and impetuous.

I traveled without direction, without hurry. I graciously

accepted rides with whomever offered them, and our lives merged for the miles we spent together. I felt no remorse in asking to be let out, nor did I feel like an imposition if our companionship was valuable and I rode with them to their final destination.

I noticed my sense of atmosphere sharpening. I could smell a situation the moment I opened the vehicle door. Humans have a musk of anger, a sweet tang of lust, a rolling bland contentment, and a hot spiking fear. I learned to balance atmospheres, to fine-tune my own vibratory emissions to counteract or augment an air, or to maintain a neutrality that allowed the emotions of the moment to roam free. The practice provided an interesting pastime; the talent eventually proved invaluable.

My traveling companions were laborers, executives, drug addicts, runaway housewives, drunks, salesmen, businessmen, families, grandparents, and rock singers. I met butlers and metermaids and razor-scarred criminals. I came to know cheating husbands and ordinary women who beat their children. I encountered bastardizations of the language, dialects from all over the country, accents from all over the world. I heard terrible jokes, revulsive propositions, and enigmatic compliments. I was told impossible stories and I came to believe them.

We traveled along freeways and highways and one-lane mountain roads. We traveled with air conditioning and with dust, in sedans and Jeeps and pickup trucks and limousines. We traveled in buses and old Checker cabs and motor homes and once in a boat being pulled by a truck. I rode long distances in tractor trailers with leather-worn wildcatters and to the corner drugstore in an antique car with a precious grandmother. The variety was infinitely surprising. And renewing.

My energy expenditure was far less than when I lived at home with Alice and Rolf. At home, I was always pacing off nervous energy, but while traveling, I was relaxed, peaceful, at ease. I had nothing to do but stand and wave my thumb at passersby. I'm a small person, under five-foot-three, and I've always been thin, so I got along fine on one solid meal a day, and I always kept an apple or an orange in my pack, just in case.

The importance of eating, I discovered, is the sociability of the act, not necessarily the nourishment. We ate at road-side stands, truck stops, cafeterias, and friendly kitchens with pastry-baking wives bustling about. We broke bread together on hilltops and over campfires and standing in parking lots. We even spent time together eating soup-kitchen broth and breadcrusts in cities large enough to have missions for the needy.

In those cities, we were swallowed by trucks and sky-scrapers and exhaust. In little burgs, we admired the freshly painted facades and pastel shingles classically designed to entice the visitor. We visited museums and saw statues. We saw clouds reflected in mirrored buildings, and we locked the car doors against the slums and the Saturday night peep-show crowds.

I was not impressed with civilization. All around, I decided, man's best shot at creation was as pitifully inade-quate as the words I have to describe it.

But we also saw square miles of cornfields, and forests with canopies so thick we felt we were indoors. In Minne-sota we camped by lakes and bathed in streams. We swam in the ocean off an Alabama beach and we stepped over the Mississippi River where it begins. We saw flatlands for miles and miles, and then slow-rolling hills and finally mountains. We saw birds and rabbits and deer and moose. There were squirrels and chipmunks, elk and bear and wild pigs. Nature spoke the loudest and the clearest, and I knew in my soul that it was the strongest. Man against the elements was a fallacy. Man looked his finest when dancing with Nature; he appeared a fool when preparing for battle.

The places I made my bed were as diverse as the sights

21

I saw. I slept in trees, in culverts, and under the stars. I slept in motels, hotels, abandoned barns, and homes with fresh linens. I stretched out, spreadeagled, on the top of a knoll in the middle of acres and acres of meadowland, and counted eighty-eight shooting stars. I slept in a train yard and in a cemetery and under a freeway.

I always slept alone.

During my nightly meditation, I contemplated the events of the day, and though tired, I renewed my enthusiasm for the adventure of the day ahead.

With every morning came my precise toilet. I washed my body thoroughly and changed to fresh clothes. Then I washed the previous day's clothes. Every day I was glad I'd always kept my blonde hair short. It was never a burden. I learned to bathe in service-station sinks; I could wash my hair and my underthings, soap up and rinse down very quickly. If I was moving, I'd pin my wet clothes to the top of my pack, where they dried in the sun before being folded away again. Otherwise, I just laid them over a tree branch, or a fence, or the rearview mirror of a parked car. Only then was I fit to make new friends. It was surprisingly easy to find accommodations for this, even in the wilderness of the big city.

For over a year I encountered the daily challenge. It was America that I saw; it was Nature that I heard; was survival that I learned. After a while it no longer challenged. I was ready for something new. And something new was delivered.

It was late September, and I was in Missouri for the second time when I encountered Earl Foster. I had returned to a place that had provided comfort in the past. This was, in fact, the first time I'd actively sought out a destination, rather than just going where life led me. I arrived mid-afternoon, found a perfectly suitable Ozark campground, and tied my hammock up between two sturdy trees, next to a picnic table.

I took off my boots and climbed into the hammock, stretched out as best I could, and pulled up my lightweight Salvation Army blanket.

The shadows stretched long, and I was suddenly very tired. Discouraged. I hadn't seen my face in anything but a rearview mirror for three days. I had only a dollar and fourteen cents left and I hadn't had anything to eat since an apple that morning.

Winter was approaching. All the animals of the woods were beginning to grow their winter coats, hoard their food, and prepare for hibernation. I felt the call, but knew not what to do. I began to wonder about my choice in life. Or my lack of choice.

For over twelve months I had been traveling, experiencing, growing in knowledge, but to what end? As I lay there in that swayback hammock, I felt as if I'd been observing, not participating. I couldn't think of a single thing I had contributed, other than a little atmosphere, to the lives of all the people who had touched me. I felt that my life had been put on hold, that a real life was a normal life—with family and responsibilities—and until I had that, I had no life. I had nothing. Nothing but the thread of a haunting echo that led me onward.

I was treading dangerous ground here. I could be free from responsibility forever, on the move forever, addicted to *lack*—and for the first time, it frightened me.

I pulled the blanket closer around my neck.

Yes, Angelina, I thought. It's time to settle in somewhere.

A memory of Rolf's face passed before my mind's eye, and the back of my throat burned for a moment, but that was not the direction my path lay. Time had passed. I had changed. Surely he had a new life by now.

A breeze came up and I set the hammock rocking just a little, while I looked up into the trees with their autumn color.

Find a place and settle down. Find a place and settle

down. Even the phrase sounded comfortable, warm, delicious. It sounded safe and secure, and I thought of looking out through crystal-clear windows at snow-covered trees from a comfortable chair in front of the fire. I would find a place and settle down. Money would come my way, I was not concerned about that—I always had the account in Wilton if I needed it. I'd get an apartment and a job and a boyfriend. Soon, before my travels turned sour and became a blot on the history of my life. My time on the road needed to be a good memory, a pleasant memory. A memory of happiness and education, of laughter and comfortable aloneness.

My tension dissolved with my decision, and I was resting on the edge of an early sleep when that dusty old blue Pontiac rattled down the road and chugged to an exhausted halt right at the picnic table beside me. There were two men in the car. They lumbered out slowly, each carrying a beer.

This was my first glimpse of Earl Foster. And a chill from Hell blew through me.

J. C. "JUICE" WICKERS: "Earl an' me pulled into the park to drink beer just like always, and right where we always goes is this camper, sleepin' in a hammock. A kid. We figured we'd give him a beer and talk for a while you know, just shoot the shit. So we pulled in and got out and the kid leaps out of that hammock and starts pulling on his boots and would you believe, it's not a kid, it's a girl! Now you tell me what a goddamned girl's doing camped out all by herself down by the lake, huh? What kind of a girl would do that?

"Well, I'll tell ya. A hippie girl, that's who. One of them stinking smelling runaway whores, that's who. Ain't got no family, ain't got no sense, just trash, you know? Filthy trash.

"But I see this look in Earl's eyes, you know? Tells me it's been too long since he's had a woman, tells me he's already had too much beer, tells me we're too far away from anybody. And hell, I figured she was just askin' for it anyway, bein' out there all by herself.

"But I'll tell ya. I'll tell ya. That look in Earl Foster's eyes was nothin', goddamned nothin' compared to the look in that girl's eyes.

"That girl was no girl, if you get my drift."

4

It had occurred to me earlier in my travels that I was indeed a single woman traveling alone; and as such, I ought not be caught by surprise or at a disadvantage. The shadows were long and it would be dark very soon, and cold. The men who had just arrived probably cared little for my privacy; certainly they would never leave after driving all the way out here just because they were an intrusion on my solitude.

I thought for a moment that I could snuggle down in my blanket and pretend that I was a man; my boots and my pack would not give my gender away, but then I would be quite defenseless and even more at their mercy. I decided to meet them as prepared as possible.

I threw the blanket to the ground and swung out of the hammock, pulling on my boots as quickly as I could, keeping one eye on the two gray-haired men. Earl hefted a six-pack of brown bottled beer onto the picnic table and watched me. I heard one of them speak to the other, but all I caught was an exclamation of surprise and the word "girl." I brushed wrinkles out of my clothes and walked toward them as they settled on either side of the table.

"Hello," I said.

"Hello. Didn't 'spect to find nobody here," said the one with the long hair. His hair was yellow-gray with a few black streaks. It hooked around his ears and hung to his shoulders in greasy strings, curling up slightly at the ends. His beard stubble was all gray, and red and purple veins had burst across his nose and cheeks like fireworks. He looked muscular in a sunken sort of way—like he used his stringy muscles, but only halfheartedly. "Beer?"

"No, thank you. I don't drink."

"Don't drink, huh?" They exchanged glances. "My name's Juice. This here's Earl Foster."

"I'm Angelina."

"Angelina." Earl Foster spoke for the first time. "Well now, that's a fine name." His voice was harsh with irony. "Wouldn't you say so, Juice? Angelina. Kind of what, rolls off the end of your tongue?" He drained his bottle of beer without taking his eyes off me. Earl had a solid round beer belly and loose stubbly jowls. His eyes were dark brown swimming in yellow and rimmed with red. His hair was thick and white and recently cut. As I stared at him with revulsion, he belched and smiled at me grotesquely. He had no teeth and his gums were red and diseased.

He tossed his beer bottle into the weeds and selected another, unscrewing the cap and flipping it to the side without looking.

"Angelina," he said again.

My sense of atmosphere reeled, trying to stabilize the feeling that flitted about me. Was it danger? I looked from one to the other, trying to decipher the rhythm of their relationship. I couldn't honestly believe either one was capable of raping me, but as I was still a virgin, I wasn't all that sure of what equipment was necessary. Juice seemed by far the physically stronger of the two, but Earl seemed in control. Earl had the brains, if there were any brains to be had between the two of them. Juice just smiled.

"Drink up, Juice," Earl said, his liquid tongue enunciating without the benefit of teeth. "We don't want to keep Juliana waitin'." He turned to me to explain, his gums clapping together, blowing the words out through his lips and spraying beer foam as he talked. "Juliana's Juice's sister. We're goin' to her house for supper. Her husband caught a mess of trout today. And the way Juliana fries up them fish . . . Ummm." He ran his tongue around the end of his forefinger, gently sucked the tip, then sipped his beer, looking at me out of the corner of his eye. "You hungry, Angelina?"

I was starving. The thought of freshly fried trout was almost too much for me to bear. I nodded.

"Want to go with us? Their house ain't more than, what, Juice, a mile away? Juliana don't like drinkin', like you, so we come here first to get a little buzz on, know what I mean?"

I looked at Juice and he just smiled his blank-faced smile and opened another beer.

"Why don't you come on as our guest? We'll go have a nice dinner and then we'll bring you right on back here. Safe and sound and full of fish."

Millions of thoughts flashed through my mind, and all of them were positive. I hadn't been hurt in over a year on the road; never even been threatened. I'd taken every ride offered, and this was just another one, with a meal at the end. Could be this was one of the countless fortunate circumstances that had befallen me all along my journey, providing me with hot showers or clean sheets once in a while. This was fresh trout.

"Whaddaya say?"

"That would be nice," I said.

Earl Foster turned to Juice and winked. "Them girls is always hungry, Juice." He reached in his pocket and pulled out a key ring, which he laid on the picnic table. "Kin you drive, Angelina?" He drew his words out in a mocking way—kin you driiiiive, Angeleeena?

I nodded. I had no driver's license, but I knew how to drive. I had taken over the task from many who needed to sleep but didn't want to stop. I would feel much better being at the controls. He stood up, belching. "C'mon, Juice. I kin hardly wait to taste me some tender white *feelay*."

I pulled down my hammock and folded my blanket, putting them into my pack. A little dark spot of wrongness poked at me from behind my ear, but my stomach was prodding me onward, and so was my sense of pride. I wanted life to be perfect and nourishing, and I needed to believe that this would turn out well. I had decided to settle down and I needed this to be an experience fit to crown my journey.

I had to adjust the car seat forward in order to reach the pedals. Earl Foster sat in the front and had to help me scoot the seat back and forth until we got it up close enough. He made a lot of grunts and moans as we rocked it, while Juice, in the backseat with my pack, giggled drunkenly. Earl sat with his arm across the back of the seat and his knees pointed in my direction.

The motor caught straightaway and I pulled on the lights. Darkness was settling in. We backed out and turned around and slowly approached the highway, where Earl indicated that our destination lay to the left. Then he looked over his shoulder at Juice and opened another beer.

We drove a short deserted distance, a mile, possibly two. Then Earl pointed at a flag, a ribbon, no, a rag tied to a tree limb, and with hard, bony fingers he gripped my arm and came toward me, huffing foul breath in my face as he leaned across, pointing to a gravel road barely visible in the under-growth. I slowed and turned in.

We bounced off the seats as I tried vainly to miss the potholes, and in fifty yards or so the road—or driveway, I assumed—smoothed out. I still drove slowly, barely more than idling down the gravel, feeling more than hearing the strip of weeds between the tire marks as they scrubbed the underbelly of the Pontiac.

The driveway curved to the right, and then to the left, and then it was a straightaway as far as the headlights could see. I began almost to dream that I was awake. The scratching from the coarse weeds became so loud it filled the car, the brush on either side of us reached higher than the roof, and the headlights illuminated a narrow tunnel through which we drove. I felt that the three of us were locked in some immortal collusion—reality had escaped us—we were out of control, sliding down the birth canal of destiny.

And then the trees disappeared and we were in the open

and the lake was silvery in front of us and another picnic table was beside us. I saw no house and no sister, smelled no fish, and fear took my mind and squished it between its gnarled fingers.

"Stop here."

I obeyed.

"Turn out the lights."

I punched the button in. Security evaporated.

"Give me the keys."

I pulled the keys from the ignition and put them in the hand that had found my thigh.

"Well, now," Earl said into the stillness. "Ain't this cozy?"

Juice giggled in the backseat.

"Too bad we ain't got a bitch in heat for you, Juice, old boy; this one'll have to do us both." His horrible fingers bruised my thigh in five round places. Then he picked up his beer and opened the car door. "C'mon, darlin'," he said. "Juice. Bring her pack."

I gripped the steering wheel until my fingers ached. I just stared ahead, trying to think, trying to decide, but the stuff with which decisions are made seemed to have fled my mind. The men sat on the benches in the starlight and spoke in low voices. They finished their six-packs, then fetched two others from the trunk of the car. Still I sat—silent, unmoving, trying to make sense of the mush inside my head.

It seemed I ought to run, yet I had a tie to my belongings. They had my entire life in their possession. The idea that two old men could rape me, kill me and throw me in the lake where no one would ever, ever, ever even *miss* me was somehow outweighed by the fact that I couldn't leave my pack. And I couldn't run down that terrible tunnel with them chasing me in the car. I didn't know where to go or what to do.

I started to cry in frustration. I couldn't think. But then from somewhere came the knowledge, the surety, that everything would end as it should. Some deeper, more powerful force was patiently at work here. My mind was befuddled for a purpose, to keep me from acting on my own. It was like tapping into a survival state, where the conscious mind is drugged so that Nature, which is infinitely wiser than man, can proceed without interference.

The car door opened and the interior light came on, blinding me for a moment. Earl stood there, his stained T-shirt stretched tight over his bulging belly.

"Now, now, little Angelina. Don't cry, darlin'."

I looked up at his repugnant face, twisted with drink and lit by an unearthly fire. Something deep within me roiled. He smiled a square smile, his lips pulled away from those awful gums, while his eyes burned into me.

"C'mon now, Angelina. Give old Earl a little kiss and he'll let you go." He grabbed my arm and pulled me from the driver's seat. I fell to the ground, rather he kick me than kiss me. I stuck my finger down my throat, hoping if I could retch, they would think me ill and take me somewhere, or leave me alone at the very least.

But there was nothing in my stomach to come up. I managed two or three gags, and Juice said, "She's sick, Earl."

His reply: "Them dirty hippies is always sick with somethin'."

So I just lay there, on the gravel, between the car and the picnic table, and I cried.

They sat at the table and drank. When my sobbing slowed, I heard Earl Foster's voice again.

"Angelina, honey, you snaggle-crotch whore, when you're through with all that pissin' and moanin', you might want to shut the car door. You wear down that Pontiac's battery and we might be here a real long time together. And you smell too bad for that."

I wiped my face on my sleeve and stood up. I got back into the driver's seat and slammed the door. What had happened to my mind? Why couldn't I think?

Seconds later, the door opened again with an explosion

of light and sound and Earl jerked me out and pulled me to him. He held me tightly against his wretched body; with one hand he pulled on my hair until my face came up, and then those beery lips came down on mine and his disgusting tongue slithered into my mouth and his whisker stubble rasped my skin.

All my muscles went slack. This is what it is to die, I thought. And then the roiling within me boiled up and out. Some primal force that Earl had unleashed by violating my soul with his filth rebelled and took control. I remember only the yell, not a scream, but a deep-throated bellow that came from way down in my guts. It surprised me more than anything else. I'd never known I was capable of that kind of sound.

Earl flew backward, as if flung.

In the light of the open car door, I saw him take tentative steps backward, then trip over a clump of scrub and land on his back. In the eye of my memory, he gets closer, so I must have approached him, although I can't exactly recall. I can only remember how good it felt to be taken care of—to have relinquished control—to know I had to do nothing but watch the drama as it unfolded.

I remember an expression of terror on Earl's pitiful face as he scrabbled back, trying to escape me. I remember the feeling of satisfaction mixed with puzzlement. I remember almost being able to grasp that elusive melody that had followed me all my life.

And then my memory fails me completely.

J.C. "JUICE" WICKERS: "So don't rush me, okay?

"So we took her to our personal drinkin' place. She was only too eager to go with us. And we get there and commence to drinkin'.

"Earl Foster, he gets a bit of a load on, and he's a little pissed that she don't join us and be sociable, she's just sittin' in the car poutin'. So he goes to get her out, come join us, have a few beers, tell a few jokes, you know?

"So Earl opens the car door, you know, to persuade her out, and she attacks him. She gives out with this yell, this—God A'mighty—it was like a cat in heat screamin' at night, you know? And Earl backs off and she jumps on him.

"I couldn't believe what I was seein'. It was dark, but the car door was open, and that old Pontiac's got good interiors. Old Earl Foster, he was down on his back and that girl was like on his chest, humpin'—humpin' up and down and old Earl was a gurglin', his arms and legs wavin' at first, then weaker, and she's slurpin', man, she's fuckin' slurpin', and drinkin' . . . God! . . . drinkin' his blood. Finally Earl give this sigh and that's the end, and I'm just sittin' at that picnic table not knowin' what to do, Jesus Christ, we pick up some scum from the beach and it's a friggin' . . .

"I didn't know what to do so I just sat there quiet like. I thought maybe when she was finished with old Earl Foster, she'd come on after me, so I just sat there, barely breathin', prayin' that the battery in the Pontiac would hold.

"Then she just rolls off him, with her eyes closed. Old Earl's neck is a mess of . . . Jesus, it was all tore up, and she's got this look on her face, like—God—like she'd just gotten laid, all peaceful and smiley, and she turns back to him, cold and dead and turnin' blue, and she strokes his cheek.

"Jesus, this makes me want to puke. She stroked his cheek, then hitched herself up and kissed him on his, his whatchacallit, his temple, and then she kinda snuggled into him and went to sleep.

"When I heard her start to snore, I snuck over and got Earl Foster's keys out of his pocket, shakin' all the time. I can tell you, nobody ever got sober faster in their life. So I got his keys without touchin' him more than I had to, and she's snorin', and got his blood smeared all over her nose and cheeks and stuff. And I got straight the hell out."

5

I shall never forget the dreams of that night. They were not dreams in the ordinary sense—with story lines and extraordinary experiences, or lifelike scenes all jumbled and confusing. That night my dreams were all sensations and feelings. Every positive emotion and pleasurable sensation I had ever had was magnified thousands of times and repeated in an endless performance all night long. The dance of life was choreographed to the most fascinating music—music that has never been heard on this earth before—fantastic music that spoke of friends and companions, shared secrets, trust.

The music was a continual stream of love and joy and togetherness. It was brotherhood and patriotism and the first sip of a cold drink on a hot day. It was the smell of baby kittens and the feel of bare toes in squishy mud. It was a hot apple pie with cheese and ice cream and being held and rocked and kissed on the forehead. It was running free on a summer's night and putting nose to cold windowpane on a rainy day. It was cozy and full, fresh and crisp, warm and soft.

It was my music, my personal music. I'd heard the strains of that symphony all my life. It was the haunting echo of that music that encouraged my journey, that led me through the adventures of life. That music had always been with me, I had heard it every time I had ever been alone, but somehow, it was never quite attainable, I'd never quite *heard* it before, it was never totally *mine* before.

Before I awakened, I knew I had finally found something worthwhile in my life. The pursuit of that music, attainment of that melody, was to be the driving force for my ambitions. The piece that had been missing from my emotions had been found, and it fit securely into place in my personality.

I had become whole.

As I slowly awoke, the feelings ebbed and flowed. I wanted them to stay with me forever, but could feel them sheeting away as my consciousness arose to the surface. I felt my brow furrow involuntarily—I wanted to stay there, in that place of pleasure—but then I heard a voice, a voice I had heard before, somewhere, sometime, a voice as familiar to me as my own name, clear and melodic, crisp and sensuous. The voice was so near and clear that I could almost visualize the lips that spoke, loudly yet gently, directly into my ear, "It is you, Angelina," and my heart pounded with joy, my spirits again soared, for the music was within me. I could know this place, could go there whenever I wanted. Peace and happiness flowed through me and I opened my eyes.

The sun was painting the sky to the east. The air was chilly, but I was not cold. The red and orange trees in their September splendor were silent. I stretched, hearing the gravel crunch beneath me. Had I slept on gravel all night? How odd. I sat up, rubbing a sore spot, and saw the body of Earl Foster next to me.

My stomach clenched in horror. What had happened? It looked as though a wild animal had had its way with him during the night. How could I have slept through that? Had I been drugged?

My pack was on the picnic table; there was no sign of Juice or the car. Could Juice have been responsible for this terrible mess? I ran to the table, grabbed my pack, and hugged it close to my chest. Then, as I looked back down on Earl Foster, pity overcame me. Poor man. As repulsive as he was, he didn't deserve a death like that.

How on earth could that have happened with me right next to him?

I looked around for a telephone, or a house, but there

was nothing but the lake, a few picnic tables in a little park area and the gravel road that led back to the highway. That was why Earl Foster had brought me here. It was deserted.

I took the blanket from my pack and covered him, as flies were waking up with the dawn. I pulled soap, shampoo, and towel from my pack and went to the edge of the lake. I dived in, clothes and all, and swam a bit, then took off my clothing, piece by piece, and washed them good, ending up naked and scrubbed. I brushed my teeth, toweled off, dressed in fresh clothes and hung the wet ones in a tree to dry. Then I sat down to contemplate Earl Foster and what action I should take.

Call the police, of course, and have something to eat.

I watched the unaccustomed stillness of the blanket on top of him. He should move, or breathe. The more I concentrated on him, the more I had a feeling that Juice was his only connection to life. Earl Foster had no family; he had no hopes, no dreams. Sad.

I shook myself and walked around for a bit, trying to push this strange intimate knowledge of him from my head, trying to remember the abuse he had done me the night before. I stood over his blanketed body and I wanted to kick him, cry for him, pray for him ... do *something,* but there was nothing to be done, so I emptied my mind of Earl Foster and concentrated instead on my freedom. I sat on the picnic table, my back to him, and read for a short time while the sun dried my clothes. Then I packed up and headed down the road, only vaguely remembering it from the night before. It looked very different in the rational light of day.

I had walked probably five miles down the main highway before a freshly waxed, late-model car stopped. I was pleased to find that the driver was in his early twenties, solidly built, with dark curly hair and delightful sparkling blue eyes. He looked like pleasant company. In the backseat were a small cooler full of ice and soft drinks and two small, clean, well-worn army-type packs, filled to a smooth, round plumpness. His name was Lewis, and he was a treasure.

In the first few minutes of our companionship, he convinced me that the West was the place to winter, and Nevada was not a bad place year 'round. He was tidy and pleasant; I felt comfortable and safe; and this one ride would take me all the way to my wintering ground. I was reluctant to give all this up to talk to the police and make statements about Earl Foster, who was such an objectionable person, and now quite beyond help. I decided somebody else could deal with Earl Foster—and I could wait to eat; I wasn't very hungry after all.

We took turns driving all day, then stopped at a run-down roadside motel for the night. Lewis arranged our accommodations, and I was so tired I said nothing. We slept in separate twin beds in the same room without incident.

I awoke at dawn to the sound of a huge truck pulling off the road, and then I smelled the cafe that shared the same parking lot with the motel. I arose silently—Lewis still slept—dressed, and went out. I spent my final dollar on two Styrofoam cups of coffee and brought them back.

Lewis woke when I returned, and he propped himself up on one elbow and looked at me, his dark hair tousled over his head, his eyes puffy from sleep. He rubbed his darkened chin and smiled boyishly at me.

" 'Morning."

"Good morning," I said, and handed him a cup. He plumped his pillows up next to the wall and sat up, bringing his sheet with him. His smooth skin contrasted pleasantly with the white of the bed linen.

"Sleep well?"

He nodded, then put his cup down in the center of a black stain on the wooden nightstand. He held his arms out to me and wiggled his finger.

"C'mere."

I sat on the edge of the bed shyly, knowing that he was about to seduce me, knowing too that I was ready. It wasn't Lewis, exactly—it was just time.

He sat forward, the sheet falling away, and kissed the side of my neck. I closed my eyes, and soon he turned me and began to unbutton my blouse. My heart was beating so fast that I could hardly breathe, not from excitement, but from fear, I think; I didn't know if this would hurt or be pleasant; I didn't know if I would like it or hate it. Sexual matters were a completely blank area and I was suddenly very anxious to learn. But I was used to being in charge of my life. And in this instance, in this sleazy motel room, Lewis was in charge, and I was about to let him be in control of my body.

My blouse off, he unbuttoned my pants and I stood and slipped them off. He stood up then, next to me, and I tried very hard to divert my eyes—for the time being at least. He rubbed himself against me, then took me in his arms and lay me on the bed, where we completed the act. I was unimpressed, although I'm sure that was no fault of Lewis's. I believe he did the absolute best he could.

I enjoyed examining his anatomy when he was finished. I asked him many questions, and he lay back with his hands behind his head while I knelt on the bed beside him and he answered me with small smiles and an occasional blush. After a while he took me again, and I tried very hard to find something enjoyable about it.

I found one thing. It was a moment of realization so intense it almost hurt; it felt like Lewis's orgasm looked. Though I've been celibate for most of my life, I can still call up that morning. I looked up into Lewis's contorted, enraptured face just at the moment of his orgasm, and I realized that while I thought I was relinquishing control to Lewis, in fact, the reverse was true. His sexual nature rendered him totally powerless. During his orgasm, *I* was in control. Total control. I could do anything to him in the space of that release. I almost laughed aloud.

So therein lies the pleasure of sex.

LEWIS GREGORY: "I loved her from the first minute I set eyes on her. She was so tiny, and a ball of fire. I think she was a virgin, although she never told me. She had wild eyes. They were always, like . . . scared, or something. They were never like other people's eyes; they were either, like, scared, or else they seemed to . . . I don't know. They seemed to understand everything about everything. I can't explain it. She was just the most exciting thing that had ever happened to me. I just loved her. I wanted to take her home and put her down in the bedroom and just take care of her for ever and ever.

"I guess I'm always wanting to tame the wild thing. When I was a kid, I always wanted to save the little birds that the cats got. I always wanted to hold them, but they always died. I was never sure if they died from fright—from the cat—or from being held by me. I wanted just one to live long enough to be a pet.

"Anyway, that's how I felt about Angelina. I was naive, I guess. I wanted to tame her but I didn't dare.

"Why'd she leave? Secrets. Wild things always have secrets, things they can't share because they don't know how. Angelina had lots of secrets, and they drew her on."

6

Lewis's house was a modern nothing, a block and wood tract-style home in Westwater, Nevada, with dreadful orange carpeting and plastic woodgrain accessories. The living room was furnished with a television on a wheeled stand, a pile of mismatched pillows, and a torn Naugahyde couch. A Formica table, covered by a green plastic table-cloth with Nevada dust ground into its quasi-seersucker pebbling and set with a plastic napkin holder and wilted napkins, stood in the corner of the kitchen. Everything in the kitchen was either harvest gold or avocado green.

Everything in the house looked as if it had been bought at a grocery store—including the bedroom furniture.

Lewis showed me his backyard, his barbecue, his toolshed. He smiled at me as we toured the house, bare walls shining down on us, like he was introducing his old mistress to his new one with expectations that they would coexist in harmony, adding pleasure upon value to his days. I had an odd feeling that I had already become one of Lewis's possessions, and that feeling was frighteningly pleasurable.

I showered while Lewis called to have our dinner delivered, then he showered while I changed the bed linen and explored the house. The refrigerator held four cans of beer, an almost-empty bottle of Tabasco sauce, a bite of fuzzy cheese in the corner of a milky plastic bag, and two sprouting potatoes. I began to make a list.

That night, we unpacked, ate, and went to bed early. Lewis stretched out next to me on his bed, then reached for me. I snuggled into a comfortable position, and we lay together while he talked of how good it was to be home, how nice it was to have a nest, unfeathered though it might currently be. Before drifting off to sleep, he talked of plans to improve it, styles of furniture, colors of paint, equity and a next-step-up neighborhood when this house had appreciated enough.

As he talked, I realized I had been wrong in thinking I wanted to find a home and settle down.

The next morning was Sunday. We read the paper in bed, then went grocery shopping at the corner market.

The trip to the grocery store stands out in my mind because for the first time I can remember, another person and I engaged in childlike play that was so much fun and so funny that I giggled uncontrollably, tears running down my cheeks. We threw groceries to each other, raced the carts, took turns pushing each other, mocked the other shoppers, read ingredients to each other with much drama, and were intentionally silly, incredibly silly, for the better part of an hour.

Then, just as I thought I would burst with joy, pleasure, and warmth toward this man, this clever, clever man, he picked me up and twirled me around, and all the gaiety disappeared. The fun was over. This close physical contact in a public place was just too distressful. I liked being in control of my own body, especially in public. The fun was over. We finished the shopping and went home.

Lewis returned to work the next day, and I was left to entertain myself, which wasn't difficult under usual circumstances, but in the barrenness of Lewis's home, I had to stretch my imagination to discover anything which had any entertainment value at all. I ended up washing all his dishes and all his clothes, and then I tackled the house.

By the time he came home from work, filled with excited chatter about his job and his friends, I was sullenly resentful. I carried in bags of sensible groceries and helped put them away, listening to his banter, then sat, chin in hand, as he fixed dinner, and daydreamed about the adventures I would have the next day. I was not cut out to lie around the house and wait for a man to come home from work. One day of that was sufficient.

The next day, as soon as Lewis had gone to work, I began to explore Westwater.

There were half a dozen chain supermarkets in town, and Lewis was the general manager of the biggest and most prosperous of these, on the north end of town. The north end was the affluent area, the goal of Lewis's real estate strategies. I stayed far from there.

This was my first experience of this area of the West; I had spent the previous winter in California, but California was nothing at all like Nevada. Westwater was truly desert—desert in the very literal meaning of the word—complete with sand, sagebrush, and cactus.

I walked from Lewis's house through his subdivision, across the highway, and into town. From the quantity of run-down motels, I gathered that Westwater was the place where Las Vegas losers came, looking to earn a decent wage in order to recoup and return. I walked through the small but respectable business district, which was filled with men in light suits and women in dresses with jackets. I kept walking, knowing that this town, as all towns, must have a seedier side, and my patience was rewarded a couple of blocks later.

I thought there was an overabundance of bars, cocktail lounges, girlie-show theaters, and adult bookstores for a town this size, until I noticed all the military haircuts parading the streets. A military installation must be nearby. I began to fantasize about this sleazy area, and soon I hungered to hear its music at night, when it would be alive, in full bloom.

But the first day I just wandered the streets, becoming familiar with Westwater.

I picked at a tuna-salad sandwich in a truck stop right next to the freeway and watched the trucks come and go, and the buses, and then I realized the building next door was a bus station, and my curiosity was piqued. I finished my meal, noticed the time, and left for Lewis's. I wanted to be home when he arrived, but the bus station drew me. I looked in through the dusty windows at the figures sitting on wooden benches, and I heard vague strains of a melody that had once been quite familiar. I agreed with myself that I would return the next day.

Initially, I explored Westwater every morning after Lewis left for work, then sat in the cool of the bus station during the heat of the afternoon, ostensibly reading a book I'd brought with me. I could never concentrate on the pages of the book; instead I watched bus-station patrons and made up my own stories about their lives.

Eventually, I all-too-anxiously saw Lewis off for work in

the morning and left for the bus station immediately after his car turned the corner.

The bus station, the fascinating bus station. It was a continual, entertaining show. My emotions roamed freely while sitting on the worn wooden bench. Some people I wanted to be with, some I wanted to travel with, some I wanted to get to know. There were others who were too obvious, some with too many children, some who angered me by their ostentatious and very assuming appearance, some who seemed, by their dress and manner, to be out of place in the seedy surroundings.

Within a week of my discovering the bus station, I was there every day, watching, watching. And the only feeling that was stronger than that which compelled me to sit there every day was this: I wanted to be there at night. I wanted to see the differences in the people; I ached to experience the atmosphere, to be with the night people in their element.

Something about the night escalates the darker side of mankind. Worries and fears weigh heavy when sensory input is slight; one can lay abed and fret over a faint sound from another room until the heart fairly bursts with the tension of it. Those terrors that overwhelm in the dark can become insignificant, even silly, in the day.

There is an excitement to being outside after dark. Even going to the corner market is different. Colors are altered, perceptions change, and the distortion of reality heightens as the darkness deepens. Things sound different in the dark.

Some thrive on it. Others hasten home and lock their doors. Most people stay home at night, not daring to venture out. I believe they are afraid of that influence that, like the tides, like two glasses of champagne, affects our baser animal natures, and pulls our minds just slightly out of kilter.

Twilight has always been the magical hour, the bewitching time that we dance around, taunting, as we wait for the dark to bend our heads, just a little—please, God, just a little—hoping against all chance of hope that the light will shine one last ray of rationality into our minds and tell us to go home and turn on the lights. But we don't. We choose the bending of our sensibilities, and soon the bend is permanent and must be fed like any habit. The night people are lovers, loners, readers, romantics. Night people are addicted.

I became obsessed with the notion of coming to this particular bus station and watching the night people in the midst of their environment during the drunkenness of the moon, the madness of the dark.

Every day for weeks I sat in the bus station. Every day I changed my seat and therefore my point of view. And every afternoon, just after the three-twenty bus disgorged its passengers from Salt Lake City, I would—so reluctantly!—leave my seat and go home, arriving just before Lewis.

I would sit at his table, chin in hand, while he made dinner and chatted on about his day, and I would fantasize about the bus station. What did it look like with the lights on? Who went there, who came in and who left, and how could I possibly arrange to be there to see them?

I never felt indebted to Lewis, nor did I feel entrapped by him. He was as pleasant a person as I have ever known, and because of that, I set careful parameters about how far to stretch his affection for me. I fancy myself to be a relatively loyal person, and Lewis was a gem of a man. He knew I was gone all day, but after the first question—when it was evident I was not interested in divulging my whereabouts, and was less excited about his pushing the issue—he respected my privacy. I believe he only wanted to be reassured that I was not seeing other men, which I found to be quite amusing and quaint. For me to go out on my own at night instead of being with him would stretch the limits not only of his affection, but of his hospitality. He would hurt and that would not please me.

So I sat with him, present in body, if not in mind, and we played cards and watched television and sometimes went out for long walks and talked about how the neighbors had valiantly and vainly tried to make their homes unique via the extravagant use of greenery.

The days went along, one after another after another. I cooked a small turkey for us at Thanksgiving, Christmas approached, and as it did, the nights became terribly cold. Space heaters were dusted off and brought out, so were the quilts and blankets. I began to get used to Lewis's sexual rhythm, and tolerated his advances with less distaste. We bought matching red sweat shirts and began to talk of Christmas presents and New Year's activities.

There was a contentment in my body; it was relaxed and well fed and exercised—but there was a hollow place in my mind and a yearning in my soul. I had to get out. I had to break away from this little-wife role, if even for a little while. I had to do something else, something more, something different—something young.

Just when I thought I could stand it no more, just when I began to seriously think about leaving Lewis, just when I thought I would burst from the frustration of forcing my true feelings to the back of my priorities—Lewis's mother died.

The call came while we were having breakfast. The telephone rarely rang; Lewis was not a gregarious person. It surprised us both when it rang, so uncharacteristically, at seven o'clock in the morning. Lewis went to the living room to answer it. I heard him gasp, then continue to listen, so I went and hugged his back while he talked, and I saw the silly Christmas tree in the corner looking out on baked desert ground, and I knew someone had died, died just in time for Christmas, died just in time for me.

He turned around and hugged me, and tears dripped onto my shoulder. It was his mother, he said. Stroke. He had to leave immediately for California and would probably be gone three or four days.

I was sorry for Lewis. My arms went around him and I held him, and while his sobs shook my whole body and he

44

sniffled and his tears wet my hair and my clothes, I tried to understand his grief. My cheek against his chest, I watched the little plastic icicles on the Christmas tree flutter in the breath of movement in the room. It matched the flutter of excitement in my belly as I thought that tonight I could go to the bus station, to let the tide of darkness once again wash over my mind.

LEWIS GREGORY: "My mother died just before Christmas. December, uh, fifteenth, I think it was. Angelina and I already had a tree up. Dad called while we were having breakfast. I called the store, packed, and left. My dad was in pretty bad shape. I helped him with the arrangements, then we buried her. He and I went out a couple of nights together; I just hated to leave him, you know, Mom was all he had. Mom and me.

"Anyway, I was gone for five days. I got back on the twentieth. I called Angelina every day, and she seemed to be doing all right. I think she even missed me. She was never big on affection or emotions, but I think she missed me while I was gone.

"She left a few weeks after I got back, you know. I tell myself that my going to the funeral without her had nothing to do with her leaving, but I just can't quite believe it. It was a real bitch, you know. Losing my mom and then Angelina, both right there together. It was a real bitch.

"But I do know what it was, really, that made Angelina leave. When I got home, she was different. There'd been those murders, you remember, those awful murders? And Angelina was alone, and didn't know anybody in town, and I know she was afraid; she must have been really afraid. So I got overly protective, and she couldn't live with that. I didn't know what else to do; I didn't know how else to act. She was so important to me, I couldn't have her out on the streets alone, at least until they'd caught whoever did those . . . I didn't handle it very well. I'd just lost Mom, and then Angelina was different. I didn't know what else to do.

"I tried to hold on tight and she slipped away, like soap.

"Like lavender soap."

7

My stomach jittered as if with cold, and even my teeth chattered a bit as I stood, arms crossed, leaning one shoulder against the door jamb as Lewis packed for his trip. He was quiet at first, wiping down the suitcases and shaking out his clothes. I could see him making a mental checklist of what he would take, and I watched silently, thinking it odd that grief-stricken men should weigh so heavily in my life.

Then Lewis began to talk. He reminisced and spoke of the special things his mother used to do when he was a child. He said, "She put pickles on sandwiches instead of lettuce." Then, "One time, I remember, she hit me. I was about fifteen. We were standing in the kitchen, and I said something stupid, something teenage, and she walked right over to me and slapped me. And then she cried and went into her bedroom. She was always just right there, just steady, nothing extravagant, just . . . Mom. That was the only time she ever hit me, and the only time I ever saw her cry. It almost killed me." His eyes glazed over with memory and tears.

I could do nothing for him, neither in support of his grief nor assistance with his packing. I had tried adjusting the mood, the way I had in so many cars. I tried lightening the air, I tried to lift my spirits at least enough that Lewis's soul wouldn't weigh so much. But I couldn't. Grief spread over the floor like a layer of molten lead. So I just watched him, and wondered at how different he was in the way he missed his mother—different from the way Rolf missed Alice, different from the way I missed her.

And then my thoughts strayed again to my freedom this coming night and my insides shivered with anticipation.

He fastened his suitcases, tucked a number of twenty-dollar bills into my jeans pocket, and hugged me. He loaded the suitcases into the trunk while I watched from the front door, and just before he got into the car, an odd expression crossed his face. He shut the door and came back to me, held me at the waist and looked at me with a fierce intensity, his green eyes cool and gentle despite the tremor in his hands. "You'll be here when I get back, won't you? I mean, I don't know how long I'll be gone—just a few days, I'm sure, but I don't really know. Please, Angelina, please promise me. I couldn't stand it if I lost you too . . . not now . . ." His voice failed and his eyes, moist in the corners, flashed with fear and longing.

I smiled what I thought to be an appropriate smile under the circumstances, sympathetic yet not pitying, and I touched his cheek. "I'll be here," I said.

And so he left. He got into the car and drove away.

I closed the door and looked around at the empty house. It was just beginning to feel like home—the little personal effects we'd added during the past few months had warmed it. But suddenly it was empty and impersonal. It was cheap and echoing and dusty. I was quite surprised. Lewis made the house sing. I cleared the breakfast dishes and sat at the kitchen table to think about him.

But all I could think of was the night ahead. My fantasy had grown to such tremendous proportions that a part of me wanted to hold back, afraid that what I would find might not live up to my expectations.

But that was silly; I had no expectations, really. I had only curiosity. Overwhelming curiosity. And it was only a bus station, I told myself. A bus station that I knew very well. It was merely a different aspect that I would see this night, like looking at an oil painting in the natural light instead of a fluorescent light. In the bus station, I would be seeing the night people in their natural light.

I went to draw a bath.

HAROLD WATERTON: "Sure, I remember her. She's one a them whatchacallits. You know the kind. They're weird about watching people. This one, I remember her. Tiny. Teeny-tiny little girl, right?

"Yep. I remember her. Used to come in about eleven, eleven-thirty, every day, stay until three. Just sit, pretend she's reading, but she's just watching.

"I been selling tickets in train and bus terminals for twenty-seven years now. And you see all kinds. I seen her kind before, too. They're getting something weird out of it, know what I mean? It ain't exactly natural to be sittin' in a bus terminal for four hours a day, just sittin', now is it? For months, now, we're talking months. I kept an eye on her, though, just waiting for her to do something. The weirdos always end up doing something. So I just waited for her to pull her stunt so's I could throw her out. I even had the maid follow her into the john, in case she's doing something in there, y'know? But nothin'. She never did nothin'.

"Then she stopped coming. I missed her, you know? You spend four hours a day looking at a pervert, watchin' them watch others, and you kind of get friendly with 'em a little bit, in your mind. So, I missed her, and went to wondering a little about where she went to get her jollies that was better than the bus station. Westwater ain't got a train station or an airport.

"Then, oh, three weeks, a month later, she shows up and buys a ticket to New Mexico. This was the best part. Them kind of people don't like to be called on their stuff, you know what I mean? They don't like other people to recognize how they get their jollies, know what I mean? So here she is, standing on tiptoes, barely able to see into the window, and I'm sitting on my stool, looking down on her, heh, and I said, get this, I said to her, 'Where you been—hidin' out from someone?' These perverts, they always is hiding from somebody, somebody who found them out. Heh. Well, she flashed them eyes at me and then backed off, real scared like. Hell, I really think she was hiding. I mean I really think she was. But you know, when she flashed them eyes at me, I almost fell backward off my stool, cuz for a second . . . well, hell.

"You know them photographs you sometimes get back and the

48

*eyes are all red? 'Specially if you take a picture of your dog? Well,
her eyes were like that, almost. I don't mean almost, I mean they
were, but only for a second.*

"Hell, I don't know what I mean."

8

I left the house at two-thirty, wanting to arrive at the station
by three in order to witness the changeover from light to
dark. The sky cast messages of late afternoon, a brisk wind
was blowing through my hair, so I turned up the collar on
my coat and only pulled my hand out of my deep pocket to
wave my thumb when a car approached. I soon got a ride
that took me right to the bus station.

I pushed open the huge doors and walked in.

Something was in the air, and it felt like adventure.

The building heat was on, and people were comfortable
in their shirt sleeves, coats piled up on the wooden seats.
The seldom-used heaters gave off a distinct odor, an old
smell, a musty, slightly moldy fragrance that was just elusive
enough to be pleasant. Someone with a little Christmas
spirit had hung a silver garland around the ticket seller's
cage, and it looked trite amid the old, authentic, run-down
condition of the building.

Some patrons were apparently waiting to meet the bus
from Salt Lake City; others were waiting to depart on that
bus or another. Two young homosexuals furtively shared
a cigarette by the water fountain. A cowboy sitting in the
corner strummed a guitar and softly sang a love song. When
he finished, the citizens of the bus station clapped for him,
which he acknowledged with a nod of his Stetson and a faint
blush. I smiled as I found a seat with an excellent view, next
to the old-fashioned coffee machine that had a yellowed
"Out of Order" sign on it. This was going to be a good night,
complete with free entertainment.

The clientele changed—a slow, steady turnover.

Drunks came in out of the cold to curl up next to the heaters. Women and children came in just in time to buy their tickets and board buses, and not a single one tarried. Old alcoholics, young people on drugs, homosexuals, social outcasts, the deformed and deprived, dirty codgers reminiscent of Earl Foster—they all came in, some stayed, some left. Police came every hour to look in and trade nods with the ticket seller. The old ticket seller was replaced by a younger, huskier man, obviously well equipped to deal with any problems that should arise among his clientele, and ever-so-slowly, the complexion of the bus station changed.

At eleven o'clock, five greasy-haired, leather-jacketed young men came in and began to berate and deride the station's denizens. Within fifteen minutes, the ticket seller had spoken with them twice, but the damage had been done. All the people, save a very few, had left, scattered to their second choice of hangouts, I assumed, leaving the station relatively empty. Then, as if they knew the schedule of police rounds, the quintet fired up their motorcycles and were gone, just before the police arrived for their next routine check. The result was pitiful: Three drunks slept in the back corner near the restrooms, one passionate couple huddled in mysterious posture under a plaid blanket, and I sat next to the coffee machine, feeling as if I had just been robbed.

I knew the night was not finished. Something told me that action would yet take place. I stretched my legs, had a drink of water, checked the schedule, and noted that there were to be no more arrivals until one-thirty, when three buses were due within ten minutes.

I reflected for a few moments on Lewis. He would have arrived at his parents' home by now, and was sleeping, probably, or sitting up talking and drinking with his father. He would have been crying, and his eyes would be puffed and his hair uncombed. I could see him, in his green-plaid wool shirt, trying to face his loss like a man, sitting next to his father, who, no doubt, made him feel like a little boy.

I looked through the artificial light, through the artificial heat of the bus station, and noticed the difference in the color of the wood at night. I noticed the outside lights had a different aura about them when seen through the old wavy-glass windows. Soft snoring came from the corner, moans of gratification came from the other side, and the ticket seller turned the pages of his paperback.

Suddenly I was starved. Ravenous.

Next to the bus station was that cafe, that truck stop, an all-night diner.

It was time.

I stood and pulled on the heavy plaid coat that Lewis had bought me and repressed the absurd notion that I ought to tell the heavy man behind the cage bars that I would return presently. I buttoned the coat, stuck my hands deep into its pockets, and leaned open the big doors.

It was absolutely frigid outside. With this cold, this close to Christmas, there should be snow. I flipped up my collar and danced for a quick moment; my breath condensed in the air. I could see the neon sign across the parking lot, high atop a pole to catch the attention of long-distance truckers. The sign, in pink neon, said, "Plain Jane's Kitchen." Under that, in flashing blue letters, it said, "Plain good cookin'." The place had always seemed right next door in the daylight, but in the nighttime distortion of reality, the cafe was clear across the parking lot, beyond the tractor-trailer rigs that were parked in remarkably orderly alignment.

I started toward it, walking briskly, head down, grateful to Lewis for the money he'd left me. I put the cold out of my mind and thought instead about what I would order to go with the cup of hot chocolate I could already taste.

I kicked a few pebbles out of my way as I walked, and decided to go out to the street, around the parking lot and the trucks that blocked my way, rather than walk between them, through the alleys they created by parking so close together. But the wind was so cold and so unpleasant that at the last minute I reconsidered, knowing the trucks would make a perfect windbreak, and I trotted between two of the rigs.

The walls created a blind maze. I could see no lights at all, save that which trickled down from Jane's neon silliness. The wheels were almost as tall as I. I felt powerless, dwarfed among all that mammoth machinery.

I threaded through, then heard a noise that stopped me dead in my tracks. Adrenaline pumped false courage and excitement through my brain and I listened for a moment longer. I heard metal on metal, a wrenching.

I watched with horror as my feet began to move toward the sound. Ears attuned to the silence, I heard more sounds; someone was trying to break open one of the containers. I approached, my feet instinctively silent. I edged around the massive end of one of the trailers and saw, under the belly of the container, three pairs of Levi-clad legs. If any of the boys bent over, to pick something up or to tie a shoe, they would see me and I would surely be dead. One walked toward the back of the truck, whispering to the others. More whisperings, then another set of footsteps echoed off toward the cab of the truck. I followed the sound, keeping the truck between us.

The footsteps turned away from me, toward the bus station. I hid as I followed, stalking, and then he stopped and unzipped his pants and I heard the splash of urine against a tire.

It was one of the leather-jacketed hoodlums who had stormed the bus station earlier in the evening. Three of them were intent on robbing the container and this one had momentarily split off from the pack.

I watched the strong stream of urine splash, steaming, as he wet the entire tire, then I could smell it, and it fired the frenzy that had already begun in my mind. Suddenly I was overcome with hunger; I felt an ancient, innate, dormant hunger awakening within. I felt my saliva glands ache with the promise of sweetness. Spittle overproduced and I wiped a corner of my mouth on my coat sleeve. I was flushed with excitement; my coat was too hot.

My nervous system tensed as the stream of urine weakened. I took two slight steps forward, balancing my weight, crouching a bit, and he shook his penis and put it back into his pants, zipping up as he turned around.

I leaped and caught his throat before he even saw me.

He went over backward, and his arms were too busy trying to do too many things—trying to break his fall, trying to pull me from his chest, trying to free his bite, trying to gouge my eyes. All were ineffective. I noted each of his slight defense attempts with as much attention as I noted the noise we made as we landed on the ground. These were things to learn from, nothing more. What was of importance at the time was my starvation, my insatiability that was only aggravated by the first swallow. Then the blood pumped hot and sweet, and my lips found the straw and tugged gently, drinking quickly, milking, staving off the final rush, the release, toying, playing, dancing around it, until I could wait no longer, and an explosion of nerve endings sparked my body, and I shuddered, quivered, and was full.

I felt faint from the exertion. I lay with my cheek against his, regaining my breath, feeling once again the cold night air. I slowly pulled back and looked down on him, on his face so pale in the muted light. He looked somewhat like Lewis, with dark curly hair hanging over his forehead. I pulled my legs under me and knelt on his chest. The terribly messy wound on his neck oozed as I watched, and I caught one drip with my finger and licked it, then caught another and wiped it gently on the side of his nose. He was beautiful.

My eyelids drooped. I heard some familiar music. I wanted to rest and slide into it, where I would be tended and cared for. I needed to lie down, snuggled up to this beautiful

53

person, this wonderful Adonis with the fragile face, and sleep the restful sleep with him. I felt warm and cozy and loved. Complete.

But the ground was hard, and the air was cold, and there were two men waiting for my fair and handsome prince to return to them. They would come here, looking for him.

With a mighty effort, I shook the webs of sleep from me, kissed the beautiful one on the lips and stood, looking down on him. His lips were red where I had kissed him; with his pale cheeks and dark hair, he looked as an English school-boy ought to look.

I loved him.

I don't recall getting home, but home I was, when I awoke with the music in my ears, surrounded by the loving feeling of being enwombed, tended, nourished, fed. I awoke and arose as if I were floating, gliding across the garish orange carpet of Lewis's home, which was somehow less objectionable today. I could recall every event of the evening before, all but my transportation home, and it was all an unbelievable adventure.

Wait until Lewis hears about this, I thought to myself, and then I realized I could never tell Lewis, or anyone else. It was a secret. This idea of such a wonderful game being such furtive stuff made me giggle into my hand, and I noticed the clock said two o'clock in the afternoon, so I went to bathe and make ready for the coming night.

Friday night.

Teen dance night at the VFW hall.

"That Friday, I couldn't keep my mind on the job, all I could think about was the dance. I'd been helping to put on those teen dances since I was sixteen—Jesus, eight years now—then when Bill got old enough and interested enough, he began helping. They're good fun, and it's a nice clean place for the kids to go and get together. I always enjoy it. But that Friday . . . that Friday . . .

"I almost quit my job, for one thing. I've been a construction foreman for a long time, and work is just one problem after another, you know? Well, that Friday, Westwater was too small a town for me, the construction industry seemed like a dead-end profession, my dad seemed like he was stuck in a rut, and if my dead-assed little brother didn't stop screwing up at work—I mean, I did him a favor by hiring him.

"It was just one of those days, I guess, but that particular day, I was ready for something else. If I didn't have the responsibility of that teen dance, I might have just taken off, quit work, grabbed my shotgun and my sleeping bag, and taken off. I was ready for some change. I was ready for some major change.

"I had no idea that going to that teen dance would change more than my life.

"It changed me."

9

Lewis called just before sundown. We spoke briefly. His father was doing all right, the funeral would be the next afternoon, he would stay a day or two longer with his father and uncles, and then come home.

I told him that his plans sounded perfect, and that I was fine—happy, in fact, was a word that I used. He told me he loved me, blew me a kiss, and then we hung up.

I turned from the phone to resume what I had been engaged in prior to Lewis's call, but I couldn't remember what it was. I knew it had been pleasurable and entertaining and engrossing—I had been *learning* something—but it had fled my mind. Surely it couldn't have been entirely in my mind, yet there was no sign of any activity in the house that would have kept me so engaged. It was a puzzle, and I felt faintly resentful that Lewis had interrupted me. I sat for a moment in the growing dusk, watching shadows deepen, watching the final orange glow recede from the sky.

I reached over and clicked on the lamp. Its harsh light rasped the room and hurt my eyes. I turned it out again and went to dress for the dance.

My face appeared to have altered a bit, I noticed as I applied a light coat of eye shadow. I examined my features individually, then stepped back to gauge the entire picture. There was a gauntness that hadn't been there before. My cheekbones stood out a touch more prominently, and so did my brow. I was pleased with the effect. My baby fat was finally dissolving. I trimmed my hair, cutting it shorter around my face, watching the white, yellow, and golden clippings fan out into the sink, then I ran a brush through my new style and dabbed lightly at my lips with a pink lipstick.

A flyer about the Friday night teen dances had been posted in the bus station, and I'd looked forward to the occasion for weeks. I swirled the hair trimmings down the drain with a gush of water.

I found my plaid coat in the hall closet and put it on, then modeled it for myself in the mirror on the door. It was stained. There was a great brown stain on the collar, it spread down the front left-hand side. I took the coat off again, went into the bathroom, and looked at it in the light.

Dried blood.

The boy's peaceful face flickered in and out of my memory; I was pleased to have given him such rest, even at the expense of the beautiful coat Lewis had given me. I rolled it up and put it in a paper bag. The trash was picked up on Mondays.

Back in the closet, I found a denim jacket with a sheepskin lining that was soft and warm and only a little too large. It would do just fine. From the linen closet I fetched an old, frayed, brown bath towel, then shrugged off the jacket and swirled the towel over my shoulders like a cape. I put the jacket back on. Now I was ready.

I stepped out into the brisk cold and shivered with anticipation.

I got a ride immediately. When I arrived at the VFW hall, I was early; there was no one about, so I scouted the neighboring area.

The hall was a large wooden building on the outskirts of town. The nearest house was hundreds of yards away. Dirt parking areas surrounded the building on three sides. In the back was a weeded lot with a few trees, and as I stomped through it, I kicked up empty beer bottles and paper trash as well as used condoms. I understood how far the chaperoning went at weekend teen dances: not beyond the glare of the lights. I imagined this area would be as populated as inside the hall by closing time.

I stuffed my hands into the high jacket pockets and pulled in the sleeves to keep out the draft as well as I could, and walked around and around the building, trying to keep my legs and feet warm.

Presently an older man arrived in a red pickup truck with a broken spotlight on the roof. He was heavyset, and walked with a hitch. He unlocked all the doors, propped them wide open, then turned on all the lights. I followed him inside for some warmth. It wasn't much warmer inside.

The man heard my footstep on the doorsill and took three steps to turn around and fix me with a watery stare.

"I'm early, I guess," I said.

"Well, you sit right there." He pointed at a row of chairs set against the wall, then checked his watch. "Boyd'll be along soon, maybe you can be helping him set up and sell tickets or something." He disappeared into the men's room.

Echoes of his cleaning activities resounded through the cavernous structure. Long ago, someone had taken pride in this building. Walls, ceilings, and rafters were once painted, the wooden floors once varnished and waxed. But that was long ago. A dusty blue banner trimmed with gold braid and covered with cobwebs stretched high across one sooty wall, saluting, in gold lettering, the Veterans of Foreign Wars. The wooden floor was worn in the center where generations of dancing shoes had done damage. A makeshift stage filled one corner of the room, piled high with amplifiers, microphones, electrical cords and equipment. At the other end of the hall was a long window into a kitchen, and a counter, presumably an area for selling soft drinks. Next to the window were the doors to the two restrooms. That wall sported the only fresh paint in the place, a light green enamel.

I tapped my toes on the floor and shivered.

A truck pulled up outside, skidding in the dirt and gravel. The engine died and two doors slammed.

"Hey, Kyle? Kyle?" a strong masculine voice called from the door. I heard answering mumblings from the men's room. Then a cowboy stepped into the room, looked around and saw me. He smiled. "Hi."

"Hi," I said, and my body began to shiver from a different excitement.

"Kyle around?"

Before I could answer, a younger version of the same man, obviously a brother, came around the corner and into the hall, rubbing his hands and blowing into them. He stopped and looked at me with the same intensity his older brother had. Then the door to the men's room opened and the old man came out, clanking a bucket and mop.

The cowboy approached him. "Hey, Kyle. I got a new table for inside the snack shop. Donated by the women at that sewing place. They got all fancy new cutting tables, and gave us one of their old ones. Bill's going to help me put it in the kitchen there, then we can use the other table for tickets, instead of the old rickety card table."

"Good. Good." Kyle opened the door to the ladies' room and propped it open with a wedge of wood. "You need help, she can help ya." He nodded at me.

I smiled up at him. He was larger than life; a more vibrant, healthier man I've yet to meet. His tan Stetson showed off his sunburned face to best advantage. He wore a brown corduroy jacket over a blue-plaid shirt with jeans and plain-toed boots. He was big, with wide shoulders, and he had deep-set green eyes, a large, open, honest face, and a scent like the forest in the spring. He smiled back at me, and I felt the ignition.

"You a friend of Kyle's?"

I shook my head. "I'm just early."

"New in town?"

I nodded. My breath was caught in my throat.

"I'm Boyd Turner. This is my brother Bill." Bill smiled, then blew on his hands again.

"Angelina Watson."

"Want to help?"

I shrugged, feeling a blush rise in my cheeks.

"You can sell tickets. There's always too much work for Bill and me. Kyle helps out with the cleaning and stuff, but"—he checked his watch—"the band will arrive soon, and—" A van pulled into the parking lot. We smiled at each other. His teeth were clean and white. "See? Help us out for a half hour? Work off your admission fee?"

He was pleading with me in a flirtatious way. He was irresistible, with his boyish charm and his wonderful eyes. I took my hands out of my pockets and stood up, ready to be directed.

In no time, activity was everywhere. The band began to set up, and as they did, volunteers arrived to work in the snack shop. Boyd recognized them, and I stamped their hands and let them pass for free. All others were to pay one dollar for a bit of black ink on their hands that said, "For Deposit Only—Wiley's Feed and Livestock."

Early arrivals began to trickle in, mostly young boys who had spent the better portion of the day deciding what to wear and preparing for this evening of meeting young girls. They paid their entrance fee, then grouped together around the doors to the restrooms. When the groups got large enough, they would all leave to go sit in cars, trade lies and plot strategies, be fortified by a beer and a smoke, and be admitted again, later, showing the stamped back of their hands.

My job was to be of service, and it brought up interesting feelings. I felt proud every time Boyd came by to pick up the receipts, when he gave me that special smile of gratitude. I felt debased when the young girls—my age, older, younger—came by and threw their dollar bills at me, or wouldn't show me their stamped hands upon reentry.

The band tuned up and played to a standing-room-only crowd. No one sat in the metal folding chairs along the walls. They stood around in their tight Western clothes, in groups of girls, groups of boys, and couples. No one danced. Everyone just shouldered through the crowd, milling about, and then, as if by signal, all of a sudden everyone was dancing. The dance floor expanded to the walls. What an odd ritual.

When the band took its first break, the hall emptied. Everyone went outside to smoke and steam off the sweat they'd garnered from dancing in close quarters. Many were becoming quite drunk and a few made lewd comments to me as they passed. Boyd brought me a cup of hot chocolate and sat on the table, looking at me.

"Bill will take over from you now. There won't be many more people coming. A few, but not many. He'll handle it."

I sipped and nodded, watching the young people divide into more and more couples, saw the flirtatious looks, heard the laughter, saw many disappear around the corner, and I knew where they had gone. I shivered and crossed my arms. Boyd was still staring at me.

"Where are you from?"

"Pennsylvania."

"Been here long?"

I shook my head.

"Here with family?"

60

"No," I said. "I'm on my own. Right now I'm house-sitting for a friend who's in California." I knew this surprised him, so I gave him my finest, most practiced defiant look, to quell the question before he asked it. He thought I was too young.

"So did you drive here?"

"Hitchhiked."

"I'll drive you home, then, after. Okay?"

I took a long time in answering. I wanted to be with him, oh, God, I wanted to be with him, but thoughts of Lewis flickered through my mind. There was no commitment here, I reminded myself—it was just a ride home. And if something better, more interesting, came along, well . . . I was not bound to him for the night, although I couldn't imagine anything more interesting than this incredible man. Was it wise to take a ride with an unknown? Oh, Angelina, I thought. You've gotten so careful in your three months of domesticity. I knew I was fully capable of handling myself.

My answer may have wavered in my mind, but my eyes never strayed from his face. I saw when shyness began to creep in. He thought I might turn him down. "Okay," I said.

His relief was evident. He smiled again, an intimate smile, a knowing smile. "So, go. Dance. Enjoy. And when we close up, I'll meet you here."

I stood up, and as I did so, he, sitting on the table, took his hands out of his pockets as if to touch me: my waist or my shoulders or my face. But he dropped them into his lap and swung his feet back and forth, then stood up and settled into the folding chair I'd been sitting in.

I went to the ladies' room. Green-painted wood covered with writing in lipstick, pen, and carvings had absorbed the smell of thousands of girls, gallons of disinfectant. The little room with two sinks, two mirrors, and two toilet stalls was stuffed with girls putting on makeup, adjusting their clothes, and combing their hair. I stood in the corner and watched them for a while, as they chatted on about the boys and their boyfriends. Then a pretty dark-haired girl with dark-red lipstick and too much rouge on her cheeks noticed me in the mirror, and she turned to me across the crowd and said, "Hi."

I shoved my hands deeper into my pockets and said, "Hello."

"You a friend of Boyd's?"

I didn't know how to answer her. "Sort of."

"You're new."

I nodded.

"I'm Catherine."

"I'm Angelina."

"Well, Angelina, if you're a friend of Boyd's, I'm a friend of yours." She turned to her friends and they all laughed, then she looked me up and down again, and returned to her creams and colors and speaking of nonsense. I watched her in the mirror for a moment longer, watched her take glances toward me without meeting my look, and I remembered that feeling, that feeling of being different, being outside the joke, outside the crowd, and I hated it. I pushed my way out, and ran directly into a drunken lad whose hands quickly felt my entire torso, inside my jacket. I shoved him from me, disgusted with the whole place, and walked outside. I wished for my space at the table again, but Bill was standing there, exchanging money and fellowship with some of his friends.

The cold air refreshed me after the steamy confines of the crowded hall. The stench of sweat, mixed with perfume, after-shaving lotions, underarm deodorant, beer and cigarette breath, was too potent for me. I took some deep breaths of fresh air and walked aimlessly around some of the cars in the parking lot. Most of the vehicles were uninhabited; a few had fogged windows, others had cigarettes glowing in the darkness as their occupants talked. I wandered among them, fists stuffed tight into my pockets. I wondered what they talked about, what it felt like to be closed up tight in someone's dad's car, with good friends and lots to talk about on a Friday night.

I heard the music start up again, the sounds of car doors slamming as the call was answered, but I listened to a different sound, responded to another summons, and found myself moving irresistibly toward the well-used vacant lot in the rear of the building. I heard a rustling in the weeds, and my heart began to pound.

I approached in the shadow of a tall bush, steadily, calling on an inborn sense of stealth, although there was probably no need. Whoever was in the vacant lot knew they were only yards away from a formidable crowd. They had, by choice, given up any right to privacy.

I wiped the corners of my mouth.

As my eyes became accustomed to the dark, I saw two shapes, two people, sitting on the ground, facing each other. As I came closer, I could hear them talking, and my sense of atmosphere picked up red vibrations of anger in their interchange. I moved ever closer, the cold forgotten, as my curiosity became overwhelming. Their voices rose to meet me.

"I trusted you," she said softly.

"You still can," he said.

"Not when you're out doing—whatever you were doing—with *her*."

"It was nothing, Julie. I told you. She needed some help, and I helped her."

"I bet." Her voice was full of scorn, of disdain.

"You know, I thought I had made you a woman, but you're still a child."

I heard a sharp intake of breath, then the girl slowly got to her feet. The boy rose, too, and they stood face-to-face for a moment before she lashed out and slapped him hard across the face. It was so loud I was sure everyone heard it, even inside the hall. I was shocked.

She turned on her heel and stomped back to the hall.

I adjusted quickly, hoping my reaction did not send out recognizable vibrations. I needn't have worried. Though she passed within brushing distance of me, her own emotions were far too loud to allow anything else near. She left without a backward glance.

His hand went to his face. I could almost see the red handprint and hear the buzzing in his ear. His face hurt, his pride hurt, his love hurt. I longed to go to him, yet I hesitated. I didn't know this person, I didn't understand the situation, what possible benefit could my presence have? I remained where I was, barely breathing, considering. Considering.

And then that voice came, that voice that I knew as well as I knew my own name, that same voice that spoke to my soul, that spoke to me with the ethereal music that supplied the foundations of my life—that voice spoke right into my ear as She had before; a clear voice, a sweet voice, rich and sensuous, and I closed my eyes and saw moist red lips as they spoke to me. "Your gift, Angelina," She said. "Give the boy your gift."

I remembered the happiness and peace; I remembered the calm and joy. Then I remembered the flood of emotions the night before, and the night in the Ozarks, and I realized that I did have a gift, I did have a mission, and my freedom came to mean a new thing to me.

In that moment, standing in the bushes, feeling new emotions, new feelings, I came to believe that I had been chosen. I had been chosen to own and use the music, that eternal, ethereal music. Why else would something—some*one*?—take charge of my life as it (She?) had? Why else would my rewards be the loving sense of peace and protection? Why else would I be obsessed with the thought of the bus station, if not to fulfill destiny by going there to pass along peace? I did ease suffering, I did bestow peace. Why else would I be here, instinctively standing in the bushes? I knew what must be done.

My freedom from responsibility was no mistake. My

freedom from family tethers, from material assets, from even the basic desires to have these things, had not been a plan gone awry. All these things were for a purpose. I had been chosen. I was special. I was to be one of the background people, accomplishing great things with little or no public recognition or acclaim. My kind of assistance would not be recognized in a good light, anyway. They wouldn't understand. Great things were afoot and I was a minor cog in a mighty wheel. Guided by Her voice.

I felt free, wonderful, and one with Nature.

Surety flooded my soul. I heard lovely strains of the music. I glimpsed through the door of eternity, and I knew that if only I could sit down and contemplate it for a moment, I would understand the elusive concept.

Later. At the moment, I had something important to accomplish.

I stepped from the bushes just as the young man sank back down to the ground, his hands over his face, his shoulders shaking.

KYLE CARMICHAEL: "Sure I remember her. She was hanging around the hall when I got there. Never seen Boyd so taken with a woman before. They flock around him, women do, big, strong, good-hearted boy like that. Flock around him, they do, he could have his pick, but he never seemed to date any of 'em seriously, not more than once or twice.

"Boyd's daddy and me were old friends—fought the war together. Never had sons myself, only daughters that my wife raised, so I kinda always felt that Boyd an' Bill were mine, too. The four of us went hunting probably every weekend. It was just a thing for the guys to do, to get together, teach the young ones about life.

"Heh. If Boyd'd taken to girls the way he'd taken to hunting, he'd probably be in a lot of trouble. That boy would not quit. Sundown didn't even stop him. He bought books and guns and loaded his own. One time he tracked a deer all weekend. Got him, too.

Kind of obsessed, it seemed to me, but it didn't worry his daddy any, and I'm not the kind to interfere.

"Always a gentleman, though, Boyd was. And his brother, too. Good sportsmen. Three of us kind of tired of hunting after a while; at first we stopped the shooting, then we stopped taking the guns, and then we stopped going altogether, but not Boyd. He kept going. Alone, even.

"Yep. Did my heart good when I saw him and that little bit of a blonde look at each other like that. 'Kyle,' I said to myself, 'Boyd's got something here that's a lot better than tracks in mountain snow. He's got a woman to chase now.' Heh. Nothing like a woman to change a boy's head."

10

I know the boy heard me approach, but he didn't lift his head until I had knelt next to him and touched his shoulder. Then his fingers parted and he wiped his wet face, first on his hands, then on the sleeve of his jacket, grief still flooding his features. As he turned to face me, I saw the cruel bruise rising on his cheek.

"What?" he said, mistaking me for an emissary from his girlfriend.

"Nothing. I just came to be with you. To ease your pain. My name's Angelina."

He nodded, sniffing, and wiped his nose on his sleeve. I began to pet him. I ran my hands lightly over his head, his brown hair frosty in the cold. I touched his swelling cheek, and fingered his chin. I unbuttoned the top button of his coat while he fiddled with his fingers in his lap. Then he looked at me, his eyes red and miserable.

"I bought her a diamond for Christmas. What am I going to do with it now?"

I unbuttoned the second button. Underneath was a red-flannel shirt, with a triangle of white T-shirt showing in the neck. I felt warm and guided, happy and healthy, and my eyes filled with warmth and love and gratitude as I held his face in my hands.

"I don't know. I don't think she deserves your love," I said, then unbuttoned my own coat.

"I guess I could just take it back." He began to wring his hands, cracking his knuckles. "I just really thought . . ." He seemed to notice me for the first time as I slipped out of the sheepskin jacket and unfurled the towel from around my shoulders. "What are you doing?"

"Shhh," I said, laying a fingertip on his lips. "I'm just going to ease your pain." I spread the towel on the frozen ground. "Here. Lie down. I'll make you forget all about her."

I could see he was nervous, and I gleefully imagined all thoughts of his broken heart fleeing in the face of a seduction. He lay back and I straddled his chest, lightly placing my knees on his arms. I began to rock back and forth, in time to the music in my ears, and I crooned softly to him as I brushed my fingers around his face.

He closed his eyes and a tiny smile flickered across his mouth. I pulled open the throat of his outerwear, exposing the tender skin, so winter-white, so virginal, unspoiled, so beautiful. Not a whisker grew here, not a mole, a freckle, barely a crease. A smooth, wide-open field with the faintest of pulses beneath.

Saliva flooded my mouth as ravenous hunger shuddered throughout my body. I leaned over and took what was mine.

His bucking was a distraction. I wished fervently that he would stop the silliness of a struggle; the victory was mine, was ours together. But soon he settled down and I quenched my thirst, sated my spirit.

The wound this time was small and precise; my technique was improving. I cleaned it with the edge of the towel, and wiped my face as well as I could without a mirror. I turned his peaceful face and traced the handprint on his cheek with a fingertip. The swelling had gone down and it was no longer red but pale blue. Then I tenderly rolled the boy child over on his side, brought his knees up to his stomach, and covered his neck with the towel. I looked down fondly at him, such a child, such a little boy, all curled up like a baby. He was irresistible in his innocence. He was beautiful and had satisfied me so completely. I felt grateful. Grateful and happy and composed; complete and very sleepy. I lay down, snuggled up to his back and slept, succumbing to the softer strains of the music that stirred me, and like a lullaby called me gently to rest.

The sounds of roaring car engines woke me, and headlights flashed at me as I sat up, rubbing my eyes, trying to get my bearings. The dance was over. I was to meet Boyd for a ride home. I kissed my lover of the evening and left him, brushing leaves and grass from my clothes as I pulled on my jacket and ran my fingers through my hair. I could not be certain whether there were telltale stains on my clothing or face, and would not know until I could find a mirror.

Head down, I bucked the exiting crowd and fought my way against the flow to the vacant ladies' room. I pushed through the door and looked in the mirror. My face reflected the peacefulness in my soul. I looked relaxed, happy, loved. Warm water washed over my hands as I watched my face in the mirror, appreciating my new look. It was the lean look of spiritual satisfaction. I dried my hands on a paper towel and checked my teeth once more in the mirror.

I turned out the light as I left.

Kyle was already sweeping a pile of cigarette butts, chewing-gum wrappers, and assorted trash ahead of his wide push-broom. The snack bar had been closed down, food put away, cleaned up, lights out. The ticket table was stowed inside. Bill and Boyd stood in the doorway, talking with some older men. I walked over.

Boyd saw me approach, smiled. "Ready?" I nodded. "Kyle

will lock up." He punched his brother in the side. "C'mon, punk." He shook hands with the two men, called his thanks to Kyle, and the three of us went back into the cold parking lot still littered with a few empty cars and plenty of empty bottles and cans.

Boyd's truck was a big, new pickup so high off the ground I thought I'd need a stepladder to get in. He lifted me by the waist to help me up, and I settled comfortably between the two brothers. The engine roared to life; he turned on the lights, the heater, and the radio, all in one practiced movement. He put the truck in gear and we were on our way.

Boyd was quiet as we drove the few miles to their house. Bill drummed on his legs, tapped his feet, and nodded his Stetson in time to the various songs that came on the radio. He even softly sang portions of one love tune. When we stopped outside his house, he jumped out with a quick thanks, closed the door, and we took off again. Boyd spoke not a word.

I slid toward the door, but not all the way. I had enjoyed being small between the shoulders of the two men. At last I had been in the position I had envied earlier in the evening. But it was so brief—and now there was a vacancy next to me, air around me, and I was anxious, for a moment, afraid that I would lose the feeling of companionship.

But the beautiful voice was with me, in the back of my mind, with me always. I felt fulfilled, and I relaxed.

It was early yet, the night stretched long before us. I didn't care to go back to Lewis's house, but what could we do, and would it be proper for me to suggest something?

We drove along, each silent with our own thoughts. I loved driving, being driven. I loved being on the road, on the move, always looking out the window at something new.

And then it occurred to me that Boyd had not asked me where I lived. My spirits lifted. So the evening had not ended. We were on our way somewhere, toward some adventure. The anxieties of facing Lewis's house alone slipped away and I relaxed. The hot air blowing on my boots made me slightly sleepy. Boyd reached over and turned down the radio, far more perceptive to the nuance of music than his younger brother, and the old songs on the radio spoke their questionable wisdom into our square, speeding universe on wheels.

We continued to drive, on the highway, on the rutted roads, past broken fences, and out onto hard-packed sand and dirt, with the moonlight actually reflecting off the desert. We drove around into town, cruised slowly through the red-light district, then idled around the quiet little neighborhoods with their houses all lined up and inhabitants blissfully unaware of the effect the darkness was having on them, even as they slept.

Still, Boyd spoke not at all. I held my silence as well.

In time, there seemed almost to be a smell in the air. It smelled like well-worn leather. I sensed loneliness mixed with love. There was relief in this togetherness—no, it wasn't really togetherness, for we were not together. No, the relief was more in discovering a camaraderie. We shared a certain passion for driving, and the night. No words were needed for Boyd and me to communicate. On a certain level, we understood each other perfectly.

The night, the heater, the music, and the eternal movie outside our wide screen bound us tighter together. I was continually surprised by the evolving tour of the town and environs. As we progressed, I marveled at Boyd's keen perception of me and of Westwater. He presented it to me in a logical sequence that surprised and delighted me at every turn. There was no need for spoken communication. The air was charged with our energy.

After hours, days, minutes, eternities, we ended up back at the VFW hall. It was dark and empty. I thought of the weeded lot in the back, and so did Boyd. But it was dark and empty, too. And so was the shell of the lad that lay therein.

Boyd slowed to a stop in the middle of the deserted

street, and looked at the building through his window. Then he rolled his window down a little way, and a frigid lick of air blew in, shattering the mood. He seemed to gather himself up with a shudder, and spoke for the first time that night.

"Out of gas," he said.

I looked at the gas gauge. The red needle rested on the empty mark.

He turned to me and looked right into me, then drew back and smiled.

"Where do you live?"

I told him.

"I never believed in soul mates or reincarnation or any of that hype, never did, thought it was all baloney, until that night. And then when Angelina and I started to talk, I recognized her. I don't mean her face, or her body, or anything, but her soul. I recognized her soul. Now I don't know how that could be, but it's true. We knew each other so well, inside and out, that we drove around—you know, after the dance?—we drove around in the truck all night long. Westwater had never looked shabbier to me. I guess I knew then that I'd be leaving, and that kind of added to the excitement.

"It was an exciting evening, all right, at least for me. We drove around until the gas stations were all closed and I had barely enough gas to get home. And we never said a word to each other. It was like the night was just so magic; it was like we were sealed in a cell together, just staring out at the world together, watching this incredibly bizarre movie of the world around us, a little microcosm of society, and we were separate from it all. We were together: No, together is not exactly the right word, we were more like one with each other in a purely gut-level sense. Soul mates, I guess, is the only way to describe it.

"When I dropped her off, I told her I'd pick her up the next night at eight, and then I drove home.

"It was funny. My whole life emptied out right there onto her driveway when she got out of the truck. On the way home, I somehow knew that not only had we known each other in the past, but *that our paths would cross many times in the future. I was already impatient. I wanted to get her and sit down with her and talk for years, and maybe uncover that ... what is it? An attraction? I don't think so. And yet when we had the chance, when we were together that night, there were no words for us. We didn't have anything to say. We were beyond words, somehow.*

"Yet the passion remained. A passion to know her, because somehow I felt that she had a lot to teach me about myself. Almost as if she were my other half."

II

I slept all the next day, until sundown, when the ringing of the phone awoke me. Again, it was Lewis. Again, he professed his love for me, but this time, I didn't respond. I *couldn't* respond. In light of the new love that had touched me—a deep love, an eternal love—I couldn't respond to Lewis's shallow words. My silence worried him and he threatened to return immediately. I had to think quickly, to assure him that I had been distracted for the moment, and that he should stay as long as he was needed. I was fine and would be fine, and anxiously awaited his return.

It troubled me to lie like that to him. To Lewis.

I wandered into the living room and sat on the plastic sofa, grateful to Lewis for waking me up in time to watch the darkness surround the house and fill the sky. The music played a mantra of calm, and time slipped away as I began to meditate, realigning myself, coming into balance with the eternal, and the next thing I knew, it was seven-thirty and I had to be quick to make ready for Boyd.

He arrived promptly at eight, dressed much as he was the night before, in jeans, plaid-flannel shirt, and corduroy jacket with tan Stetson. He stood uncomfortably inside the door of Lewis's house, and the sight of him there horrified me. Boyd did not belong in a house like this. He belonged in a barn, in a rustic ranch, in a little cozy den of some kind, next to a campfire maybe, but never in a quasi-modern, up-and-coming, awaiting-appreciation tract home.

I hurried to the hall, opened the coat closet, then paused. Feeling a little bit strange, I opened the linen closet and took from it a blue-flowered towel and draped it over my shoulders before putting on the sheepskin jacket that I had worn the night before.

In two steps, Boyd was helping me with the jacket, and he asked, "Why the towel?"

I paused again before answering him, because I didn't know exactly how to respond. I wanted to pour all of it out to him, all about my mission, my place of calm, the feelings that were mine when I lived up to my potential. But I dared not. Then I wanted to explain about the meditations, and how sometimes I heard voices in my ear, and sometimes I just instinctively knew things, and one of the instinctive things I knew was that tonight I should have a towel around my shoulders. But that explanation sounded crazy in my head before the words got out.

So instead I said, "This jacket is too big and sometimes the cold goes up my sleeves and settles on top of my shoulders." He smiled at this, as if he understood my deception.

The truck was still warm. I climbed in the passenger side by myself, and could feel Boyd smiling behind me as he watched me hurry to do it; to establish once and for all that I was able to care for myself, that he needn't lift me in and out like a child. The solid door closed behind me and I centered myself on the bench seat as he walked around the front and got in. When he shut his door, the familiar space closed about us and all my anxieties fled. We sat in the silence, in the darkness, for a long time. Then he reached up, fired the ignition, and turned on lights, heater, and radio in that same grooved motion. I was fond of it already.

Acceleration pressed me to the seat as we escaped Lewis's neighborhood.

I resisted the impulse to ask where we were going. I knew that I could trust Boyd, that he would find something for us to do that would be mutually pleasurable. As we drove toward town, I began to pick up a difference about him, a bit of emptiness. There swirled about his head a trouble, so I sat next to him in the warm cab and tried to ease the space around us.

Eventually, he spoke, his deep voice startling in the confined area. I knew Boyd's silent conversation; his speaking voice was foreign to my ears. I took a moment to digest the sound before what he said had any meaning. And then I was quite shocked.

"A kid was murdered at the dance last night," he said.

Murdered!

"But we were the last to leave," I said.

"I know. He was out back, in the vacant lot. It's an old weedy place where some of the kids go to drink or smoke or fool around. I spent all afternoon with Julie, his girlfriend. They'd gone back there to make love and had a big fight, and the next thing we know, he's dead. Had his throat torn out. The sheriff thinks there's a wild dog or something on the loose. Same thing got a biker kid out by Jane's Cafe on Thursday night."

Murder, he said. Murder. The word careened off the interior walls of my skull and I was unable to think of anything else. Murder. The word went around and around; I could almost see it as it passed across the back of my eyeballs. Murder. My mind caught on the snag and repeated it and repeated it until it was a meaningless assortment of sounds. Murder.

I hadn't murdered the lad at all. I had loved him. I had loved him totally and completely, with my entire body and soul. I had loved him to his reward, to his peace. He's away from that spiteful wench, they had not gone there to make love, she had lured him there to break his heart. Somehow, I knew the essence of her character. The boy had seen through her, but he had been in love with the idea of love. He wanted so much to be able to love her. Now he has real love. Now he's at peace; he has his eternal resting place deep in the bosom of the place of calm. What right have they to use that terrible word—murder?

And by a wild dog! My work was clean that night. I tidied up with a towel, and left him clean and respectable. How *dare* they! My face flushed red and hot, and I shoved my hands deep into the jacket pockets. I dared not speak, for I knew that my voice would shake with indignation.

The silence fell around us again, but the air in the truck was different. It was tinged with anger—mine—and Boyd's sorrow. Finally I could stand it no longer. I had to know more.

"Did you know him?" I couldn't keep the tremor from my voice.

"Not well. Knew who he was. Knew his girl, Julie. She's a real nice kid, but of course she thinks it's all her fault. The guilt is eating her alive."

And so it should, I thought.

"Dan was my brother's age. Bill knew him pretty well. In the same class and all."

Boyd turned down the main street and pulled the truck into a parking space in front of the Ford dealership. He killed the engine, then turned in the seat to look at me. For the first time, I noticed a brown spot on the iris of his right eye. It was a little dab of brown, right atop the pupil of his green eye. It gave him a curious look, it was a focal point, a very individual characteristic. I wanted to sit and look at it forever, look deeply into his eyes and learn more about Dan's death and its repercussions in the community, learn more about Boyd and his gentleness, but he lifted his hand toward my face, which alarmed me in my suddenly paranoid state, and I jumped back.

"Hey," he smiled. "Relax." Then a gentle forefinger stroked my cheek and my chin. His voice was soft and

mesmerizing. "C'mon. Let's go see a movie. I need a laugh."
He came closer. The rim of his hat caught the light from the
string of bulbs over the used-car lot and cast a deepening
shadow over his eyes. "Come laugh with me," he said as he
turned his head, and very gently, his lips brushed my cheek.
His cologne was strong and deep—a very basic scent, quite
opposite the light, almost feminine stuff Lewis used.

He backed away and the shadow receded and I saw the
pain in his eyes, and the question just fell from my lips,
"Why do you hurt so?"

"Because he was so young," Boyd said, almost whispering, his hurting eyes looking directly into my own. "Because
he had so much to look forward to in life. Because he was
robbed of all of the pleasures of growing up and getting
married and having kids and a career. And because we've
all been robbed of having him and his kids around. Danny
was a good guy. He would have been a good man, a good
citizen, an asset. And now some senseless thing has . . ." He
turned away from me and gripped the steering wheel. "Do
you want to go to the movies or not?"

I could see that I had upset him, I could hear it in his
voice, feel it in the air, but I could not stop myself now. This
was too intriguing.

"Maybe it was right for him to die."

Boyd's eyes blazed at me. "That's a lot of fundamentalist
crap. People have been saying that to me, you know. 'God
works in mysterious ways,' and 'Somehow it's all for the
best.' That's all a bunch of crap. The God I know doesn't go
around ripping the throats out of kids."

I laid a hand on his jacketed shoulder. The cold was
beginning to penetrate the cab. "Don't you think that sometimes people bring things on themselves?"

"What the hell is the matter with you? Don't you
understand?"

My face flushed hot in reflection of his sudden anger.

"A boy's throat was ripped out by wild dogs last night

while we were inside dancing and having a good time. I spent all day with his girlfriend, who was wearing a diamond ring that his mother found in his dresser. He was going to give it to her for Christmas. It's December eighteenth today. I say that's a fine Christmas for a lot of people. And you're sitting here telling me that probably because Julie got a little pushy with him out in the vacant lot, when he saw the monster he said, 'Here, doggy, doggy'?" He pounded the steering wheel, the aura of his grief smelling sour. "You're a pretty unfeeling person, Angelina. I thought I had you pegged, but now I don't know."

"I'm not unfeeling, Boyd, I'm just detached. I'm trying to find a perspective here. I'm sure there's a larger picture, if only we'll . . ."

"No. I've found my reason. We've got a hunting party set to go at midnight tonight. We're going to track that thing down and blow it to bits."

It was my turn to recoil in horror. Boyd grinned at me when he said that, grinned without mirth, grinned with the bloodthirsty grimace of a death's head. Of course. He was a hunter. A hunter.

And so was I.

I opened the door and jumped to the sidewalk, to the harsh brightness of the used-car lot. The theater marquee spilled light over the opposite side of the street, and a line was beginning to form at the door.

Boyd jumped out and ran around the truck to me, but I turned from him and walked away.

He hunted for pleasure, for sport, for recreation. He found beautiful wild animals and killed them. I hunted for pain. I found the confused, the hurting, the oppressed, and I loved them into death, into peace, into calm, into eternity. And I was hated and he commended.

"Angelina." I heard his heavy steps behind me, and one big hand caught at the shoulder of my jacket. He spun me around. "Angelina?" The brown spot over his iris looked at me and I saw it as a bull's-eye. "Please. I'll drive you home." I shook his hand off and began walking again. "Please. It's dangerous!" I continued to walk, trying to stomp a little bit, make my steps a little louder on the concrete, wishing I was larger and heavier and not so laughably petite.

I pushed my hands into my jacket pockets, steeling myself for a long, cold walk home. It would be good for me. The early night air chilled me into shivers. I felt vibrant and alive.

My feet took me down the main street, toward the seedier side of town. Prostitutes stood about on the corners, most of them scantily clad. If they were fortunate, a heated car would pull to the curb and they would climb in with a paying customer. If not, they would wobble on their high heels into a heated barroom, where they would warm their knees and try to stir up some activity inside. It was hard weather for hookers, especially this close to Christmas.

I sauntered past them, ignoring their glares, ignoring the noisy warmth that exploded onto the street every time a saloon door opened, ignored the long dirty boys who stood passing plastic packets between themselves, ignored the short-haired men in uniform who made rude comments as they roamed the streets in packs.

I noticed these things merely as peripheral details. My mind was busy with Boyd as I walked down the gritty sidewalk, past the adult bookstores and peep shows.

As I walked, I recounted our conversation in the truck. I tried to make sense of it. I tried to find a thread of reason to pull the conversation together. Boyd and I were too close; we were too much of the same fabric. We were like identical pieces of cloth from different dye lots; they are too different to match, yet too close to contrast. It was a peculiar situation. I could understand his point of view. At least, I could comprehend understanding it. Boyd would not allow my point of view at all.

Not at all.

Who is he to disallow my opinion? For some reason, my

indignation snapped up this rationalization for resentment and began to nurture it. By the time I was deep into the hollowed and empty downtown area of Westwater, I was burning with a furious rage at Boyd and his brother and the sniveling wimp Julie and the entire posse they had arranged to track and mutilate Dan's killer. If only they knew. If only they knew. If only . . .

Maybe I should volunteer to go with them.

Don't get too crazy, Angelina, I told myself. Let's not go off the deep end here.

I had to stop and look at myself in a storefront reflection. I looked at my diminutive stature, my tiny little face and features, my short-cut blonde hair, and I thought of stalking the stalkers who beat through the bush trying to scare up a crazed coyote. The thought made me smile in spite of my rage, and sanity again flooded in. Forget it, Angelina, I told my reflection. My mirrored self nodded back and I resumed walking.

But, as is the way with many resentments, my mind would not let it go. By the time I had walked out of downtown, passed the library, and was headed toward the bus station, my chest was knotted again and my temperature was rising. I began to run to burn excess energy.

Hands in pockets, I trotted past the bus station, past Jane's, feeling the cold air rasp at my throat as my breathing came harder from the unaccustomed exertion. It felt wonderful. I crossed the freeway into Lewis's subdivision and turned left instead of right toward Lewis's house. I wasn't ready to go home yet, I wanted to continued to run, to run faster and harder, to wear out all the built-up tensions, resentments, and anger. My feet pounding the pavement became the only sound, a hypnotizing rhythm, almost like my meditations, and softly the music came and my feet landed lightly, and the place of peace, it was there, just ahead, just out of reach; it glittered tantalizingly just ahead. Why not try it Boyd's way for once, Angelina, the music said. Don't be too spiteful until you've seen his entire point of view. Understanding lay just ahead.

Just ahead was a man walking his dog. He was in the middle of the field that bordered the outer row of houses. He had walked down a mown path, and without breaking stride, my feet light, my speed incredible, I ran, I almost flew down the path, and in slow motion, I saw him hesitate, and turn, saw the dog cower, the look on the man's face, then I heard the wildcat scream, the scream of victory, of bravery, of competence, of exhultation.

And I brought down my kill.

The dog ran off, growling and snarling, and came back as I finished. I stood and backed away from the man and looked down on him—my first kill purely for pleasure. The dog licked the man's cold, wrinkled face with sidelong glances at me, then found the leaking wound. The mutt's brow furrowed and he began to whimper, forgetting all about me as he lapped at his owner's flaccid neck. He worried the wound a bit with his teeth, chewing gingerly on the edges with his little ineffectual front teeth, and I chased him away, then brought the towel from across my shoulders and covered the man with it.

Then I put one boot atop the man's chest and looked to the sky in a great dramatic urge. I brought my arms up as if to embrace the cold night sky with its zillion sparkling stars, and I shouted to them. "I see now, Boyd! I understand! You and I are two of a kind!" And then I laughed, because Boyd had yet to learn this. And I laughed again, knowing that the pleasures of the universe, the delights of eternity, belonged to me.

I tucked the towel around the man's neck, just above the beaver collar on his coat, like a muffler. I feinted at the dog one more time, clapping my hands to chase him off, and then I walked back home to Lewis's little house, where I showered and fell into bed, wondering at the pleasure of the kill, wondering who it was I was trying to please.

"I was pretty keyed up that night. I'd been sitting all day long with Julie, while she cried and rubbed that diamond on her finger, and also, I was anticipating the hunt that night. I was pretty tense.

"Angelina was pretty young, too, when you think about it. She was only about . . . well, I don't know, but she was young. Just a kid, actually. If I hadn't been so keyed up, I probably would have noticed that and cut her a little slack. But I didn't. I didn't.

"So we argued. It's hard to say exactly what it was we were arguing about, but she ended up jumping out of the truck and taking off down the street. I tried to stop her, but she's pretty stubborn. I can get that stubborn, so I knew when to give up. There wouldn't be any changing her mind.

"See, this is where I have trouble. Sometimes you find orphaned pups—foxes, coyotes—and they make good pets, because they're young enough. But there comes a time in the life of a wild pup when it's too old to tame, and trying to keep it is just a waste. I keep thinking that maybe if I hadn't let her go . . . she was still so young . . . Then again, maybe it was my instincts that told me she was already past that point.

"That was the last I saw of her for a long time. Things got pretty busy around town, I hardly had time to think about her, although she was never out of my thoughts. I even drove by that house a couple of times. Anyway, I was helping out the sheriff, doing a little footwork for him on the case, and that's when, you know, when I got the word about the towel, Jesus, the towel, and then I knew. I couldn't believe it, that's why I didn't tell anybody else. But I knew. That's when I seriously started trying to find her. It took a long time. But I found her."

12

I soared from dizzying heights to stomach-clenching depths in great sweeping glides. Wind washed my face and some flimsy chiffon garment tickled my skin into goose bumps. I flew over mountains and hills, looked down upon cemeteries and churches, little towns with their tangles of wires atop toy poles. I looked up and saw the night on the other side of the daylight; it was always there, patient, comforting, lending support and guidance. It was my security, my safety. I knew I could not fall.

The daylight began to ring. This was a wrong sound, harsh, flat against my flight's sweeping, soaring musical accompaniment. The air became thick and hard to glide through as the shrill bells poisoned the music. My body shuddered and twitched in uncomfortable resonance. I wished for the darkness, for the light to go away, and I swooped down, searching the countryside for sign of a cave, a hideout, even a valley with shade.

But the daylight was fading, I was fading, and then I was on the ground, pulling tufts of ... sheets to my chin, and I opened my eyes and Lewis's telephone on the bedstand rang again.

I sat up, stomach queasy, uncomfortable, cleared my throat several times, then picked up the receiver. I noticed dusk descending around the house. Again, I had slept through the day.

"Angelina?" It was Lewis.

"Hello," I said.

"Where have you been all day? I've called and called. Out having fun?"

"No, I've been here. The phone hasn't rung."

"Oh. Well, maybe there's been some trouble on the line. Listen, I'm coming home tomorrow. God, I can't wait to see you."

"Tomorrow?"

"Yeah. I'll be leaving here mid-morning, so I should be there late afternoon."

"How's your father?"

"He's doing fine. He's got some good friends here, so he'll be all right. I just can't wait to see you. God, I've missed you so much."

I was silent.

"Angelina?"

"Yes?"

"Are you all right?"

"Of course."

"Have you missed me?"

"Yes, Lewis, I have."

"Well, get a good night's sleep tonight, sweetheart. I'll see you tomorrow."

"Okay."

"Bye, love."

"Good-bye."

I hung up the phone. Lewis would be home tomorrow. I tried to luxuriate in a cat-like stretch, but anxiety nibbled at the edges of my consciousness. I had enjoyed Boyd, enjoyed the bus station, enjoyed my freedom, and now Lewis was coming home to put an end to it.

I plumped the pillow and pulled the sheet up over me again, feeling vaguely wrong for sleeping all day long. Mother would never approve.

The clock said five-thirty, winter dusk was deepening. Odd that the phone had not worked all day. Must have been a problem at the main station, a neighborhood-wide outage that had just been fixed.

Surely I could not have slept through the ringing.

I closed my eyes and thought about Lewis coming home. He would want me to submit to sex with him again, something that interested me not at all. I had changed in the days since Lewis had been gone. I felt anxiety about his return, the same anxiety I felt as a schoolgirl, as if I were going to class to take a test for which I felt I was not prepared.

Lewis had standards, requirements.

He would want me to be home every night.

My anxiety turned to anger. Again, I had allowed myself to become enmeshed with responsibilities. Now I had to cut loose from this restrictive web. I had no desire to submit to any test, any scrutiny. I would have to leave him; the only question was when.

Darkness deepened outside, and I became wide awake and restless. My freedom drew nigh, the decision was made: I would soon be traveling again, alone, unburdened. Yet for now, I had to wait. I had to wait.

I went to the kitchen, feeling leaden and sad.

Lewis would be home tomorrow. The phrase continued to run through my mind. Each time I paused in my mundane chores—dusting, cleaning the bathroom, vacuuming—the words would zing through my brain and anxiety would follow on their heels.

I ran out of busy work at nine o'clock. The two living-room lamps emitted a yellow light that reflected weirdly from the dark-black picture window in Lewis's front room. I paced. I sat on the edge of his couch. I paced. I sat. I felt stiff, wound tight. My hands pulled and twisted on each other, fighting a war in my lap.

Lewis would be home tomorrow.

I wanted to go out. Into the darkness. I wanted to surrender myself to it, give myself up to the strangeness, the altered side of my personality that came so alive after sunset.

I wanted to go find Boyd, to see if they had tracked and killed anything that they could calmly blame for the deaths.

Boyd.

I wanted to see Boyd. I *ached* to see Boyd.

My hands fell apart and lay on my thighs like two broken birds.

Boyd.

I leaned back into Lewis's stiff couch and closed my eyes. I remembered being in the cab of Boyd's truck, snugly bookended by the brothers. The scratchy feel of the forced hot air, the music on the radio, the spotless windshield . . . I remembered his smell, woodsy and alert.

I remembered our fight.

My fingernails dug deeply into my palms as a jabbing nausea fired up behind my breastbone. It would not take long for Boyd to discover who was responsible for those deaths.

I began to pace again. Just below the surface, feelings were prodding me, poking, trying to get through. New emotional plateaus were about to be reached in my upward climb to adulthood.

Boyd was the only one who understood me. He was the only one who could leash my passions.

I wanted Boyd—

Dear God, I wanted Boyd to stop me.

With this thought, my breath whooshed out of me as if I had been kicked. My stomach cramped and I fell to my knees. After a few moments the pain eased and I made my way back to the couch, feeling frail and delicate. I lay down, suppressing urges to bolt. Compelling urges born of panic insisted that I pack my bag and leave Lewis's house that very night. "Go," my insides said, "without even packing a bag." As soon as that thought was clear in my mind, it was replaced by another that said, "Go to the bus station. Entertain yourself." And another devil on my shoulder said, "Find someone in need."

My body seemed to throb with each new idea, but it would not respond with action. I felt bloated and heavy, as if the excesses of the past three nights had finally wreaked havoc with my internal system.

I closed my eyes, and laid my flushed cheek against the cool plastic of the couch. I was hoping to sleep, hoping to bypass the maddening internal dialogue that I knew would plague me as long as I denied myself the darkness.

I closed my eyes and began to search for a place inside, the meditation place, the one place that had aided me before. I heard the music, the beautiful music, and the yammering inside my head was stilled.

I listened to the music, relaxed into the meditation,

swayed back and forth with the rhythm. Just as I felt centered again, the music parted and I heard Her voice, the clear, beautiful female voice that spoke with delicious lips right next to my ear. The voice was crisp and cool like a mountain stream, and the words massaged my heart and I melted into them. She said,

"It is time, Angelina. Come. Follow me."

I saw a wisp of something ethereal slip down the corridor of my mind, and I followed.

I awoke at three-thirty in the morning. The night was waning and I felt in need of a bath. My confining clothes had left imprints on my sticky skin. I stretched some, then drew a hot tub and soaked a long time while I pondered. I remembered little of my meeting with Her. I knew only the feelings.

I watched the bath water lap at the edges of my body as I examined the feelings, pulling up one after another. The most potent came first. It centered in my solar plexus, it jittered in my stomach and at the bottom of my throat. I recognized it as something secret, something fun, something just a tad naughty, something not to tell our parents, but to giggle over in our bedrooms, with the doors closed and the lights out. At night.

She and I had a secret, but I didn't know what it was.

The second feeling was of responsibility. I could feel slight tension in my shoulders and I knew I had made a commitment, possibly a lifetime agreement. With that feeling was another . . . a feeling of security.

I would serve Her and she would care for me.

With these feelings came a new freedom. I could relax. I had only to carry out my assigned tasks. I felt lighter and freer than I ever had. Life would be easier from now on. I would be told where to go and when. I had no urgencies, no worries. I had an important mission, and as a Chosen One, I was here at Lewis's for a purpose. I would be told when to leave.

Lewis would be home tomorrow.

I poured more lavender skin softener into the bath and began to scrub and shave.

I would be leaving Lewis. But not quite yet.

LEWIS GREGORY: "I got home about four in the afternoon and she was asleep in the bedroom. At first I thought she was drunk, or drugged or something. I couldn't wake her up. I shook her and slapped her a little bit, gently, you know, not hard or anything. I really started to get scared. She was barely breathing. When I put a cold washcloth on her forehead, her eyelids flickered a little bit, and I got a few sounds out of her. I checked the medicine cabinets, and the kitchen, and couldn't find anything she could have eaten, or taken, that would do this to her, so I just kind of waited. I brought my suitcase in and sat down and watched her. And slowly she woke up. She just woke up. Jeez, I've seen heavy sleepers before, but . . .

"By five-thirty, she was pretty aware, and by dinnertime she was active and nervous. It was strange. It was like watching something . . . regenerate. A flicker of the eyelids, and then slow, groggy movement, and finally awareness. It was strange. Reptilian, I guess you'd say.

"I was tired from driving, and by nine, I was ready to go to bed. She said she wasn't, and stayed up all night watching television, I think. Anyway, in the early morning hours, I felt her crawl into bed with me. When the alarm went off at six-thirty, I tried to wake her up, I was . . . you know . . . glad to see her, but she was out again.

"I'd never seen anyone sleep like that before. She didn't sleep like that before I left for California. I had time to get used to it, though, because it never changed. Up all night watching television, asleep all day long. She slept right through Christmas Day. New Year's, too. I'd be up half the night just trying to be with her . . . I got so run down, I almost got fired.

"I loved her very much, but she'd changed. She was too different. And I loved her for staying as long as she did, after I just lost my mom and all. When it was time for her to go, we both knew it."

13

I stayed with Lewis for a little over two weeks after he returned from California. Those weeks were very difficult for both of us. I wanted Boyd. I wanted to hear him, to see him, to touch him. At times I imagined I saw his truck drive by outside Lewis's house as I sat alone at night, the television chattering mindlessly into the empty room. The television was on for Lewis, a special effect so he might be comforted, thinking I was being entertained.

I was not entertained. I was tortured. All night long I paced the front room, waiting . . . waiting. I would meditate for hours, delving into the internal music, losing myself in that peaceful place, but the longer I kept myself imprisoned at night—confined to Lewis's dreadful living room—the less frequently I could locate that place where I mentally soaked my feet and renewed my strength. I hated staying there, yet I was not ready to leave. My emotions and, undoubtedly, Lewis's were in constant, painful turmoil.

And then one evening when I awoke, it was time to go. I believed that mysterious forces had been busy, the delay had been fruitful; arrangements had been made, contacts had been activated, the path had been cleared. My prudent behavior in waiting would be rewarded. This Truth rang true. There was a power in the music, a power in the universe. The forces that controlled all things reassured me that I truly owned my own place in the world. As different as I might be, my niche had been gently carved and prepared.

I dined with Lewis that night, then held his hands and looked into his eyes. All my will focused right there, at that moment, wishing for a happy and fulfilling life for Lewis. He was a good man. I wished for rapid appreciation on his home, and a wife and sons to keep his level of respectability right where he felt most comfortable.

No words were necessary between us. We hugged, then I packed. I declined his offer of a ride to the bus station, but took the offered sheepskin jacket and a hundred dollars.

At the door we kissed, and I stepped down the walk, then down the sidewalk, willing myself not to look back and not to run, but to walk calmly. I heard Lewis's front door close behind me, and I had a moment of sadness as I imagined him entering his lonesome living room with the plastic couch and orange carpeting and the little touches of life he and I had bought when times were better between us.

But that tiny moment passed, and the door had shut, severing the cords that bound me to him, and suddenly my feet were free, my breath came clear and strong, and I jumped into the air as high as I could and fairly skipped through the cold, clear air of Westwater, flying with the freedom of the newly unburdened. Again I resolved, no more entanglements. I had a commitment, one comfortable commitment, a tightly bound agreement that anchored my soul to the forces that be, and that one was enough.

I heard my boot heels echo off the exterior walls of the houses, and then the buildings, as my stride took me confidently toward the bus station, where I bought a bus ticket to a warmer clime.

"When Angelina left Westwater, I knew it. I felt her drawing away from me as if she were draining out my life. The attraction between us was more powerful than anything I'd ever heard of. I tried to keep busy—I tried to go hunting, I tried to work, but she'd ruined me. She'd ruined me. I felt that if we could just sit down and talk, if I could really just talk to her, to find out more about her and the way she thought, then maybe I could let her go her own way.

"But she was too damned different. I'd known some different people before, but Angelina was different in a way that was so opposite that we matched. Like two halves of something torn apart, the terrain of her soul seemed exactly the opposite of my own. And I thought we would fit together, if we could, and make a whole.

"When I thought about her sitting right there next to me in the truck, after killing those people, and then trying to tell me that maybe Danny had asked for it, at first I was furious. I mean, how dare she? And then I was amazed that she could do that. Kill someone, I mean, and be curious about people's reactions, instead of remorseful. Curious! Shit. I've felt funny about shooting a rabbit for dinner ever since Dad and Kyle and Bill hung up their shotguns. And then I was a little afraid. Afraid for the others out there, afraid, in retrospect, that maybe she could have killed me, right there in front of the movie theater. And wrapped a towel around my neck. Or in that field instead of old Mr. Simpson. But I knew she would never kill me. She would never kill me.

"And then I was lonely. I was lonely for whatever it was that she sucked out of me when she left, leaving an empty hole in my gut. I just wanted to sit her down and talk to her for a while. For my own sanity.

"So, you see, I had all kinds of motives for trying to track her down. I believed I was the only one who could. I guess I still believe that."

14

There were only three other passengers on the bus, and it pulled into the darkness while I slid into a depression. I felt as if I had been suspended in a colorless, odorless solution. The bus nosed its way toward the freeway, then picked up speed, carrying me away from Westwater, away from Boyd.

I shrugged up my shoulders until the padded shell of overcoat arose about my ears, and I pressed the back of my hand to the fogged window as telephone poles whipped past in the night. My pack was on the seat next to me. A black soldier smoked a foul-smelling cigarette in the very rear seat; a middle-aged woman dozed in the safe seat directly behind the driver. The cavernous emptiness of our passenger tube echoed around me. This was not how freedom was supposed to feel.

I thought momentarily about Lewis. He and I were surely members of different species. I had great respect for Lewis; I admired his ideals, his drive, the all-around tidiness of his affairs, but there was nothing the two of us had in common at all. Nothing at all.

My mind was filled with Boyd, my whole being was filled with Boyd. He pulled on me like the tides. I thought I needed to escape him, to get farther away, and farther still, out of his range of influence.

But that was silly. The influence was in me, not in him, not in the air. Nevertheless, the pull was real, and I felt it all night long.

Dawn soothed the desert and I had just enough energy left to admire it before I nodded off. I slept through the day and awakened at twilight, refreshed, alive and tired of the bus. I disembarked at the next rest stop and took a look at Red Creek, New Mexico. Impulsively, I told the driver he would be going on without me. I washed up in the cafeteria facilities and had a bite to eat before hitching up my pack and heading back out to the road.

The blacktop stretched forever in both directions. I had no need to imagine which way we had come. To the northwest lay Westwater. Its force still pulled on me. I began walking east, the sound of my boots a comforting, familiar sound on the shoulder of the road. I had not known I had mourned that sound until now; there was no other sound like it.

I took long, rapid strides in the early evening air, getting my energy up, pumping hot blood through my muscles. I breathed deeply and swung my arms. It felt good. The flush of freedom was beginning to come back again; maybe I had snapped the string that held me to Westwater, had finally outrun the magnetic influence.

The moon rose over the low hills; there was barely any traffic. The desert gleamed in the moonshine. I walked down the middle of the deserted road, tapping out a pattern with my boot heels, feeling the light of the moon bathing me in its cool warmth as it gleamed off the wide stripe of road ahead. I imagined I was walking down a canal, clicking my heels along on top of the water.

My thoughts returned to Boyd. What made him so different from Lewis? I wasn't thinking about individual differences, like hair color and tastes in furniture. I meant *fundamental* differences—the way I was different from my classmates, the way I was different from everybody else. Boyd had that difference as well. He and I were different from each other, yet there was some common . . . there was something similar . . .

We were in the vast minority, Boyd and I. Most people were basically the same, showing healthy expressions of their individual differences. They married, had best friends, served on committees, and played bridge. All those activities seemed so foreign, their motivations so alien, to me.

My freedom fled. Frustration loomed before me, showing me an eternal search, a quest as hopeless as that for the Holy Grail. I would search for inner peace, for a common bond, normalcy, and never find any of it. It seemed my destiny was to be a futile search for answers to questions that were barely asked.

My frustration seemed as endless as the road that stretched before me, silvery and shining in the moonlight. As endless as the path of my life, as endless as the fence that stretched alongside the road, as endless as the herd of sheep that bedded on the other side of the fence.

As soon as I conceived the idea, blood raced to each capillary in my body. My whole being flushed. It had been weeks. Weeks. Suddenly, right here, was an antidote to my frustration. I could feel the relief already, creeping in around the edges. How could I have ever forgotten? The music was my companionship, my eternal friend. I needed only to evoke it.

I jumped the fence and caught up a lamb from next to its mother. I ripped at it furiously and drank, knowing at the time that it tasted wrong, it tasted . . . bad, but I was helpless to stop myself.

When I was finished, I was disgusted with my behavior. There was no relief in the act at all. I found the sheep's trough and washed myself, noticing the thick medicinal smell in the water and then the official quarantine sign posted nearby. I noticed how oddly calm the entire flock seemed to be. They had hardly reacted, even as the little one bleated in the face of its death. I had thought it peculiar how little noise and struggle the lamb had put up—and there was none at all from its mother. I found myself faintly amused but too wrapped up in my own loneliness to pay much attention. I washed and anticipated the sleepiness—and the music, the heavenly music—that always accompanied a kill. It didn't come.

A mile farther down the road, the sickness struck. I vomited until there was nothing left, and still I heaved. By sunrise, my eyes had swollen shut and my fingers were as thick as stuffed sausages. I could barely lift my head. I lay in a shady dry drainage ditch all day, feeling my skin stretch tighter and tighter until I thought it would pop, thirst overwhelming me, waiting to die.

As evening cooled the air, I felt slightly better, and by moonrise I could stand. I propped myself against a signpost, and when a car finally came along, I staggered to the side of the road. It was a young woman with a child. She stopped for me. When she saw my face in the interior light of her car, she gasped, then took me home with her, fed me, bathed me, and put me to bed.

Her name was Sarah.

I stayed with her for three days while the allergic reaction to the medicated lamb passed. The opening of her home to me was an act of charity and selflessness that was to follow me for a long, long time.

Sarah Monroe. She was a swarthy-skinned, tightly muscled dance instructor. Sarah lived with Samuel, her three-year-old son, in a tiny one-bedroom house. The boy's large brown eyes were curious and questioning, calm and patient; I had never before met such a child.

The first night, I slept. I woke frequently, but the illness was still with me, and I soon slipped back into the healing sleep my body demanded.

I slept until nightfall, when Sarah came home from work. She encouraged me to sit up and talk.

This was my first real view of Sarah, Samuel, and their environment. Her house was furnished with Indian-print cloths as wall hangings, window covers, bedspreads—one even billowed down from the ceiling. The brightly patterned cloths comprised her wardrobe as well. She wrapped them around her body and her short dark hair in comfortable fashion. The effect was slightly claustrophobic, but colorful and lively. Pillows of all sizes and descriptions were scattered about the carpeted floor and piled into mounds in the corner. Shelves of raw wood were separated by bricks; these shelves were filled with books on dance, movement, therapy, and mysticism. In one corner of the small living room was a mattress, neatly covered with a flowered fabric.

Sarah looked like an exotic mix of nationalities. I watched her move about her tiny kitchen as she brewed tea for us. She propped me up against the wall, helped me get comfortable; Samuel sat on the mattress and quietly watched us. His eyes were the same dark color as hers.

Sarah unwound her sarong to reveal a yellow leotard and tights. She sat on the carpeting in the middle of the room and began stretching exercises. I'd never seen anything so beautiful or fascinating in my life.

As she worked, she talked. She was thirty-four, taught dance in the high school, movement in the preschool, and spent two afternoons a week with the elderly in town, giving them gentle exercises to keep the ravages of age to a minimum. On Saturdays she helped in the physical-therapy clinic.

The local high school had put on a dance exhibition four years earlier and Sarah's classes had danced, and so had Sarah. She danced with an invited guest: a handsome boy from San Francisco, who had come to dance and left behind a child growing in her womb.

"It was quite a scandal," Sarah laughed as she lowered her throat to one knee, fingers gracefully holding one foot.

She spoke of raising a son, of teaching high school girls; with sidelong glances at my reactions, spoke of her love of life and the freedom of commitment to one's own beliefs.

I could follow her for only moments at a time, and then my mind would sprint away, chasing a thought or an idea, and upon returning, the topic would be different and I would have to pretend I was following, until I caught up and she said something else that sent me running after a new concept.

It was exhausting work. I slumped in the corner, sick, still feverish, weak and unhappy, while in front of me a healthy, happy, well-adjusted woman exercised with a flushed face and a feminine sheen of perspiration covering her face and chest. She stopped and looked at me.

"Drink your tea," she said. "It will help you heal."

With a clap of thunder in my bowels, I realized I was not only different—I was inferior. I drank my tea and weakly made my way back to bed—Sarah's bed, which she had generously given up for my use. She bedded down in the front room, on the mattress, with her son.

On the third day, we followed the same routine—I slept through the day and arose at dusk, when she came home from work. I reclined against pillows, and Samuel sat on his mattress and we both watched his mother end her professional day stretching. Only this time, because I was obviously better, Sarah began asking me of my life.

I told her lies.

She knew I lied, I could tell it by her movements, and it became a sort of a game to me, to tell her something terribly untrue and go on to the next question, my imagination taking me into strange realms. I didn't even care if my stories conflicted with one another.

Sarah stopped asking questions. Samuel turned from me and put his thumb in his mouth. It was this action that made me stop. I stood and stretched, then showered while Sarah finished her exercises. She showered then, while I tried to play with Samuel, but he only looked at me with those liquid brown eyes and made it obvious he would rather amuse himself. So I packed, feeling vague resentment and remorse. She had been so kind to me and I had only lied to her. When Sarah had finished in the bathroom, I was ready to move on.

She saw me to the door, her eyes understanding and forgiving, and said, "When you learn to be true to yourself, Angelina, let me know." I turned and walked away.

"It was at least six months, maybe closer to a year, before I got all the information about those three deaths in Westwater. When I found out the truth—like that the teeth marks were human—there was no doubt in my mind about Angelina being the one. The police were so freaked out that they concocted the wild-dog theory on the night that Danny's body was found. They thought it better that the community believe there was a pack of murderous dogs roaming the streets than a homicidal maniac. When in truth, they'd found a towel tucked neatly around his wounds. Jesus.

"I couldn't believe it, though. I mean, I knew it was true—if it was anybody, it was Angelina . . . but how could any person do something like that? God.

"Anyway, she was long gone by the time I put it all together. I

96

was the only one who could know. No one else knew her attitudes, her . . . personality twist, I guess I'd have to call it. She was just a little bit different. No one else knew about the towel. I saw it right out of her closet, and then saw it again, covered with Mr. Simpson's blood.

"I began to think about her. I wrote down everything I could remember about her, everything she said, and I began to subscribe to different newspapers, looking for something suspicious, some murder with her M.O., any lead to follow up on, any clue to her whereabouts. I stashed money and kept a suitcase packed and ready, just waiting for a lead. I slacked off at work, even took a demotion from construction foreman to flunkie so I could cut out at the whistle and go hang out at the police station. The cops kind of enjoyed the fact that I was so fascinated with the case.

"I knew that Angelina and I'd meet up again someday. And every morning when I woke up, I wondered if this would be the day, and I'd look at that suitcase waiting there by my bedroom door, and I prayed for it.

"But it didn't happen. For almost a year, I waited.

"The more I thought about her, though, the more I began to dream about her, the more my imagination got carried away. There were times when I could have sworn I was with her . . ."

15

For five months after leaving Sarah's cottage, serendipity pushed and pulled me around the West. I grew increasingly frustrated and angry over feelings for which I had no names. There were no definitions, no dividing lines, no labels for the torrents of emotion that ravaged my soul.

I knew I was special, I knew I had a purpose, a calling—but during this confusing time I hated it, hated the thought of it. I raged against God, against Nature; I thought of myself as a joke. There was nothing, *nothing*, for which I was suited.

I tried to keep on the move and away from Westwater, Nevada. It continued to haunt me; my weird attraction for Boyd continued to pull on me.

My life was a disaster. My memories of this period are foggy, like looking back through warped, smoked glass. I moved all the time, barely resting, barely eating. I dared not get caught up with anything, dared not become attached to anyone or anything. There was no joy in my life; there was no companionship. I heard no music, no words of sweetness were whispered delicately into my ear; I learned little, except about misery.

I kept thinking about Sarah and Samuel. The words "healthy" and "balanced" always came to mind. Sarah had made mistakes, even public ones, and she continued to live, work, *thrive*, in the same community. I tried to remember all the things she told me, but my shame kept interfering. I had lied to her, accepted her hospitality, and acted like a fool. Even more discouraging was the gentleness with which she let me go. She forgave me.

Someday, I thought, I will have balance. Someday I will have health, and my skin will glow like Sarah's and my eyes will shine like Samuel's. Then I will return to Red Creek, New Mexico, and thank her for the profound influence she had on me.

Someday, I thought.

In the meantime, my skin was papery, my hair lifeless, my eyes either heavy-lidded or half-vacant. I tried meditating, whenever I stopped working long enough, but there was nothing, nothing.

I must have been insane, I thought, to believe that there was someone who loved me, someone who was committed to me, someone who would take care of me.

I couldn't believe I had really killed those people. Three people. Three *people!* Three people and a lamb. And Earl Foster.

I must have been insane.

My nights were filled with bizarre nightmares. I dreamed about those three people in Westwater. I dreamed with sad tenderness about the old man's retarded daughter; I dreamed about the young boy's intended fiancée. I dreamed about the punk's mystified parents. These dreams held over into the daytime, until at times I thought of the dead as characters I would occasionally play. Their memories lived within me and occasionally I answered questions as one or the other of them. I was losing my identity. Isn't that part of insanity?

For five months after leaving Sarah's, I worked at odd jobs for cash. I either worked or traveled restlessly, compulsively, during the day, and then fell into exhausted sleep at night.

And then, late one afternoon in mid-June, I walked into Seven Slopes, Colorado. I was tired, hungry, dirty, and discouraged. Though my emotions still raged out of control, I knew it was time to release them, stop feeling sorry for myself and do something positive. Settle down.

Settling down, I realized in a flash of wisdom, didn't have to mean bondage. Again I thought of Sarah, and for the first time I understood that a routine itself could be liberating . . . If I didn't spend all my time and energy looking for a new place to sleep every night, maybe I could successfully rest, or meditate, or—heaven knows—maybe enjoy something.

At the gas station I got directions to the laundromat, then walked through the quiet little town with its Swiss-chalet shops. As I walked, I admired, and as I admired, I felt my face relax, felt the scowl fade away. Seven Slopes would probably be as perfect a home as I could find.

Suddenly a lifestyle of normalcy was the most attractive thing I could imagine. I wanted yellow kitchen curtains, just as Alice had once had.

Seven Slopes, Colorado, was nestled in a bowl where six valleys converged. The seven slopes rose dramatically on three sides of the little town, and while they were green and pleasant in June, they surely were awesome snow-skiing territory in the winter.

A winter trade would mean transient outsiders from October through April. Tourists. Where a small town might get stale after a while, outsiders would probably sate my appetite for newness, freshness, aliveness.

As I walked, I noticed that the gondola ski lifts were still operating on one slope. Summer tourists. The quiet little townspeople in the off-season probably had their noses in each other's pockets from May through September, but I could stay aloof, apart. I could have an orderly life without becoming overly involved. I could live here and enjoy the visitors. Year 'round.

I found the laundromat, and availed myself of the restroom to clean my body while the machines cleaned my clothes. When I was again tidy and refreshed, I hiked up the hillside to spend the night. I walked through waist-high grass and wildflowers, my boots kicking up a fresh, green smell. My heart felt lighter in this place; I was anxious for the morning. In the morning I would begin to settle down and make this magnificent setting my home.

I watched the sun set behind the Rockies, and felt the excitement of living. I barely had time to wonder where that excitement had been before falling asleep with the sweet smell of fresh mountain air all around me.

In the morning, I awoke to the song of the birds and the dramatic vision of the sun on the mountains.

I knew this was home. I felt it in my bones.

The apartment I could afford was a converted basement under a clothing warehouse. It was dismal, the only windows little push-out ones next to the ceiling along one side, but it had two bedrooms, a living room, bathroom and kitchen, and nondescript gray-brown carpeting throughout. The smaller bedroom and bathroom had no windows at all, but I loved the place. It was my first apartment, my first home, my first step on the road to responsible adulthood. After I paid the landlord, I walked through the empty space, touching the walls, and I felt proud.

Within the week, I had spent the last of my odd-job money scrounging the basics for my apartment—mattress, chest of drawers, linen, kitchen table, and chairs. I needed a job.

My luck was running. The first day out, I was hired as an operator for a telephone-answering service.

The weeks went by. A new life unfolded before me, and I began to understand Lewis's point of view for the first time. There was pleasure to be found in responsibility. There was pleasure—almost animalistic pleasure—in nesting and feathering one's nest. Other animalistic urges filled my dreams and much of my waking hours, but I had not forgotten the sickness with the medicated lamb, nor had I forgotten the feeling of inferiority when I sat, sick and confused, in the corner while Sarah and her perfect baby radiated such health before me.

I avoided the night. I was afraid, for the first time, of the night, of its hold over me, its relentless patience. I could see where I had been crazy once—seriously mentally ill—but I had put all that behind me. I had a chance to make a new start in life, and I was pursuing it. I had a life in the daytime; I wanted no part of the night tide that turned my mind.

I bought furnishings for my small apartment, bought new clothes for myself. I began to dress like a young lady, with nice summer dresses and jackets and slacks and tops that were becoming to my petite figure. My apartment began to assume a personality of its own, with draperies and creative use of some discarded materials and plenty of fabric. It was not fancy—it was just all mine.

The answering service consisted of five switchboards filled with message lights and holes, and we used old-fashioned cords, plugs, and headsets. I enjoyed my work, talking with the faceless population, taking messages.

Three of us worked during the peak morning and evening hours, two during the daytime, and one at night. Mrs. Gardener and her secretary worked in the office on the other side of a glass window, where they kept an eagle's eye on us.

Most surprising to me was how much I could enjoy the companionship of the girls with whom I worked. Eventually I even began to feel as one of them.

I learned to laugh.

In my off-hours, I explored the town, which seemed small only at first glance. Behind Main Street, with its facade and after-ski entertainment for the visitors, were the shopping malls and warehouses and little suburbs where the local people lived. There was little poverty. It was a pleasant place; it appealed to my latent snobbery.

One day it occurred to me that I no longer felt different. I felt like a person; I even felt that soon I would consider myself "normal." The thought even passed through my mind that one day I would erase the past and find a young man and settle down to a family. The idea made me smile. It didn't seem likely, but I felt my options widening; I felt it was important for me to leave the doors to my mind open. I was young.

I was very young.

The evenings turned cool. Soon the days shortened; the nights lengthened. I was afraid for my new lifestyle. I knew what could happen if the night took me again. I carefully guarded myself against it. At times I felt that since I would not go to the night, it was coming for me.

Strangers began to roam the streets; whole vacant areas of town opened up and made ready for the season. The answering service took on extra help, as did everyone else in town, and the air of excitement intensified. The lazy summer was over. The winter, and its attendant darkness, was about to descend.

I guardedly enjoyed it all; I enjoyed the changes in the town, in the people. I felt happier and healthier than I ever had in my life. My dreams were of normal things, I thought rarely of Boyd. I busied myself planning a trip back to Red Creek, to see Sarah and Samuel in the spring, after the visitor season waned.

And then the first big snowfall came. The town filled to overflowing. Condominiums that I had never noticed before suddenly swept to life, and the mountains dazzled their white brilliance by both sunlight and moonlight.

Fashion ski wear was everywhere; even the clerks in the stores were so attired. Sunburned fresh faces with flashing white teeth were everywhere. Bars and restaurants were loud with celebration: music, singing, happy voices. Pairs of skis lined both sides of Main Street as they stood in racks, leaned against buildings and cars, were carried on shoulders, and on the sides of great huge buses. It was a fascinating spectacle, twenty-four hours a day.

All the girls at work were avid skiers; each was horrified to learn that I had never strapped a pair to my feet; each vowed to introduce me to what she considered the highest form of sport. I continued to excuse myself from their forays into the powder, but I could not keep my eyes off the main street of town.

It was the after-ski activity that fascinated me.

The sky was darkening as I finished work, and I plunged my hands deep into my pockets and hurried home, afraid to be out in the growing night, afraid of the attraction it held for me, afraid of the fascination that I had with all the parties. At times I would find myself standing in the snow, staring through the windows at the fireplaces, the colorful sweaters, the charming alcoholic glow on the sunburned faces, and I would have to shake myself and run home before the darkness turned me past the point of good sense, past the point of no return.

The day before Thanksgiving, one of the girls at work attempted to ski "Sucker," one of the most difficult of the third-slope ski runs. Thereafter she was put into a cast from armpit to toes, and I was called in to assume her hours at work.

She worked the midnight shift.

At first, I was all right. I felt the pull, and resisted it. I knew what normal behavior consisted of, and I practiced it all night long. I tried my best to sleep from four in the afternoon until nine, then get up, go out and have breakfast, and then get to work at midnight, where I would work until eight in the morning. The routine was simple, and I had no problem with it. My only problem was with the tug, the tug from the other side.

I kept the fluorescent lights brightly lit, kept the draperies drawn. I wanted no dark influence to touch my switchboards.

But of course it did. It was there the first time I walked in at night. The girl I relieved from duty was tainted. I rushed her out the door and double bolted it. The switchboard room was quiet, empty; the office was dark, the desks cleared, the typewriters and calculators covered. The darkness was already inside.

The darkness was already inside, and more of it seeped in through the calls that I had to answer. The personalities of those people—customers, clients whom I had talked to during the daytime—were obviously altered by the night, and at night, when they assumed I was not busy, they wanted to talk.

And as they talked, I knew the influence the night had on them, and soon I began to sway with the motion.

Within weeks, the darkness owned me again.

GLORIA GARDENER: "She was a good worker. I hated to have to put her on midnight when Becky broke her leg, but she was really the only candidate. All the other girls had families, or boyfriends, or something, and Angelina was all alone. She didn't seem to mind too much, at least she didn't say anything to me about it. I gave her a big raise for the inconvenience.

"She got along just fine with the other girls. A little shy at first, I think she'd been through some pretty rough times, didn't like to talk much about her past. I mean she was just a little thing, young and all, but her face had no innocence left, if you know what I mean. I thought I was giving her a break, when I, you know, hired her, so young and all—and an orphan at that. She worked out real well. The other girls, well, they're just precious, and they made her feel real welcome. I didn't have any idea at all that Angelina would give me any problems here at night. But then, I guess, well, young girls have their temptations, don't they?

"Anyway, Becky was out of work flat on her back for six months. It was six months full before she came back to work. By that time, of course, Angelina didn't want to give up her shift, so Becky started back daytime. But Becky wanted her night work, so she's the one who discovered what-all Angelina'd been doing at night, and then told me about it. The other girls had been covering for her, I guess, because apparently she'd been at it a while, and I'd never had a clue."

16

During the night shift I worked steadily, with no breaks. I answered calls, tallied the day's totals, refreshed and updated client information, spoke with lonesome clients and drunk clients, answered burglar alarms with calls to the police, dealt with emergencies of different kinds—all in a state of frenzied activity, worry, and self-restricted movement. I kept my emotions drawn as tight as the draperies and avoided too much talk with the customers.

I felt the dawn rather than saw it—the pull relaxed, I eased my grip on reality, and began to breathe again. I had passed through another night—had beaten it one more time.

I was exhausted every morning.

At six o'clock, another girl, usually Theresa, joined me

at the switchboard. Together we would make the scheduled wakeup calls, start the coffee for Mrs. Gardener, tidy the boards, and make ready for the onslaught of incoming calls.

Theresa was a lively redhead who was forever fighting with her boyfriend and then staying up all night to make up. I enjoyed her rather remarkable reminiscences over her first cup of coffee. Her very presence enlivened me; I saw in her the complete embodiment of daytime: sunshine, health, happiness, love. Even her terribly puzzling relationship with her boyfriend brought light to the room.

At six-thirty Judy arrived, and by then the board was lighting up with calls. This was the home stretch, and with the daylight, my humor was much improved. At eight, Suzanne came in and relieved me. I punched my time onto a card, stored my headset, filed my daily report, and left, exhausted.

The morning I met Cap Nicks, I walked with weary legs from the building into the frosty December air. All night long I had waged my battle with the patient, patient darkness, working all the while, and then emerged into the sunshine filled with avid skiers marching down the snow-packed sidewalks, skis resting on shoulders, looking far too active, healthy, and lively for eight o'clock in the morning. I remember watching their parade, feeling exhaustion leaden in every cell, thinking that a cup of hot chocolate or even coffee would sit well with me.

Instead of turning left, to go down the street and home to my basement apartment, I turned right and went up toward Main Street, to a popular little breakfast spot.

I should have known better. The line of tourists waiting for breakfast wound out the door and down two shops. It is the visitor season, Angelina, I told myself. It was a hard concept, that of seasonal populace, and I was unaccustomed to it.

As I stood there, I realized that coffee or hot chocolate was not really the issue. What I wanted was companionship,

I wanted to be with someone interesting. Anything to keep me from going home to an empty apartment.

The loneliness was suddenly overwhelming. I felt a need to share with someone the terrors of the night, the confusion about my past that strangled my thoughts. I needed someone to talk to, to be with. I needed to learn not just the definition of the word *remorse,* but to see how other people lived with it. And remorse wasn't the only word I didn't understand. Altruism was another. So were compromise, and sacrifice. All those social words.

Loneliness wrapped around me like a leper's shroud. There was no one for me. No one but Boyd, and he was impossible. Someday, though, someday I would return to Boyd, someday when I could hold my head up and be *clean.*

I kept walking, past the warehouses, beyond the service entrance of the shopping mall. I heard my boot heels on the frozen ground and on the hard-packed snow, on the ice and even on the pavement, but it didn't sound the same. It sounded low.

The air was crisp and cold and my nose began to run. I shoved my hands deep into my pockets, where one shredded an old Kleenex and the other toyed with a penny and a smooth pebble. The sun was bright as it reflected off the snow, and I stopped for a moment, letting sadness and loneliness mix with my exhaustion. I kicked through the soot-blackened plow bank at the side of the road and felt sorry for myself.

I felt like giving up. Life was just too hard. I had to fight the darkness and do it all alone, and it was too much, it was too hard, I felt used up.

I wanted to lie down in the snowbank and wait for someone to come and rescue me. I wanted someone to take me away from all this, to take care of me. I was tired of doing it by myself.

Instead, I just kept kicking at that snowbank, and when I'd expended a little excess energy, I decided that home was indeed the place to be. There, I could brew myself a nice hot cup of tea and get comfortable. And sleep. I was so tired.

Feeling the hot sun on my back and the cold on my face, I put my head down and began to walk toward home. Suddenly the sanctuary of my little apartment was ever so appealing. I could hide there. My pace quickened.

I had crossed the street, hearing new life in my footsteps, when I heard a husky, whiskey-honed voice boom a greeting.

"Good mornin'! Ain't she a beauty?"

A man, a big man with flesh rolling over his trousers, stood in the corner doorway of a warehouse. He was barefoot and balding and wearing a stretch-necked T-shirt, and he was clapping his hands against the cold and dancing a little, his bare pink toes finding fault with the hard nuggets of salt atop the cold sidewalk.

"You keep looking at your feet while you walk, you'll miss the whole day!" He stopped fidgeting for a moment, rubbed his hands together briskly, then rubbed his reddening arms. "You in a hurry?" He smiled again, big, clean white teeth. I shook my head no. "Well, hell, come on in then, get out of that cold." He suddenly started to shiver convulsively, doing a strange little dance in his bare feet, his belly jiggling obscenely. "God damn, it's cold out here." He opened the door and I walked through, smiling at his odd appeal.

He followed me in and closed the door behind him. "Well, pretty thing, what can I offer you? Coffee? Tea? A friend? That's what I need, anyway, a little personal company. A little female company. Name's Nicks. Captain of this here club. Most call me Cap."

"I'm Angelina Watson. Tea would be fine."

"One cup coming up." He turned away, then paused and waved an arm around the warehouse. "Welcome to the Seven Slopes Anti-Tourist Yacht Club."

The room occupied the entire vast end of a warehouse.

The roof with its skylights and metal rafters stretched far overhead. A metal partition divided the Yacht Club from the rest of the warehouse building, but the wall reached only twelve or fourteen feet high.

The Yacht Club, for all its space, was decently furnished and looked not only comfortable, but livable. Several sets of living-room groupings were scattered about the floor, complete with lamps, rugs, and homey atmosphere; a kitchen with three refrigerators and a serving bar separated the rest of the room from Cap's personal living quarters, which I could see consisted of an unmade bed, a freestanding closet, and several cardboard boxes. A long bar ran the length of two walls, an eclectic assortment of bar stools waiting in front of it. All the exposed plumbing was nicely painted, and the result was the oddest interior I had ever seen, but not unpleasant. Not unpleasant at all.

Cap came back with an unbuttoned plaid shirt on over his bulging T-shirt, carrying a teacup on a saucer. He set it down on a coffee table where a mug of steaming coffee waited, and motioned me over.

"Here, here, come sit here. Heater's right under this table. Makes this whole area nice and cozy. So. Now. What do you think of my club?"

"It's most unusual," I said.

"Hah. Hah. Ain't it the truth. We call it a 'loft.' That gives it a little more class, don't you think?"

"What exactly is this place?"

He sat heavily on the couch, both elbows winged out over the top. "Before there were tourists, we had a nice little town. A man could go into a neighborhood bar and have a quiet little drink, take his girlfriend along, you know, maybe get a sandwich or something."

I sipped my tea. Cinnamon.

"And then Seven Slopes was *discovered*. Ta-da. Big news coverage, write-ups in all the ski magazines, condominiums went up and ski facilities, and now all the bars are full of cocaine and stupid people on vacation. So some of us got together and established the Yacht Club. It's open all the time, except Mondays, that's my day off, and now and then when I sleep." He grunted toward the coffee table and took a sip of his coffee. "So you are my first customer today."

"And you're the captain."

"That's right. Captain. Before they called me Cap, they called me Boss. I retired from the railroad line down in Denver."

"Does this club have memberships?"

"Yes, indeedy. No tourists here. We're all anti-tourist, but not officially. Tourists are good for the economy, you know. They're just not good for our social life. All our members are full-time, bona fide residents." He looked at me, and again I noticed the kind features, the humor in the eyes. "Are you a resident?"

"Yes, I live on Wharton Street. I work at the answering service."

"You work for Gloria? Gloria Gardener?"

I nodded.

"Ha. Good for you. Bet she keeps you hopping, doesn't she? Gloria's a good old broad. Her husband's a charter member of the Yacht Club here. Maybe that's why she doesn't have any use for me at all. Hah. Gloria. Give her my love . . . no, better not." He winked at me as he noisily gulped the last of his coffee.

Suddenly, all the energy ran out of my limbs like warm water. I needed to go home.

I stood and thanked Cap, parrying his insistence that I stay and have breakfast. I explained my working hours, and he invited me back that night as his guest, to have a little late dinner before work, to see the club in action, to meet his friends.

In my anxiety to get away, I agreed. Later, I was sorry, and thought about not going. On the other hand, it was a perfect excuse to see some of the local side of social life in

Seven Slopes, and I, too, was lonely for companionship.

"I began to hate Angelina. After such a long time with no word
of her, I figured she must be dead. I tried to tell myself that she
was either dead or reformed, but I knew better. I knew deep down
inside myself that if Angelina died, I'd know about it. She was all
I could think about, and it was ruining my life. I prayed for word
of her so I could stop her. And then I prayed for word of her so I
could see her again. I had to talk to her, I had to ask her 'Why?'
And finally I prayed for word of her so I could have an excuse to
leave Westwater. It was suddenly too damned small-town for me. I
hated it, and I hated everybody's demands on me. Another winter
and I thought I'd die of boredom. I was restless like I'd never
known before. Really restless. I just wanted to get out, see some
new things, meet some new people. I just wanted to get out.

But this is the address where my newspapers come, and it was
from here that I'd started my network trying to find her, so I didn't
dare leave. I was trapped here because of Angelina. She'd tied me
down here in Westwater, and I really hated her for it."

17

I slept through the day and awoke about four in the afternoon. It was already dark outside. I turned on the radio to
hear Christmas music, and I couldn't help but reminisce.
One year ago I had been with Lewis; the Christmas before
that, I had been with my mother and Rolf. Would the
holiday season ever again be as it used to be? Probably not.
Christmas was for children.

I fixed some toast and a cup of tea and sat at my rickety
table, worried about the coming evening at the Yacht Club.
I would be socializing with older people, people of experience, people with wisdom. How would I appear to them?

I worried that the darkness would overcome me in the
midst of a mature crowd, that my behavior would turn

bizarre; I worried that this, my first actual social event, would turn bad, and I would have to leave Seven Slopes in fear and shame, like I had left so many places before.

I spread marmalade on my toast and regarded it. My appetite had fled. How on earth did people accomplish their social obligations? Didn't the stress and tension of it all ruin the experience? Did anyone truly find pleasure in it?

Maybe others just accepted life. Maybe they just accepted their behavior as the manifestation of their personality, and nothing to be ashamed of. Well, it was certainly worth a try. I had made so many strides in Seven Slopes, keeping a tight rein on myself. I couldn't let fear of my behavior cripple me.

I would go to the Yacht Club and let whatever would happen ... happen. With this decision, the burden of life seemed to lift from my shoulders. I had no need to fight anymore, I could relax. I began to look forward to the approaching evening.

Then it happened.

I was barely awake, toying with my toast, still groggy from my long sleep. I was feeling a bit of Christmas melancholy, reminiscent, wrapped in a cocoon of my own thoughts, when suddenly it felt like the bottom of my mind dropped out and I fell through, down into a huge void. My stomach lurched, and then—I was face-to-face with Boyd. We saw each other only long enough to both register astonishment, and then like a yo-yo, I was snapped back, the trapdoor slammed shut, and I was sitting in front of my cold toast, sweat gushing from my pores and my head reeling.

I thought for a moment that I would faint.

I made my way back to my bed and lay down, filled with wonder at the vivid hallucination, wondering what possible significance it could have.

The next thing I knew, it was eight o'clock.

Four hours had passed. Four hours with no memory. I hadn't slept; I knew I hadn't slept. Panic gripped me. I knew where I'd been. I'd just spent four hours with Her—four hours with the owner of those lips, with the voice of the dark, the music of my dreams. Four hours with the force that had driven me insane in Westwater. Four hours with no memory of it. What had she done to me?

Oh, God, what now? I tried so hard to outrun it; I tried everything I knew to keep the dark away, but what match was I for this voice, this force, this female Mesmer that stole my conscious mind and bent it to her will?

I began to pace. My mind was filled with possibilities, ways to divert Her, things to do to keep Her influence from me. I couldn't go to work. The darkness filled that answering service. I couldn't stay home, for it was dark, and I'd slept the day away. I couldn't go out, I couldn't stay in, the world began to close in on me. I felt helpless in the face of Her power, helpless, hopeless, tiny, lost . . .

I know, I thought. The Yacht Club.

Yes! The Yacht Club. There was light there, and people, and conversation. That's what I need, that's exactly what I need. She wouldn't dare . . .

She wouldn't dare.

It was eight o'clock.

I showered and changed and made ready.

I was still deeply troubled, and quite anxious, as I walked along the streets toward the club. I could hear club activity from more than a block away, and could see muted lights coming through the high warehouse windows, but She was on my mind. She and Boyd and that strange, strange experience of seeing him, or recognizing his essence, being so close as to almost smell him, for that one instant. And then, instead of letting me ponder the situation, She captured my attention for four hours. She'd left me alone for months, now, months. And now, all of a sudden, four hours gone. I was truly afraid.

I knocked hard enough on the Yacht Club door to hurt my knuckles. When the door opened, however, I forgot all that had been troubling me. The room was transformed with the warming auras of the people inside. It was like a vast informal cocktail party.

People stood drinking at the wall bar, talking in small groups, or sitting alone. Clusters congregated at the living-room sets, or stood about, munching snacks, eating sandwiches, drinking beer, sodas, coffee. It really looked like a club—actually, it looked more like a Christmas party—not like a bar at all.

A tall gentleman who introduced himself as Kent offered to take my coat, so I peeled it off, then took the brown towel from my shoulders and slipped it down one sleeve. He hung my coat on a long, brass rack behind the door. He questioned me as to my membership status, and when I told him I was Cap's guest, he smiled in apparent recognition and escorted me to the back, where Cap was tending bar.

"Angelina!" Cap came around the end of the bar and hugged me. I wondered at his fierce affection as I was forced into his folds of flab, then as he released me, I realized he had been drinking, and for some reason had need to show me off. I suppressed the comical urge to look to see if the impression my bony body had made in his great stomach had stayed—a permanent outline of Angelina pressed in flesh.

He was dressed nicely, in a clean flannel shirt and jeans, and he smelled good. He was happy, deep within his element.

"What can I get you to drink? This is a private club; we don't worry about IDs here."

"Oh, I don't drink. Just tea. Please."

While I waited, I looked around and noticed a singular lack of women. There were several present whom I assumed were wives; most were playing cards with husbands or partners at card tables set up in the far corner. A couple of women were engaged in sofa conversation with their dates, and there were two women deep in animated discussion at the wall bar, but the rest were men. An astonishing assortment of men.

I swallowed.

Cap brought my tea. "Gee, I'm glad you came," he said. "I wasn't sure you would. Next thing, we'll have to make you a member. We need some ladies to brighten the place up a bit. Add a little color." I smiled at him. He was a delightful person. "You have a good time now, you hear? I'm stuck behind the bar tonight, or I'd meetcha to some folks. I know you go to work at midnight, but maybe you could stop back by and have some coffee with me when you get off your shift?"

I told him I would, took my tea, and went off to explore this very interesting male territory.

As I shouldered my way through the passages, my nose attuned to the male odor, I listened to snatches of conversation, hearing pauses in the conversation as I passed. I became aware of what people were drinking. After a few leading remarks by some of the men, I realized that my criteria for companionship this night was a man who didn't drink. A man who didn't pollute his body. I graciously declined offers of all kinds as I roamed, attentive, searching.

As I slowly walked around, looking, listening, inviting myself in and then out again, introducing myself as necessary, I began to settle down. I felt calm, I felt comforted. I felt a presence again, a guiding, loving presence that warmed me. It was a familiar feeling, one that had been missing from my cold, lonely life for too long, and it felt marvelous. I continued to wander through the Yacht Club, enjoying the atmosphere, feeling confident and relaxed.

I made almost one entire circuit of the room, feeling better and happier all the time. The struggle was over. I was protected, and relieved. And free to let the evening take its course, free to enjoy myself.

Then I saw him. He stood in the corner where the two wall bars met, talking with another man. It was him, there was no doubt. My man for the evening.

He was tall, and gray-haired. His deeply lined face

showed years of humor and adventure. He was lean and handsome, with a straight nose and clear, clean eyes.

He drank mineral water. I walked to his side and stood there, tacitly interrupting his conversation.

"Hello," my gentleman offered.

"Hello," I said. "My name is Angelina Watson."

"I'm Fred Bertow," he said, his eyes registering immediate interest. "This is Carl."

"Nice to meet you," Carl said. "I'll see you later, Fred." Carl made a shrewd and speedy exit.

"I haven't seen you here before," Fred said, leaning closer. He smelled of soap and water. His hands were strong and hairy, the nails neatly manicured. My saliva glands began to ache.

"This is my first time here."

"Are you new in town?"

"I've been here a few months."

"Maybe I could buy you a drink."

"No, thank you. I have tea. Maybe I should get straight to the point."

His smile of amusement was genuine. He was intrigued. And interested. "You look like a nice person; clean, sober, and—I assume—healthy . . ." I waited for his response.

He lifted an eyebrow and confirmed my impressions with a slight nod.

"I find that very attractive."

"Do you?"

"Yes," I said simply, and sipped my tea.

He swigged his mineral water from the short bottle as we regarded each other for a long moment. I could visualize his mind racing with the implications and strategies of the next move, which was clearly his. My heart pounded. I tried to keep my knees from shaking or my mouth from grinning stupidly. Men are an easy lot.

When he knew his next move, he smiled. "Are you as squeaky clean as you expect?"

"I take care," I said. "And look to associate with those who do the same."

"Shall we associate, then?"

"I'd like that." For a split second, I looked at this man's face and couldn't believe I was saying these things. Then he spoke again, and I fell back into character.

"Now?"

I looked at my watch. It was nine-twenty. I set my teacup on the bar and walked toward the coatrack. I dared not turn around to see if he followed me, but when I took my coat from its hook, he took it from me and helped me into it. I slid the towel through the sleeve and into my oversize coat pocket.

Together we walked out into the crisp cold night, plumes of hot breath preceding us. I found I had nothing to say; I let myself be guided by his large hand in the middle of my back, letting the evening take its course. Surely She had something in mind.

DEDRICK "CAP" NICKS: *"Angelina seemed like a nice girl. A little rough around the edges, maybe, but—hey, you gotta be, these days. Especially girls out on their own. They've got to be tough.*

"She came by a couple of mornings, we sat and had coffee together. But she was always real tired after work. She came by at night a couple of times, too, you know, before her shift, but I was real busy then, and we didn't get a chance to talk much, so we never really got to know each other. Hey, maybe that's a good thing, huh?

"No, we just traveled in different circles. The Yacht Club wasn't her kind of place, although it seemed so at first. She seemed fascinated. Well, hell, we old geezers are pretty fascinating, I must admit. But we weren't her style. The young ones, they need to go for those tanned athletic young skiers. The tourists. They would be more to Angelina's liking, I think.

"Hey, I was wondering if you could tell me. I mean I've leveled with you, and in my business you hear a lot of rumors. Is it true, I

mean, did they really find all that, well, you know, all that stuff in
her apartment after she left?"

18

Fred's apartment was beautifully decorated in expensive and tasteful furnishings. It looked like a magazine advertisement, complete with muted pastel colors, original artwork, and a sweeping view of the snow-covered ski runs and the night-lighted storybook village.

His two little dogs greeted him with wagging tails and wiggling bodies, snuffling and dancing their excitement. I felt like stepping on them, nasty little things. They surely sensed my opinion, for they completely ignored me, took their token loving and greeting from their master, then upon his order disappeared into a far room of the apartment.

Then I had Fred's attention. All of it.

His large hands seemed to cover every inch of me as he helped me off with my coat, and to my amazement, I found myself moving into his caress, excitement raising goose bumps from toes to fingers, my nipples shrinking to hard little nuts. He poured two glasses of mineral water with slices of lemon, then dimmed the lights and we cozied on the couch to watch the view. I felt completely comfortable by his side; I was amenable and excited by his touch.

I was becoming a woman.

"Sometimes," he said, "I sit here, right here on this couch, and watch the skiers all day long." His hand began to play with the hair at the back of my neck. I could feel my temperature rising. "And on the holidays, at night, all the ski patrol people go up to the top and ski down with torches. They come down in a line, and crisscross, and ski different patterns, all holding up these flames in the black night against the white snow." He kissed behind my ear. I wanted to see the torch skiers. I wanted to see them so much that I almost could; I could almost pluck them right from his memory and see them in my mind's eye.

He took my glass and set it on the coffee table, then brought me closer to him. His embrace was nothing like Cap's, or Lewis's. He was lean and hard, and my skin ached to be next to his.

He must have heard my thought, for he unbuttoned his shirt and pulled my blouse up from my jeans and with a hand on my lower back, pressed my exposed belly skin to his. The contact was zinged with an electric vibration. I felt the quiver run through us both, and our breathing stopped for a moment. Then he pulled away and looked deeply at me. Slowly he began to unbutton my blouse while I sat there, gazing at his face, remembering the details, and he began to talk again.

"There's something magic about skiing fast. Skiing so fast down the slopes that you're afraid to fall." His feather touch did away with my blouse quickly as the intensity of his passion grew. "It's so exhilarating that you can't stop, don't want to stop, don't want to fall." His face began to change and his fingers became harder in his excitement. "Because if you fall, the ice crystals just might slice you to pieces. What a way to go, huh, Angelina? In a burst of orgasmic glory, a red smear on the slide of your favorite ski run."

He was working on his own clothes now, my blouse off and jeans undone. We were leaning our way toward a horizontal position on the couch, incongruously warm with the huge cold eye of a window right in front of us, showing us winter in all its attendant splendor.

Suddenly he pinched me hard, bringing a bruise on my waist, then he lay me down on the couch and with one hand pulled my jeans to my knees, and his finger, hot and dry, probed into me and I cried out with the suddenness of it. He hesitated a moment, smiling at me with heat, then stood and shed the rest of his clothes, pulled the jeans from my legs, then scooped me up and carried me the length of the living room and into the bedroom beyond.

We lay together on the smooth comforter, our hands busy with each other, our mouths as well, tasting, licking, speaking in low, soft tones. It was choreographed beautifully; it felt as if we had danced together like this many times before.

Our legs entwined, then rearranged. He attempted to mount me, a move I parried with little difficulty, and we continued our dance, wrestling more and more intensely. The physical friction rose and our waltz became a match—a contest of two wills—testing, tasting, delaying, his frustration growing with each of my denials, my excitement exploding with each new emphasis of his frustration.

Our contest grew fiercer—pain became legal—and I felt one wrist and an ankle burn in skin friction as I twisted from his grasp.

Then the music rose in my ears, and it seemed as though it had been there all night, playing soft background accompaniment to our courtship, and now the volume rose with an appropriate shift in depth.

The musical strains were memorable, monumental, the arrangement was unique, it was ours, it lifted in chorus, building, building, the crescendo almost deafening, and I heard my part orchestrated, knew when it ceased to become a *pas de deux* and became a solo, and Fred flipped to his back. I sat astride his chest and gripped his pectoral muscles, fingers digging into his armpits, holding, holding, holding one final moment longer, and at the crash of cymbals, I saw the look on his face—the flash of questioning, the instant of knowing and the bit of regret, and I dove for the giant worm that pulsed just below his ear.

The lullaby that wove about my head as I drank was the sweetest, most innocent music I had ever heard. It told the story of peace and harmony and life and life after life. Fred quieted, and my breathing slowed. I sucked more, I was full, but he was so pure, so delicious, it was like fresh spring water on a hot day—I couldn't bear to waste any. I wrapped my legs around his heavy limbs and hummed along with the lullaby, teasing the nipple of my nourishment with my teeth, and my hands roamed his hairy chest and massaged his facial muscles until they relaxed.

I closed my eyes and saw the torch skiers, criss-crossing the mountain. My face softened into a smile as I thought of Fred's expression when he talked of skiing fast, so fast he was afraid to fall, and I knew the sensation. I felt the exhilaration, saw Death flying down the mountain by my side. I knew Fred in that moment, and I loved him.

It wasn't until I felt in danger of sleeping that I noticed we had fallen to the floor in our violent struggle, and brought half the quilt down with us. I sat up and tickled the cold flesh with my fingertips as my passions cooled even further, and as I ran my fingertips over his knees, it happened again.

I broke through and saw Boyd.

I felt him looking out through my eyes, seeing what I saw, the beautiful, lean body of Fred Bertow, resting in the ultimate sleep, neck open and sore, quilt pulled cockeyed from the bed. And it wasn't beautiful through Boyd's eyes. It was pagan and disgusting.

Then it was soft again, and loving, and I turned inward, and looked directly into Boyd's shocked and repulsed expression, and I said to him, "Do you love them before you kill them, Boyd? The defenseless animals you slaughter with automatic weapons? Do you give them pleasure, or at least a fair chance? Do you love them, Boyd? Do you love them like I do?" And then I began to laugh and I wiped my chin and felt the slippery ooze, and noticed that it had dripped down my front, between my breasts, and mixed in with my blonde pubic hair. And I laughed harder and harder, and then he was gone and I came back into the room, the silent bedroom, with just Fred and me, and I heard the dogs whining in the other room, and suddenly the humor disappeared.

It was as if I'd just awakened, and I was shocked at what I'd done. I was horrified. How had this happened? How could I have let this happen? Not only did I let it happen, but I pursued him. I *made* it happen.

My soul twisted inside me. Despair flooded in. I realized I had absolutely no control over my life. Everything I had done in the past months to keep the darkness from my life was all in vain. All in vain. All of it. I couldn't believe I had killed again.

I was cold then, and afraid.

I arrived at work on time that night, but my mind was fogged and I slept off and on during my shift.

In the morning, I dragged myself around, and when eight o'clock finally came, I went to the Yacht Club to keep my breakfast date with Cap. I begged off, pleading exhaustion, but it was really shame that tired me so. He winked at me as if he understood that I'd had a wild night, and let me go.

The police didn't come by for six days. By that time, Fred's dogs had found the only thing there was for them to eat, mutilating what clues the police might have had as to cause of death. Since I was obviously the last to see him alive, they came to ask me if he had been complaining of indigestion or chest pains of any kind.

He had not, to me, and I told them this.

"I really began to rage out of control when I began to see Angelina, I mean actually see her.

"Angelina and I had some kind of weird connection. I can't really describe it, it's like . . .

"When I was a kid, we used to spend a lot of time calling people on the phone. Well, one girl's phone number was always busy, but the rest of us discovered that if we shouted into the phone between the busy signal tones, we could talk to other people

calling her number and hearing the same busy signal. It was like a weird conference call.

"Well, that's kind of what it was like with Angelina and me. We just kind of fell into some sort of a void, like that place where the busy signal existed, and we saw each other. Sometimes I could see right out through her eyes, like bright little windows in the vast dark void, windows to the outside world.

"And, like that busy signal thing, I think there was more going on in there, but there was never enough time to look around. It always took me by surprise. And Angelina'd usually just done something . . . you know.

"The first time it happened, I almost shit. But then it began to happen more frequently. I had to quit my job. I was afraid it would happen when I was working with a saw or something. Or driving. I kind of quit driving. The connection lasted for only a second or two. Just long enough to shock me, I guess. I don't know why. I don't think Angelina did it on purpose; I think she was just as shocked as I was.

"I soon got tired of looking at her victims and listening to her lunacy, and I started looking for clues as to where she was. I mostly just stayed home and waited for it to happen again so I could concentrate on what else I could see from her point of view—a landmark, a street sign, anything. I stayed home and waited for word of strange murders on TV, in the papers, on the wire service. I lived for clues to her whereabouts.

"She knew when I started looking for her, too. At first she was pretty crafty about it, but as time went on, she warped right out of control. She got careless and began to leave a trail."

19

I returned to the Yacht Club several mornings in a row after I finished working, but I was not able to keep up with Cap, who was always bright-eyed and well rested. My jaw hurt continually from keeping such a drastically tight rein on myself. I was not pleasant company. After about a week, my anxieties got the better of me, and I began going straight home. I never merely arrived home from work; I felt as though I barely escaped with my life every day. When the door at the top of the stairs was bolted, I was almost safe. When the door at the bottom of the stairs was bolted, I heaved a sigh of relief. I could relax.

Home. My apartment was my refuge. It was comfortable and mine. It had its own peculiar scent: basement, bordering on damp. The odor was pleasant, it was distinctive, it was familiar; it smelled like home. The apartment had my personality, all furnishings I had made or scrounged or bought. Lighting was kept low, soft and soothing. I could be myself within those cool walls; I needed no pretenses. I came to view it almost as a friend, a protector, a companion.

The first thing I did when I got home was think about Sarah. I would feel the scant meat on my arms and think about her, round, muscular, healthy, glowing. I would set my jaw again and vow to behave the way I needed to behave to get on a straight course to a lifestyle as healthy as Sarah's.

I thought at times that I was on the verge of a breakdown, that my personality might be unstable enough to crack. The thought was vague but ever-present, lurking in the back of my mind. I felt at all times I was under tremendous pressure. I had no idea what the pressure was from, nor what I was to do about it, nor did I closely examine the feeling. The possibility of going completely berserk had always been with me—indeed, I knew I had occasionally been insane— and the possibility increased in my mind when I had bizarre flashes that related to nothing in my experience.

I would be eating breakfast, for example, and wondering if Mary Lou ever finished her college degree after she divorced Al, and I would have warm feelings toward her, and then realize that I knew no Mary Lou; I knew no Al. These, to me, seemed like symptoms of a breakdown. I had no idea what a breakdown meant or what I might do should that happen. I wasn't sure I would recognize one if I had it, but I did know that I could at least do it in privacy, if not safety, if it happened at home. As a result, I rushed home after work and never invited guests.

And then She began to woo me.

This was a private matter, and one I was not anxious to share, or even admit. I wasn't sure who She was or what Her powers or interests in me were, but Her attention was so flattering, so sensual, so particular, that I was quite drawn to Her. Quite attracted. Quite infatuated. I began to let my defenses down, despite my better judgment.

My first glimpse of Her had been at Lewis's house. Up until this time She rarely let me remember our conversations, much less see Her face. I knew Her only as the ethereal essence that appeared in the depths of my meditations. The One that lives within the music. And now, after Fred, She came after me, She wanted me, She desired me, and I was . . .

I was young. Very young. And the young know no danger.

I found myself acting for Her approval. Eventually, thoughts of becoming well enough for Sarah fled. This was too flattering, too encouraging, too much fun. I searched for the witty thing to say, and discovered that I did so for Her entertainment. I knew, somehow, that She was watching me all the time. I knew that anyone who loved me as much as She did would want to be with me all the time. I began to live with Her thought as closely as I lived with the color of my hair.

And I knew what pleased Her.

She was pleased when I made dates with the people who called the answering service in the middle of the night, and when I left the office unmanned to go meet them.

She was the one who told me about the pond, and the old shack where I took them, and then took them, and buried their remains in the snow for spring to find if the hungry small animals did not discover them first.

She directed me to the areas most populated with eligible tourists. She helped me pick out attractive clothes, say clever, attractive things to those people She chose for me—when before I had been a tongue-tied simp.

And while She was directing me, I took great pride in showing Her that I was learning from Her, that Her teachings were not wasted, that I was intelligent and eager to please, and soon my imagination took over and I began inventing creative ways to show off my newly acquired skills at seduction.

I made a cape of dark blue terrycloth, machine washable, to wear under my coat and keep my work neat, and She delighted in this. I said and did outrageous things, basking in her approval. I carried on lustful conversations with clients, complete with base innuendos, in front of the other morning-shift girls, much to their shock and Her enthusiasm. I became more outgoing, more enthusiastic.

And then I would go home and lock the door and feed the cat, eat if I was hungry, delaying the time, the moment, teasing myself.

And then the time would come when I had no other obligations, and I would lie on my mattress on the floor and slide into meditation. The lips would speak into my ear—the full, red, glistening lips—and She spoke with clarity and purpose, gently, and told me of the pleasure I had given Her that night.

And She proceeded to give me pleasure in return.

She appeared to me always in one of two forms. When I was awake, meditating, the lips would speak to me, and while I saw them only in my mind's eye, I knew each crease, each wrinkle, in her lip, each curve of white tooth, each glistening dot on the tip of her tongue.

And when we scampered through the void together, listening to music, She was merely a whisper of fog, mutable fog that danced and swirled and tickled as gleefully as any playmate.

Sometimes in the void we would just listen to the music, and I would calmly sit while She acted out the sounds, as if She, the fog, was the very substance of the tones. She changed as the music soared; She swirled as a delicate mist; She expanded to great mounds of rolling fog and obscured my sight as She fell on me and wrapped about me, tickling, teasing. The music must have been of Her creation; no one else could possibly have imagined something so beautiful, so perfect, so essentially suited to our relationship, our experiences, our personalities, our togetherness and love.

Other times we would just talk, Her wit, experience, and lightning-quick anecdotes a joy to be around. But mostly Her essence was that of love, and when I was with Her, I was loved, totally and completely.

It seems incomprehensible now, but it was a long, long time before I realized that I had no name for Her, nor did I really know Her. My loneliness and longing to touch another's soul became confused in the light of this brilliant and loving personality, and I thought I had found what I had been looking for.

Maybe I had, indeed.

She, certainly, had found what She had been looking for when She found me, and She milked my devotion as completely as I milked the lifeblood from Her victims.

In the name of love.

The days lengthened, Easter came and went, the belching buses ceased to bring tourists, and brown patches began to appear on the mountainsides. I came out of the winter as if arising from a deep sleep, awakening from a slumber so fraught with night terrors and strange sounds that reality held little but suspicion.

Melted snow ran in the streets, down the hills, and great floods and mud slides were the plight of those who lived below us.

Spring brought to me a sense of renewal. I saw the grass

turn green, the leaves sprout on the trees. I walked along the streets at twilight, both morning and evening, and, inspired by it all, wished for a life in the daylight—to come into the sunshine and laugh in the warmth of it.

But I slept through the day instead. And from sundown to sunup, I let the darkness enter my mind. I was continually busy, puzzling over my strangeness, aching over my loneliness, wanting so much, but afraid. I searched for friendship, camaraderie. I found, instead, only victims.

My health began to fail. I was afraid I would not survive the nights and the toll they were taking on my body. I barely recognized myself in the mirror anymore. I needed to make some changes.

The first thing I did was to leave the answering service. Permanently. I didn't need the job. It was too . . . too . . . confining. Leaving felt like a great relief. I could now do exactly as I pleased, with no time constraints, no guilt. I could spend my time as I pleased. I could live on my savings and the account in Pennsylvania for a long, long time.

But that first night, instead of sleeping and beginning to rearrange my odd schedule to coincide more with normal waking hours, I was up with Spartacus, the cat that had adopted me when I was so eager for adulthood and responsibility, petting her as she gave birth to a litter of four kittens, two yellow-striped toms, one calico, and one tiger female just like her mother. I held the newborn babies in my hand, still wet from their birthing juices, and I petted them and talked to them, smelling them, and feeling them. They were so pure, the little ones. They had never eaten, they had never meowed, they had never really even thought. How clean. How nice. How tasty. I licked one's face, tasting its wetness—salty, like tears—tasting its life. Then I put it in the box with its family.

But then there was also Her, and at first I was afraid of Her reaction to my leaving the answering service. I was afraid that She would no longer find me humorous, or exciting, or attractive, when in fact, those fears lived only in my mind. Her affection was uninterrupted and consistent.

My petty insecurities, my fears and wishes for a different life, in fact, paled before the immensity of Her affection, Her consistency, Her solidly based strength.

There was something every night that kept me entertained, kept me awake, kept me from adjusting my schedule. My struggle against it was little more than wishful thinking, for always She had the final say, and when I was bunched up in my bedclothes, fists clenched against my eyes, She would come and whisper in my ear and my touch-starved body responded. I was lost. Again, lost.

As the night paled and the blackness of my little basement windows turned milky, exhaustion overtook me and I could no longer hold my head up. Sleep would finally come, dreamless sleep that held no rest.

REBECCA DEL ROSARIO: "I didn't really want to bust Angelina, but she was really getting out of control. I took my time before turning her in, because I didn't want it to sound like sour grapes, you know? I mean I really wanted my shift back—my boyfriend works midnights, too, so it's just perfect, and it's a total waste when I have to work days, I mean total.

"But Angelina was really getting out there. I mean, at first I thought she was just not doing her work, logging in the calls and that. I figured she was sleeping. Girls always used to sleep on the midnight shift, that's one of the problems Mrs. Gardener has always had.

"So we covered her a little, I mean, we all cover for each other sometimes, and then the morning-shift girls started telling me these weird stories about the way Angelina was acting. She must have been on some drugs or something. They said she'd talk real loud. You know with the headphones we wear, a whisper gets the point across real well, but they said she'd pace back and forth behind them, her phone cord hooked up to the board, and she'd answer calls and yell at the people and talk real loud and say terrible things.

"Once she told a customer that she would never date him because he was Italian, and everybody knows Italians eat garlic and she can't stand to taste garlic on a man. God. Can you imagine? I mean, she was totally out of control.

"And when I found out she'd been leaving at night, well, that was it. I just had to tell Mrs. Gardener. I mean, Mrs. Gardener could lose a lot of clients, and that would be everybody's job, right? Angelina had no right to rip us off like that.

"I saw her the day Mrs. Gardener fired her. I showed up early, because I knew that Mrs. Gardener would have to come in early to see Angelina before she went home, and I had all the evidence. I was surprised at how she looked. In fact, I hardly recognized her. She'd been on midnights just over six months, and boy, it had really taken its toll on her. She was as skinny as a bag of bones; her eyes seemed dark and sunken; her blonde hair didn't even look blonde anymore, it looked kind of gray. She seemed anxious to get away, and when Mrs. Gardener fired her, she just took the check and left. Didn't say anything. In fact, I thought she was having a hard time keeping her eyes open. Getting fired would wake me up, that's for sure. But not Angelina. I don't know what drugs she was taking, but she was really strung out. I mean, I've seen strung-out people before, and she was, like, totally done.

"I kind of worried about her a little bit, you know? I mean, she lived in a basement under a warehouse down in the light-industrial side of town, kind of a spooky place. I went by to talk to her, to see if she was all right, but she never answered the door. That was okay, though, really, because I didn't really want to go in that place, it was too creepy. I just wanted to check on her, you know? I never really wanted to be her friend."

20

As a compromise between Her vigorous demands of me and my own desperate need for companionship, I developed a sort of system as I picked over the town for suitable company. I spent a certain amount of time at Alcoholics Anonymous meetings, PTA meetings, Parents Without Partners, high-school dances, and other such gatherings. Occasionally I'd find a loner, preferably a visitor, and we would pair up, providing his nutritional habits were suitable. Publicity and town security made this difficult at times; the local residents seemed a bit hysterical over the missing-persons scandal, but my persistence always won out.

The spring floods tidily disposed of the little shack by the pond, flushed out my little amusement park, cleansing the entire area in general. I heard rumors of officials conducting investigations in town, but I was not worried because the general consensus assumed the disappearances were drug-related. In addition, I was pleasing Her, and surrounded by the protection of Her powerful influence, I felt safe.

For the summer months, She had shown me a small cave, just a short hike from up behind the Snowson Hotel. It seemed to excite them, my friends, my lovers, to be led by the hand up through waist-high grass by moonlight to a cave in the mountains. Many times the talk turned to the famed Seven Slopes murderer. The idea of meeting up with him in the hills added excitement, added tang. The walk gave us both time to savor the anticipation, to feel the exhilaration of the physical exertion in the hike, heightening the senses, honing the appreciation, keening the edge between pleasure and pain.

Indeed, I received an extra bonus, as the taste of adrenaline is much like tart honey. I became as a sorcerer, who controls his realm so totally that he need merely raise his arms and the tides leap to his command. I controlled the tides of fear, and my sweet tooth savored the taste of it.

The cave was always clean when I got there; I assumed the wildlife in the area was well fed, a fortunate by-product of my habits. I enjoyed being merely another convenient link in the food chain.

In one of my more lucid moments, however, when the odor of plasma was not throbbing in my nostrils, when my mind was not crazed with the thought of the hunt, or of the kill, or of the reward beyond, when I was not sleeping the drugged sleep of the sated beast, when I was not reveling in Her wallowsome pleasures, I had an occasional thought that I was the last to be seen with too many missing persons.

I knew I would soon be leaving Seven Slopes.

I pushed these thoughts away. They were cumbersome and unpleasant.

The time came, however, when they would not be pushed away.

The night was young, the kittens had grown to gangly adolescent cats, and they frolicked with each other around my feet, wide-eyed and hunter-wary, as I sat at the table, reading.

I perused the newspaper once each week to discern the popular gathering places, events, socials, and the like—anywhere I could meet new people, find new friends. I had before me a steaming cup of tea, my cape soaked in the sink, and my world was at peace.

I turned the page, feeling the little smile on my face, my body remembering the intense flooding of pleasure from the night before, when I felt the elevator feeling in my stomach again. It lurched, as if one floor, then stopped.

I knew that feeling. It was the dropping through, it was the fall into the void that could not be controlled. It was meeting Boyd face-to-face and shame-to-shame.

But I only dropped one story and then things focused again. I took a deep breath and folded the newspaper, looked at it again in horror. Boyd could never see the name of the newspaper! I turned it upside down, and as I did, my mind fell through, and there he was, and She was with him.

She hovered behind him, fog spread out behind him as an umbrella, or more like wings, like a giant bat. He did not see Her, did not know Her, would not know Her. But I did, and I knew that She had warned me to hide the newspaper, which meant that She controlled these meetings.

For a second, I saw Boyd look through my eyes, around the apartment, felt the cat licking my hand, and then I was in his truck, headlights careening as it rolled slowly off the side of the road onto the shoulder, wheels humping over clumps of weeds in the gravel, and then we were face-to-face again, and I saw that he knew of my nocturnal activities, and that all he felt was scorn. Fury burned up my chest. Then it was over, and I was again calmly seated at the kitchen table.

I knew, then, that She was threatening me, testing me. This was Her ultimate checkmate to squelch any rebellious thoughts that might remain. She wanted me to have no friends, no companions. She wanted Her hold to be absolute. She wanted all of me, all the time.

She controlled these meetings with Boyd. *She* kept him foremost in my mind. And now She was threatening to reveal my location to him, as easily as letting him read the name of the local newspaper.

Well, it would not work.

She would not have me. She would not have me.

I took a series of deep breaths and tried to calm my trembling. I knew I had to renounce Her, had to fight Her, and I could win, I *would* win, because I had something that I don't think She counted on. I had my free will. And it was strong. I would defeat Her.

I intuitively knew my next step. I dressed quickly, kissed each cat, assured them all that I would return, then left my apartment. I stepped into the comfortable summer night of the deserted industrial area. In the garage at the end of the street, the night crew provided maintenance to buses and trucks, but the other buildings were nighttime-deserted; only ghostly security lights were brave enough to show their beacons through the darkness, through deadeye windows and down ragged alleys.

I knew right where to go.

I avoided the lighted places, dodging down side streets, not wishing to be seen, stopped, or questioned. I found a pile of trash by the curb waiting to be picked up. Leaning against it was a beautiful plank. I ripped another from a boarded-up window on a recently vacated building, and found some small plywood scraps blown up next to a fence by the airstrip. I made a small pile of all of these finds just two blocks from my home, and as a pack rat scurries along the gutters at night finding shiny objects, so I looked for lumber to build my defense.

I had to return to my apartment for my hammer, and with it removed some molding from empty doorways, and at last I thought I had what I needed. It took seven trips to take it all into my basement, but once there, I began to work in a fever, the plans coming to me automatically, the tools feeling like old friends. My tool box consisted of only a hammer, a bent handsaw, a couple of screwdrivers, and some nails. They would have to do, and they worked. My frustration reached frenzied proportions at times, and as I perspired in my work and the sweat began to turn sour in my clothes, I stripped down and preferred the sawdust covering to the cotton.

My measurements proved right, my intuition flawless. I dared not think that I was being guided in this endeavor. This was my act of rebellion, one so strong She could not ignore it or deny it. I knew She would at least take note of the drastic measures I was taking to avoid Her contact, the dedication with which I was putting Her from my life. Once

She realized how important this was to me, I knew She would leave me alone, to rediscover the daylight and find my way among people again—someday to meet Boyd face-to-face in the flesh again, in the light, eye-to-eye.

And then it was finished. I dragged the kitchen table into the bedroom and placed the box atop it.

Unaccustomed to manual work of this magnitude, I felt as if lead flowed in my veins. I returned to the kitchen to find the kittens all sleeping in a pile next to the stove, and I saw the light begin to come in through the windows. Dawn. I had worked the night through, and She had not touched me. I had beaten Her this night, and I would again the next night and the next. I would no longer be Her puppet, Her pawn. Her ideas for me were not wholesome and I would have no part of them ever again.

Ever again.

I looked down at myself, covered completely with a sawdust-and-sweat paste, gritty and distasteful. I saw my ribs and my hip bones protruding, and I knew that my health would return, and my apartment would be cleaned, and I would get another job and return to normal. Soon. Very soon.

I leaned against the stove for support. The dawn was breaking and I was becoming faint. I took a long drink of water from the tap, and then, without taking the time or energy to shower, I crawled into my box and brought the lid down. The fit was perfect.

She will see what I have done to keep Her from me, and She will leave me alone.

And I will miss Her.

"I thought I was going insane. God, my flesh crawls whenever I think about it. I began to understand what real evil is. I mean, I saw it. When these things happened, when I punched through and met her on . . . on what is that place, a different plane? Anyway, it was like there were always two Angelinas. One the victim, the

essentially good girl, the one that I knew here in Westwater, and then there was the other one, the evil one, the one that lived inside the dark place and pulled the strings to make her dance.

"God, I don't know. Maybe that other one wasn't Angelina. Maybe it was something else altogether. I guess I'm just afraid to let my imagination dwell on what it might be. But one thing's for certain: There were two of them there, and together they were awful.

"I began to get a sense of where she was, though. Every time I broke through, I kind of felt mountains. I knew she was up in the mountains, somewhere. I looked at maps all day long, subscribed to more newspapers. I knew that it wouldn't be long. She'd make a mistake and I'd have her.

"Then, of course, that big story broke, and I was on my way."

21

One night went by and She didn't contact me. Then another night, then a whole week. My emotions were so intense they were physical. I ached to see Her again; I wanted with all my being to be with Her, to laugh and watch Her, to feel Her next to me, with me, inside me, around me. I missed Her so much that I felt like hurting myself in order to outdo the pain, I felt like curling up in the corner and rocking back and forth with the ache of it.

Simultaneously, I shivered with the excitement of being free of Her. My teeth chattered and I wore heavy sweaters and bulky socks, even during the warm summer nights, and my arms and legs were always cold. I could hardly believe that I had really done it, that I had beaten that which threatened to destroy my soul.

In the back of my mind I didn't think She would give up that easily, I thought that She had just withdrawn and was watching me, that I was fooling myself into thinking that

I had even a modicum of power over Her vast personality. But I refused to dwell on those thoughts. I just wrapped the blanket of my resolve a little tighter and made yet another set of plans for my life.

Eventually the shivering stopped. My internal thermostat seemed to return to normal; I did without the blankets and sweaters. Still, my schedule was nocturnal, but that was fine—one thing at a time, and I knew that eventually this too would change.

I ventured out now and again to the convenience market for supplies, and I tried my hand at baking breads and things in my little oven. The nights stretched long before me, and I bought extra lamps to chase the darkness away from my apartment. I avoided the warping influence of the night as best I could, and each dawn, when exhausted from the effort of it, I would crawl into my box and congratulate myself on another successful night.

After several weeks had gone by and still I hadn't heard from Her, I began to feel much better about myself; my boldness grew and I began to leave the house in the early evening and spend some time with Cap before the crowd accumulated at the Yacht Club.

He was always genuinely delighted to see me; his enthusiasm I found hard to believe at first, but I grew fond of it over time. He seemed concerned over my appearance, always discussing vitamins and the benefits of rare meat, and it was an odd occasion indeed when I escaped the Yacht Club without something to eat in my stomach, or at least in my pocket. My appetite was poor, there was no doubt. I baked and cooked, but one or two bites would sate me. Most of the food went to the cats, or in the case of the baked goods, to the family of rats that had moved into the spare bedroom.

I begged off explanations by telling Cap that I'd been down with the flu, and was having a hard time regaining my weight. He would boom his laughter to the rafters and polish tables and talk about how much he could eat at a real family-type Thanksgiving dinner. Cap loved food. His eyes glazed over when he talked about brown roasted turkeys and crunchy nutty cranberry relish, and I helped him sweep the floor and laughed at his preoccupation with that which would most likely prove to be his downfall. Heart trouble was no stranger to Cap, and he knew he was digging his own grave with his fork.

And when the locals would start coming in for their evening drinks, I would kiss Cap on the cheek and slip out the door to go for a walk.

I began to roam the little town each night, thinking at every corner about returning home to try to sleep, to try to break the routine, sleep a little bit each night to regain a normal schedule, to be awake a little bit each day. But eventually, as the weeks passed and the nights grew longer, the darkness seeped back in through my pores, and I gave up on the idea; became content, instead, to leave the majority of the shops to the daylight personnel, to leave the average, normal life to the nine-to-fivers.

I roamed the streets every night, speaking in night language to the other regulars I met.

And the nights turned chill, and Spartacus and her daughters each had a litter, and I no longer turned the lights on at home. I roamed from sundown to sunup, restlessly, relentlessly, searching for something, anything, that would give me peace, that would fill the nameless void that screamed with emptiness, hollowness.

I knew She waited for me, and I desperately sought a diversion, an alternate path, a way to outwait Her, though I knew Her patience was eternal. I could see it as clearly as I could see the face of the full moon.

In November, the snow began to fly, the visitors flocked back, and the Yacht Club was packed from opening to closing. I avoided it entirely.

I felt brittle, as if my bones had bleached, and my coats

and warm clothes were no longer enough to keep the cold out as I wandered through the night and the snow. Even my apartment was cold. The broken window the cats used for a door was always breathing cold air on us.

One evening, I drew my cape from the closet and unfolded it. It felt heavy, heavier than I remembered it. A weird thrill of dreaded anticipation zinged through me as I fingered the material. It had been a long time. I swung it about my shoulders and tied it at the throat.

For warmth, I said, for warmth, and I put my down coat over it and went out into the night, into the winter, and hated the fact that the darkness outside had begun to feel more like home.

I shoved my hands deep into the pockets, my fingers automatically closing on the pocket toys, and I unconsciously rubbed them as I strode along the darkened warehouse street. It was barely ten o'clock at night, but the evening was wickedly cold and my nose was red and running before I had gone three blocks. Snow hung unfallen and heavy in the air, muffling the sounds, distorting them so that the crunch of ice beneath my boot heels had a fourth-dimension sound, and the yellow lights on the white snow, and the freezing cold all added to a surrealistic aura in the town. It felt deserted.

I felt deserted.

The restaurants and bars were filled to overflowing in town, so I avoided the main street, not wanting to deal with drunks or happy talk. I didn't feel like being lured into the coziness of a fire and brightly colored sweaters worn by people with fresh hair and rosy cheeks.

I scuffled my boots against the packed snow of the sidewalk on the street that paralleled Main.

As I came to the corner of Jack and Poplar streets, I saw Joshua's little shop, lit up all warm and inviting. In a couple more strides, I saw Joshua, sitting in his customary posture behind the cash register, hefting a paper bag to his lips, then wiping the overflow onto the filthy, ragged cuff of his army jacket.

Visiting with Joshua was an irregular occurrence, but not necessarily an unpleasant one. I pushed the door open and almost gagged in the warm, humid air that smelled like cheap wine and Joshua.

"Hey, Angelina! How are you on this raw night?"

"Cold, Joshua, thank you. And you?"

"Mindin' the store. Mindin' the store. Come by for some reading material, or just to jaw?"

"Just some company, if you don't mind."

"Mind? Gets lonesome here. Listen. Look around. I gotta go in the back a minute. Help any customers out if they come in, okay?" He cackled and grabbed his steel crutches from where they leaned against the wall, then made his crippled way through the striped curtain that separated the front of the newsstand from the back room.

The back room, I knew from previous visits, consisted of a filthy toilet, singular washbasin, and stacks and stacks of old magazines and newspapers. The front of the shop was similar—only the magazines and newspapers were somewhat fresher, more current, and the cash register was new. Joshua had told me that the merchants' association came in every now and then and cleaned up the front for him, washed the floor, painted it up a bit, but they never bothered with the back.

Behind the counter were candy, gum, and cigarettes, to the left and right were big magazine stands. Four free-standing paperback-book racks, heavy on war novels, stood about, and the picture-window display area was piled high with comic books. Newspapers were stacked on the floor around the front counter, so in order to make a purchase, one had to stand several feet from the counter and lean over. Joshua liked that, putting people off balance.

He had all the local trade. This tidy, pretty little town supported its local embarrassment, its local war hero, its token broken Vietnam vet that it fed and cared for like a pet. Joshua slopped up its charity like gravy with a big, chewy crust of scorn.

And it had made him old.

I had stacked two bundles of newspapers and was sitting on them, loosening my coat, when I heard Joshua finish on the toilet, heard the clank of his metal crutches, and soon he swung back through the curtain.

"Did you take care of that run of customers for me?" He smiled. I felt somehow as if I were the only one in town whom Joshua didn't make fun of. He threw me a paper bag, which I caught in surprise reflex. "Eat something, willya?"

I opened the bag and found two hardening doughnuts.

"Oh, thank you, Joshua. I'm not hungry."

"Wasting away. What the hell's the matter with you, anyway?"

"I've been ill lately, I think, but I'm over it now."

"Well, that's good. Don't know anyone else who'd come sit with me at night." There was a long pause while Joshua focused his attention on the bottle in the paper bag. He never drank while I was with him, but he stared at his liquor as if it were his only reference point. "Why do you?"

"I like you."

"Bullshit. Nobody likes me. I'm crude."

"I like you."

"Yeah?" I almost saw the flicker of a smile in the corners of his mouth, but he wouldn't allow himself that. "What do you like about me?"

"What's on the other side of your crude front. What you could be if you took off that face and put on one that's more human."

"You don't know what the fuck you're talking about. You lose both your legs and your balls and then let's talk again about being human." The expression on his face never changed. This, too, was a part of his front.

"Does nothing touch you? Have you sealed yourself so

141

tightly that nothing can touch you?" Suddenly I felt as if Joshua were me, and I was confronting myself, a strange, inconceivable part of myself.

"Maybe you better go."

"I've touched you, then, haven't I?"

"Get outta here, Angelina. You're boring tonight."

I took off my coat. "I care about you, Joshua. I care that you sit here night after night and drink and moan to yourself." This, too, was a part of myself. "I'd like to touch you . . . in a different way."

His look never wavered. I felt a flicker of interest flash across the back of his eyes, *felt* it, as if it were my own, my own wish to change, to merge with a better portion of myself, but on Joshua, it was a hope too radical to be real, the hope that a girl, a real girl, would ever look at him, ever touch him in a loving way again. He continued to stare at me, and I realized that I did care for him. I cared for Joshua, and I cared for myself, my own well-being. His face was suddenly young and innocent, my own superimposed upon it, as in some accidental photograph, both wrapped up in the ravages of disappointment.

A shudder ran through my body and I rubbed my arms. When I looked back at him, he was again Joshua, dirty, nasty, bitter Joshua. I had closed the door on the frightening face of affection.

He groped for his crutches and stood up, coming toward me. His face showed the ache of longing. The soft touch of a woman's hands on his skin would be enough to change his life. I had this power, and had to use it this moment. I stood, knocked the stacks of comic books into red and blue rivers of slick covers, and spread my coat atop them in the display window, smoothing them out and rearranging their sliding mass.

I separated from myself at this point. I felt powerless over what I was doing, not understanding my motives, not understanding what I was about to do, even. I knew only that Joshua needed hope; he had lived too long with fear. I dissuaded him from locking the door with a touch of my hand on his arm. He turned off the lights, and a moment later, I turned them on again, feeling a weird, agitated excitement growing in my stomach.

He sat on my coat, on the edge of the display, stood his crutches against the wall, and as I reached for the ribbon that tied the cape around my neck, my saliva glands began to flow. It was then that I knew my purpose, and the hunger that had been growing in me all these months; the ravenous, starving ache had been for Joshua, not for Her, not for anything else but him. Him.

And there he sat, looking small and fragile. Frail. Anxious. Waiting. Knowing.

I twirled my cape around him and gave him my love. In the window. In the light. And I tasted the aspirin, oh, how his pain never receded. And I tasted the wine he drank and the sugar in the food he ate, I tasted the pain and more pain and the isolation and anguish, and the comics crinkled and shifted wetly beneath us and Boyd looked on at it all, and I didn't care.

And neither did Joshua.

"As soon as I saw the headlines in the Denver paper, I found Seven Slopes on the map and took off. I didn't sleep much the night before, so I was kind of spacey as I drove. I just remember two things from that trip. One is that I drove too fucking fast, I knew it at the time, but I just wanted to catch her, to have it be over, to nail her and have her put away. Away from society and out of my mind. I was too tired and I drove too fast. Luckily, I didn't have any problems.

"The other thing I remember was a phrase that kept running through my mind. Know how sometimes a song will get stuck in your head? Well, from the time I saw that headline, grabbed my suitcase, and was out the door, until the time I pulled into Seven Slopes, the thought that wound around my head was this: How

could she ... How could she snuggle up so warm and close to a
guy and then just suck him dry? In the front window of a store, for
Christ's sake."

22

Faint strains of music with a melancholy cant hung suspended in the air above me. They moved slowly, sluggishly;
I urged them with a little nudge of my psyche: Liven up,
become more, give me, give me ... praise. Let me soar, take
me with you and let us sing the music of the spheres!

But instead, it felt as if it were dying, it slowly wound
down with a sickening grate, like a scratched phonograph
record when the plug has been pulled.

I awakened slowly, feeling first the cold that had seeped
into my bones during my sleep. I felt the darkness around
me and it was good, it was comfortable, and I felt the hard
wood beneath me and around me and it was secure, it was
close, it was good.

And then I remembered Joshua, and my stomach lurched
with a vile shudder. I saw his face, not in peace, but with a
gruesome grin at death.

I pushed the lid of my box open and gulped fresh air. My
apartment was pitch-black. My head swirled in sweeps of
dizziness, I had to hold it with both hands to still it. Slowly I
climbed out of the box and down from the table, steadying
myself for a moment before dashing into the bathroom to
lose everything my stomach contained.

Black it was, the vile stuff that poured forth from my
mouth and splashed in the toilet. The sweet, tangy ambrosia
that had been mine the night before had turned black and
diseased and hateful during the course of the day, during
my sleep, bloating my stomach, now to be spewed forth in a
raging gush of acid.

Boyd's word came to mind. Murder. I had murdered

Joshua; there was no question. I had not acted to ease his pain; I had not acted in carefree delight; I had not acted to please Her. There had been no musical pleasure, no warmth or friendly aftermath. I had sealed Her from my life and killed anyway. I had murdered Joshua, and in so doing had lain waste my own soul.

I lay my cheek against the stained porcelain and watched the thread of saliva that connected my lips to the swirling black mass in the water. My stomach continued to lurch convulsively with small dry heaves. I waited, beads of sweat cooling my skin as my breath echoed back from inside the bowl.

My stick-thin arms were the same color as the toilet; they had not seen the light of day in a year.

I had renounced Her and yet continued to live in Her manner.

She was gone and Joshua was gone and I had no one, no one, no one.

No one except . . . the Boyd of my fantasies.

Depression and despair stiffened my joints. I rested my face on arms crossed over the bowl and felt the hurt from the inside out.

It was time to go. My time at Seven Slopes had ended. I would soon hear my footfalls on the highway again.

Slowly I got up, showered, and dressed warmly. What had happened here? It seemed as though the past year and a half had been no more than a weird memory. I had come to Seven Slopes seeking employment, fun, friends. Life had been new and exciting. My future had been shining and filled with anticipatory delight, and now it was dark and ugly and frightening.

What had I done wrong? My intentions were good, at least they felt right; I had never wanted to hurt anyone, and look at what I had done . . . oh, look . . .

My knees sagged as I considered my life in Seven Slopes. It was as if I looked at it for the very first time. Had I never considered my motives before? Had I never been honest with myself before? Had I lied and cheated and sinned like this of my own volition all this time?

It seemed incredible.

And right now I had a choice. I could stay and be caught; turn myself in. Or, I could leave, straighten up, and try to lessen my debt to society by becoming a contributing member. The debate wanted to go on, but I had already made my choice.

I pulled my backpack from the closet shelf and loaded it with warm, practical clothes, leaving all the bright, spring clothes that had been so pleasurable once, but had hung, musty, for a long time. I emptied the refrigerator and fed the contents to the cats and the rats. I walked through my apartment, touching all the things, remembering how I'd acquired them, the thrill of furnishing my first apartment, paying my own way, and I felt sad to be leaving it all.

Especially . . .

I spread my cape over the top of the box, smoothed it out where it was stiff and crusty with Joshua's blood. The cape on top of the box on top of the wooden table looked like a shrine. And, in a way, it was. It was a shrine to adulthood, to growing up and leaving the things of childhood behind. It was a symbol of seeking truth, and justice, and making good all wrongs.

I would come back to Seven Slopes someday, and when I did, it would be as a good person, a nice person, an adult, and I would join the Yacht Club and play bridge and do all the right and proper things adults do.

I opened the window in the second bedroom so the rats could climb up and out, then shut the bedroom door so the cats would not eat them as they tried to leave. I said my good-byes to each of the cats and kittens, my friends, their yowling voices dear to me, their feline smell pleasant and comfortable. I would miss them.

In a final gesture of farewell, I walked one last time

into the bedroom, I suppose to convince myself that I was leaving, that there was no hope in staying, and as I did, I saw what they would see when they came in.

Indignation rose through me, knowing they would soon violate my space, enter my domain, my kingdom, and they would see before them just what I was seeing now.

Well, they would not. I swept my cape from the lid of the box, wadded it up, and stuffed it into the last space of my pack.

Wait, Angelina, I told myself. You won't be needing the cape. Leave it.

And then I thought of Boyd seeing my little shrine, for surely he would, and I smiled, and returned the cape to its dramatic place atop the box. Then I hefted the pack to my shoulders, and without a backward glance, I left.

At the top of the stairs, the frozen air fell upon my face like a mask. I looked from left to right down the deserted street. My breath plumed out before me as I tried to make a decision. Where to go. Which way. Right or left.

The cold began to gnaw at me, and I wished for a little more meat on my bones. South. I would go to the warmer south.

Westwater.

Lewis.

My boot heels quickly regained their familiar rhythmic beat; my stride had purpose, and I headed for the pay telephone next to the library. Small change jangled in my pocket and I thought there would probably be enough for a quick conversation. All the way there, I argued with myself about whether to call or to just show up. If I called, he could tell me not to come. If I just arrived at his house, he could refuse me in person. Which would be worse? But surely he would want to see me. Lewis had loved me once, there had to be residue from that. I had to at least offer him the opportunity. Maybe we could regain what we had . . . maybe we had both grown, changed.

As I deposited the coins, my mind flickered back to Westwater, to the teen dance, to Boyd's truck and that haunting, magical night we spent together, to the bus station and the man in the coat with the beaver collar. Could I really return?

Then the line was ringing, and a female voice answered.

"Hello?"

I was shocked into silence for a moment, and she repeated, "Hello?" It was the voice of a woman; I could see her, tall and thin, with raven-dark hair, a good cook and probably a tennis player. She and Lewis were young and healthy together, a good match, an up-and-coming pair, the beginnings of a lifetime of family. What on earth was I doing?

I cleared my throat, and in a voice that sounded so young, so weak, so inferior, I said, "Is Lewis home?"

"No, I'm afraid he's not. May I take a message? Are you calling long-distance?"

"Yes, I'm a friend of his from a long time ago . . ." A baby cried in the background. ". . . and I just wanted to talk with him for a moment."

"Well, can he call you back?" Not an ounce of jealousy in her voice. She's secure.

"No, no, is this his wife?"

"Yes."

"No, no message. Tell me, is he well?"

"Yes, he's fine. We're all fine."

"That's good," I said. "That's all I really wanted to know."

"Well, okay. You're sure . . ."

"I'm sure. Thank you. Good-bye." I hung up, and pressed my forehead to the side of the booth.

Up-and-coming Lewis. Housing appreciation. No, he and I could never, never.

I was headed back on the road again, with no destination, with no direction, knowing no one, starting over again, fighting not only myself and the adolescent pressures of growing up, but fighting the elements and the social conditions of life as well.

It was almost too much to carry.

I thought briefly of Rolf, thought of going to Pennsylvania. I thought of Boyd, I knew he would not be married with a child. I thought of the local police station, of a warm cup of chocolate and someone to confide in.

I turned away from the phone booth, already exhausted, shoulders aching from the psychological load, and looked into the winter sky, saw a few snowflakes falling by the streetlight. The town was deserted. Of course. It was Christmas Eve.

I needed a place in which to heal, to change. I needed someone to help me, to teach me, to show me how.

And all of a sudden I knew where to go. Sarah. Surely her invitation was still good. She probably even had a Christmas tree.

"The police opened her apartment as soon as I arrived, which was about three days loo late. I, like, saw it when she killed that poor guy, that newspaper vendor, and when I read about it, I knew where she was and drove up there right away. Seems everybody in town knew Angelina, and everybody had nice things to say about her. About the worst comment I got was that she was a little odd, but nobody would believe that she could've done the damage she had.

"Until we opened her apartment.

"God, it was awful. The whole place was black. Walls, table, curtains, all black. It smelled like a den, or a lair, or a bat cave. There were the remnants of apparently what the cats had been eating for the days since she'd been gone. The cats smelled bad enough, but ... well, it was pretty hard to take. The place was absolutely filthy, with the window open and the cats in and out, and more cats, and cats in heat and fighting and litters under the table, and oh, Jesus.

"The window in the back bedroom had been left open and rats had come in and nested in there, but the police chased them out and closed the window behind them.

"In the other bedroom was a mattress on the floor, all torn up and clawed, and a table with a coffin on it, for Christ's sake. The policeman in front of me backed out of that room so fast he almost knocked me over. He crossed himself and wouldn't go near it. I was afraid too, but knew it had to be opened. The other policemen were happy to let me do it.

"A yellow tom cat had draped himself across the top. I shooed him away and he spit at me and jumped down. The box was covered with a piece of blue or black terrycloth. I pulled it off—one side was all stiff, hardened. The police put it into a plastic bag. Underneath was the coffin.

"The coffin was patched together with bent nails and rough edges, it was no more than a coffin-shaped box—a crate, actually. I looked at that thing and knew I was going to open it, and wondered what the hell I was doing there. I tried to steel myself, and lifted the lid.

"It was empty, but not completely. My initial rush of relief that there wasn't somebody inside was quickly overcome when I smelled the scent from the box. I leaned over and sniffed, and it was unmistakable. Then I knew. I knew for sure. There was no doubt. It was Angelina's scent. I knew it from memory, she'd left it inside of my truck, impressed on my coat, everywhere. She had a particular smell, as we all do, but it always smelled like perfume in my mind.

"Now, here, it smelled the same, there was no mistake. It was strong, but it was also different, it was more . . . God, how do I describe it? Feral? Animal? It's like once you've smelled a foxhole, you never forget it. Like that.

"So I knew in that moment that finding Angelina would be no small task. She had turned, all right. She'd be crafty. But I also had some important things on my side. She was really sick. Really sick. Sick enough to sleep in a . . . God.

"Sick people, unless they get well, keep getting sicker."

23

There was little traffic that Christmas Eve. I walked the highway bearing southwest out of Seven Slopes, quickly leaving the entire experience behind me. I walked into the endless night, freezing cold, with only the stars for light. My body was heavy, burdened with sadness, with loneliness.

Two miles down the highway, I connected with the main freeway. A light snow fell and I kicked pebbles out of my way and felt through the soles of my boots for the vibration that indicated an approaching truck. With each one that passed me by, I stepped more boldly into their paths so they inevitably honked their monstrous air horns and had to steer around me. Couldn't they see that I needed a ride? It was Christmas, after all. Where had Christianity gone? Then the truck would roar past, the backwash nearly knocking me from my feet, sucking me into the giant tires, and just for a moment, it would be warm, warm from the friction, and then it was cold again, in the freezing wind, and soon the silence returned, always deeper than before, and then even the asphalt vibration ceased. The world was a desperately lonely place.

I walked on, trying to keep my mind on my stride, on the miles going by, on the next town, which surely couldn't be far away. My destination seemed abominably distant—so distant that it was not even a reality, it was a farfetched goal. I don't think I really believed that I'd make it all the way to New Mexico. It was too cold, I was too tired, too used up.

And then I noticed a glow in the sky ahead. I looked behind me to make sure, yes, the sky was definitely lighter ahead. A town. Soon I'd come over a ridge and see a cafe sign, the first truck stop this side of town, and it would be warm and serve hot chocolate and I could stay in there and rest, warm up and maybe even get a ride south, maybe one ride all the way, all the way to New Mexico.

Then I heard my boot heels, felt their rhythm, and the old feeling washed through me. I felt it, but was reluctant to give in to it; my misery had kept me warm all these miles. But there it was, undeniable excitement. I had left Her behind; I was getting out of town, making a new start. What on earth had I to be morose about? Life was good; I was free. I was intelligent and able; my past need not haunt me.

I skipped a few steps as the glow in the sky became brighter. My whole body tingled in freedom. I felt the tremble in the ground, it grew to a rumble, and the next truck stopped and gave me a ride.

It was warm in the cab, and the driver had a thermos of hot coffee that he shared. We drove right through that town, and the next, my teeth chattering in the warmth of the truck. I had no conception of how cold I'd been until I started to warm up, and then the task seemed impossible. Frost had etched the marrow of my bones.

The driver's name was Ned, and he was a nice boy. I often caught him peering at me with curiosity, and while I was loath to be rude to him—he was, after all, giving me a ride, warmth, and coffee—I did not appreciate his overt interest. I located a blanket behind my seat and wrapped up in it.

"You a runaway?"

"From what?"

"You know. School. Family."

"No. I have no family."

"Where you headed?"

Exasperating, his questions. "New Mexico."

"Got family there?"

"I have no family, as I said. I have friends there."

"Aren't you awful young?"

This was too much. I turned to look right into his face, so

he needn't keep sneaking peeks around my coat collar. "I'm not too young," I said.

"Oh," he said, obviously embarrassed. "I'm sorry. At first you seemed a lot younger. I see now . . ." His voice trailed off.

Silent miles rolled by.

"So when was the last time you ate?"

"I'm not hungry."

"That wasn't the question."

"What is your interest here? Are you trying to make conversation or be my keeper?"

"Listen. I pick up what I think is a half-frozen, starving little kid on the side of the road. I ain't supposed to pick up riders anyway. I'm just trying to help you out and all you do is give me lip."

He was right. I retreated into the folds of blanket.

"I'm going to stop for something to eat. I'll buy you a sandwich if you like; maybe eating will take some of the meanness out of you. Or you can see if you can find another ride. I don't know why your attitude is so bad, but I don't need it."

I wasn't at all hungry; my stomach shivered with cold.

Eventually he pulled his rig into a cafe parking lot, parked it with skill, and shut it down. "Junction a mile ahead," he said. "You can catch a southbound ride there. Good luck."

"Thank you," I said, and with trembling fingers unwrapped myself from the blanket and felt for the door handle.

"Keep the blanket."

"Oh, no, that's all right. Listen," I said, folding the blanket and stowing it behind the seat. "I'm sorry if I was a bother."

"No bother, just no fun. I can have a better time alone," he said, then jumped down, waited for me to get out, then turned his back on me and walked into the cafe.

He turned his back on me and walked into the cafe.

He turned his back on me.

153

I watched him go, trying to raise enough indignation to go after him, but I couldn't.

Again, life was hard; it settled heavily on my shoulders. I watched him go, thought of running after him, apologizing. I thought of following him into the cafe, ordering a cup of hot chocolate, but I wouldn't be mistaken for begging another chance. I watched him go, then settled my pack on my shoulders, adjusting it away from the tender spot where it had been rubbing, and began walking. Next time I would be nicer.

Steadily moving, placing one foot in front of the other, eventually I could make out the junction. It was one lone streetlight shining a yellow pool of light at a lonely crossroads. As I got closer, it seemed lonelier and more barren with a light snow falling diagonally through the spill of light.

I felt more and more depressed as I looked at that little cone of light, with the silence of the night and the closeness of the snow surrounding me. I finally arrived at the crossroads, stood on the curb under the light, and that was the end of my endurance. I dropped my pack to my feet and locked my frozen knees, standing up as straight as I could, my shivers bordering on convulsions. I could not go on.

It would have been better if Ned had never picked me up at all. Becoming semi-warm and then freezing again was much worse. My down coat was no match for this biting wind; the portion of leg between my coat and my boots had no feeling, nor did my toes. My fingers were stiff.

I put each hand up the opposite sleeve, and stood straight, shoulders hunched up about my ears. If I remembered the fireside talk in Seven Slopes correctly, I would soon become sleepy as my blood thickened and ran sluggishly through my brain, and I would just lie down to rest, to take a little nap.

Such a pleasant notion. I closed my eyes. Taking a little sleep sounded like a wonderful idea. I could almost imagine a nice, friendly little dream, and maybe, maybe when I woke up, I would be at home, in bed, cuddled down soft and warm, this whole thing having been a terrible nightmare.

Or maybe not. Maybe dying right here, right now, would be best. There would be no more running. No more loneliness. No more being the stranger, the different one. I wouldn't have to get well, or get better, or strive to try to stay awake during the daylight hours. I wouldn't have to worry about my past, or my future. Or Her. I felt myself teeter. I thought I'd better lie down before I fell down, but my mind was too busy to hold that thought long enough to act. Why did everybody think of slitting wrists or hanging? This was so superior. Just go outside on Christmas Eve and take a little nap.

Even the cold lost its threat. The concept of cold ceased to exist. The cold became my friend, my companion. Come in, come in. You and I will rest together for a long time. How comforting. How luxurious.

Then there was a terrible noise, and I opened my eyes and a car was in front of me, honking. A man looked out the window, and I wanted to wave him on, no thank you, I'm fine now, but my arms were too tired, so I just closed my eyes again.

My arms were too tired to resist him, too, when he came around and pushed me into the front seat of his car. My knees wouldn't bend, and I was afraid he'd break my bones, but even that didn't matter too much. Sitting was an improvement over standing. I rested my head on his shoulder, feeling the vibrations of his voice, and slept.

"I showed the police in Seven Slopes all the information I had on those three murders from Westwater. I got their attention.

"Then one cop started to tell me about all those missing-persons reports that had been filed, up about five hundred and seventy percent in the last year. Damn these little towns. They keep their cards held so close to the chest—they're afraid for their precious

tourist industry. Their lid on publicity kept Angelina in business. It let her slip away, too.

"Drugs, they thought, or flakey people who were not where they said they would be. Transient place, during the season, they said. Can't be held accountable for tourists.

"But I knew better. I knew better. Angelina. Damn.

"I spent a while in Seven Slopes, talking to people—people where she worked, people where she hung out, waiting for another clue, combing through the newspapers, the wire press, the police reports. Just waiting for another clue. We started to get a little press on the situation, and some national cooperation, and I finally felt like I was doing something positive.

"And every time I saw hitchhikers on the road, I stopped and yelled at them. Jesus, kids out there accepting rides with strangers. They have no idea, they have no fucking idea at all what's out there.

" 'Things can happen to you just because you're in the wrong place at the wrong time,' I'd tell them. 'You keep hitchhiking and you're putting yourself right smack dab in the center of harm's way. You're asking for it. Don't flirt with danger. Stay the hell out of its way.

" 'Go home,' I said. 'Lock your doors.' "

24

When I awakened, I was naked in limp, white sheets, and glad the nightmare was over. I could sleep the rest of the night in peace. I pulled the blankets up and rolled over.

Simultaneously I smelled the rank odor on the pillow next to mine and felt the gnawing ache in my legs. It hadn't been a nightmare. I became instantly awake and alert. On guard.

I checked quickly around me, noted the sleazy motel room, noted also that I was alone. Then I examined myself.

I seemed to be untouched; at least the creature who had

slept next to me had had the decency not to deposit his odor on me, or in me, as I slept. My feet and legs ached, the meat of my calves felt squishy as I pinched it. The pinch didn't hurt, I couldn't even feel it, but the ache remained. Fear sank into my bowels. My legs had been frozen and thawed. I swung them out of bed and tried to stand up. Fire flushed through me, but I stood.

I found my clothes folded neatly on top of the dresser next to his briefcase. He hadn't deserted me. He would return. The neon from the motel sign cast pink through the window. The evening felt early.

By the time I finished showering, I was light-headed and weak-kneed. I came dripping from the bathroom and with blackening vision made my way to the bed. Once down, with deep breaths, my sight cleared and I saw the weasel of a man standing over me, holding a paper bag of foul-smelling food.

"Here," he said. "Better eat something."

I took the bag from him, but had no stomach for what it contained. I picked at it while he watched me; I listened to him talk as he sat on the edge of the bed. I hoped to discern who he was, what he wanted, where we were, and where he was going.

"I drive nights. That's the best time. I usually stop where I'm going and get a couple hours of early morning sleep, freshen up a bit and I'm ready for my sales calls. I guess you're lucky I drive nights, otherwise you might still be out there. Storm hit pretty bad up there, too. You'd still be standing there, up to your nose in snow."

My gratitude was less than overwhelming.

"Anyway, I'm glad to see you awake and eating. I was afraid for a while I was going to have to call an ambulance. I mean, you sure sleep soundly, but then I've never seen anyone frozen like that before." His smile was fleeting, nervous.

I tired of the food and dropped it to the floor.

"How do you feel?"

"I'm healing."

"Well, listen, I've got to get back on the road." He checked his watch. "It's after five. I hate to leave you here, but it's either that or take you with me, at least as far as a hospital, but I can't be responsible for your bills."

"I don't need a hospital. Where are you going?"

"Texas."

"Driving through New Mexico?"

"Hope to make it the whole way through tonight."

I pulled myself out of bed and staggered toward the dresser.

"Hey, wait."

"I'm going with you, if you don't mind."

"I mind. I think you need medical attention. Listen. Right after I leave, you call the hospital to come get you." He approached me. "I know about these things. You can't pay, but they'll treat you. If you're with me, they'll stick me with the bills and I've got a wife . . ." His hand went around my wrist.

"Don't touch me," I said flatly, and his hand jerked back. I sat on the edge of the bed and began to dress. "I don't need a hospital; I need to get to New Mexico. I'll go with you."

"I don't think so. I think you're trouble all the way around." He took his briefcase and little traveling bag from the dresser and opened the door.

I was powerless to stop him. I sat on the edge of the bed, not even knowing if he'd paid the motel bill, and watched him go through the door—the man who'd saved my life. He set his bags on the sidewalk outside and looked in at me as he reached to close the door. My jeans were on but unzipped, one boot was on, my shirt was unbuttoned, my hair was wet. My body ached and I was bone weary.

In that split moment, I saw myself as he must see me, alone, forlorn, and abandoned, and instinctively I knew how to play my hand.

"Please?"

His pointed face softened and his shoulders sagged. He turned to face the parking lot, hands on hips, and I knew I had him. He turned back.

"All right. Two conditions."

I finished dressing.

"One, you're out of my car before morning, and two, if you get sick, I'm dumping you on the side of the road."

He came in and picked up my pack, carried all three bags to the car. I followed, each step painful from my toes to my hip joints. The darkness outside was fresh and new; it welcomed me. I was on my way to Sarah's. I would be there, if not tonight, then the next.

Riding in his car was harder than I thought. His continual chatter rasped my nerves, particularly because every minute or two he asked some kind of question that required some answer, and therefore effort was expended in listening and understanding. This was very hard with most of my attention on the overwhelming, frightening ache in my legs.

I tried every imaginable position, but nothing helped. It didn't matter if I was cross-legged, sitting on my heels, or lying on the backseat with my feet elevated. The ache was the same. I could not get comfortable, and the pain made me restless. I could not sit still.

Around midnight, we crossed over into New Mexico and stopped at a standard, twenty-four-hour truck stop for something to eat. He helped me to a booth, where I sat, pale and trembling, while my traitorous legs screamed at me, and he went in to wash his hands. It was a foolishly long time before I realized he wasn't coming back. When the knowledge finally struck, a stone plopped into the pit of my stomach and sat there, amid the emptiness and bile, and I lifted the greasy menu and found that he'd slipped ten dollars beneath it before slipping out the back.

I ordered hot chocolate and sipped at it, avoiding the

curious eyes of the resident night people. My legs radiated so much pain they seemed to warm the booth.

I had been abandoned. I was on the run, alone, half-crippled, in the middle of nowhere. He had left me cold, without so much as a good-bye. My self-pity flamed into anger. How dare he! Hadn't we shared . . . What?

Just exactly what had you shared, Angelina, I asked myself, and then I realized the worst. The man had saved my life, fed me and driven me, and I had never even asked his name.

The pain in my legs was momentarily forgotten as I marveled at this. What had I become, that I could be so insensitive? My face burned, I held a mouthful of cocoa on my tongue until I could swallow it past the clump of self-pity in my throat, my vision blurred under the wash of unfallen tears.

Don't stop now, Angelina, I told myself. I blinked away the tears, swallowed the chocolate, and swooned slightly with the onslaught of pain from my legs. Sarah. Sarah will know what to do and how to do it. The vision of Sarah stretching on her floor, every fiber tight and smooth, her skin glowing with perspiration and the flush of health made me smile. That is what I want, I thought. And Sarah will know how to give it to me.

I ordered another cup of chocolate and a rare steak, rubbed my legs, and began to look around. The first thing I noticed was the placemat. It was a map of the state of New Mexico, with a big star in the northwest corner that said, "New Mexico State Cafe!" in outlined, dramatic letters. It matched the lettering on the menu. This version of "You Are Here" on the map probably saved the bored waitresses thousands of questions. It lifted my spirits; I hadn't far to go.

I drank the second cup of chocolate and ate small bites of the overcooked steak. The cafe was fairly empty on this cold Christmas night. Truck drivers were at home with their families. I would be fortunate indeed to find a ride.

And if I didn't?

The flush ran through me again. Where would I spend the day? Where could I sleep and not freeze? I needed shelter, darkness, a box—I needed to remember that She was still lurking, just waiting for me to give in, just watching, patiently, oh so patiently.

I calmed myself, rubbing my thighs, and tried to remember, not so long ago, when I was younger, more adventurous, when I never had to worry about where I would sleep—I was One With Creation, and I belonged wherever I happened to be. What had happened to those days?

I was not sure. But something had. Carefree life was for children—the child I had been at that time—that time before Earl Foster, before Lewis, before Boyd.

Three men sat on round green swivel stools at the Formica counter in the New Mexico State Cafe. One boy chain-smoked cigarettes in a corner booth while his rat-haired girlfriend slept with her head on his shoulder. A tiny woman sipped coffee and patted her lipstick with a handkerchief after each swallow, and I began to focus on her. Once I saw the flask she tipped into her coffee each time the tired waitress filled her cup.

She saw me watching and raised an eyebrow, offering me a nip. I smiled, amid my very personal pain, and declined. In a moment, she had joined me, uninvited, but I was too weary to protest. Her reddish-brown hair was so neatly coiffed that I thought she'd tamed it with a hair net. Bright spots of rouge dotted her powdered cheeks, and her eyebrows had been drawn on in a fine line. Brown eyes twinkled out of a wrinkled face with precise lips. She was no larger than I—an elf, I thought—and I smiled at her.

She patted my hand with her old spotted one. "Traveling alone?" she asked. I nodded. "Me, too. This is my Christmas trip, a little Christmas present I give myself every year. I just love to travel. At night, that is. The daytime is too scary for me, all those trucks and buses and ... things." She tipped again into her coffee, then screwed the thimble top on tight and slipped the silver flask into her purse. "Do you like . . . the night?" And her bright little eyes turned predatory as she hooked them into me over the rim of her coffee cup.

I nodded.

"Thought so. Ever wish you were different?" The thrumming in my legs lessened. I couldn't believe this woman. She spoke to my soul.

"Yes. I do."

"Forget it." She waved her hand across the table. "We are the way we are. You're young enough to accept it and enjoy your life in the night. I wasted mine trying to change." Her hands made little piano-playing motions on either side of her coffee as she looked into it, brow furrowed, thinking. "So what do you want?"

"I beg your pardon?"

"What is it you want? Night people always want something. They're always going somewhere or seeking something or just plain out to get something. What's yours?"

I thought for a moment. "I need to get—" I shoved my plate over and pointed at the map on the placemat. "Here."

"I can drive you," she said. "What do you want there?"

I was torn between being incensed at her probing questions and being nice and cooperative in exchange for the ride.

"Friends," I finally choked out. "I have friends to visit there."

"Ah." She chuckled and signaled the worn waitress for more coffee. "A life raft. Someone to save you? That's fine. I'll drive you. You will find that it won't work. But I'll drive you." She paused while the girl filled her cup, then she emptied the last dribble of liquor into it and stirred the black liquid with a spoon. "Will you let me?"

I nodded. She smiled at me, turning her head this way and that, looking me over, and I sipped my cold cocoa and felt the ache in my legs and was glad this woman, this old, strange, intriguing woman, would take care of me, all the way to Sarah's house. We sat in silence for a long time, almost too long. And then, with a gasp, I remembered.

"My name's Angelina Watson. What's yours?"

"Rosemary. Rose." Her sharp eyes glittered at me as she finished her coffee in silence. Then, with lips tight, she drew money from her leather handbag and set it on the table. "Shall we be on our way, then?"

Obediently I followed, hiding the pain that rocked the top of my skull as I stood, feeling very small and inexperienced. It didn't occur to me until later—until it was too late—that she had told me that night people were always out looking for something. Instead of asking her name, I should have asked what she wanted in return for the ride.

But by then I already knew.

"I felt her moving away from me. I felt her moving south, and it was all I could do to stay in Seven Slopes and wait. I itched to be back on the road, back on the trail, but all my information was routed here, and I had to wait. Waiting is the hardest part of the hunt. I just prayed to have one of those experiences where I could see out of her eyes so I could look around and maybe recognize a landmark or something . . . It was hard, that waiting. The hardest waiting I've ever done. To be so close . . .

"And then I felt Angelina hurting, hurting real bad, and all the disgust and all the hate I'd felt for her melted, as if . . . well, it just melted. Then I didn't want to hunt her anymore, I wanted to hold her. I wanted to stop her from hurting, stop her from hurting others. I felt that if I could stop one, the other would automatically stop. If she didn't hurt anybody else, she wouldn't hurt herself.

"I spent most of my time in the Hot-Dogger Bar, trying to figure out my life, and that's where they found me when they finally got word."

25

Her suit was tailored, her coat leather, her car luxurious. Rosemary took old-lady steps over packed snow to her car, got in, and started it up with a wild cloud of frosty exhaust. I walked slowly, more like an old man, and by the time I was able to swing my deadening legs inside, the interior was warming quickly. The pain clouded my brain, I leaned my head back and closed my eyes. If it had been a pain I could press, a pain I could grit my teeth against, an acute pain, one I could scream over, it might have been easier. But it was just an infernal ache, a continual, inescapable, nauseating ache.

The miles rolled beneath us as I agonized, trying everything I knew to rid myself of the pain, or at least to ease it. Rosemary's presence was comforting, I could feel her shiny eyes on me as she checked me every now and again, sometimes patting my shoulder as she did.

It was a long time before I could speak, before I could offer Rosemary any company. And that was only after She came for me, to offer me bribes, to lure me back to the old ways.

I fell through, for the briefest of moments, into the void, and She was there. She cupped my chin in Her hands, ever so delicately, and Her touch was like velvet. Her love and warmth surrounded my delirious head, She cooled my forehead with Her breath, lay Her cheek next to mine, and I knew Her offer.

She would lift the pain.

It was such a compelling idea, to have normal, pain-free legs. I dwelled for a moment on how wonderful it would be, and for another moment on how much I had missed Her (oh, yes, that was the ache that I felt) and I opened my eyes to look upon Her loving face. Boyd stared at me from over Her shoulder, *he judged me,* and reality slammed me back into the car, by Rosemary's side, into the pain of my frostbitten legs.

"*No!*" I said, teeth gritted. "I won't pay that price!"

Rosemary's eyes were wide with alarm and I began to talk—began to talk about Sarah.

Sarah. She had made it on her own. Lived, loved, raised her son, held a job, cooked meals. Adult. Responsible. Led a healthy life. Sarah would show me how. She was a good person, a kind person. She had helped me once; she would save me now.

Sarah. The very thought of her swarthy, part-Indian, maybe part-Oriental, complexion, and her broad, straight teeth in a big unself-conscious smile, was enough to make me sit up straight. She had everything I wanted. She had feelings, she had love. She had friends, and knew how to be a friend. She had family—a son. I wanted a son someday; I wanted a place of my own filled with bright colors and patterns and light. Fresh air. I wanted a stove and a singing teapot. I wanted a job and a car and a way to help strangers in need.

I looked at Rosemary, hooked over the steering wheel like a little bird. I didn't always want to be the one who needed help.

My legs ached.

The miles rolled by and so did the hours. Eventually patches of city lights began to shine down on me, curled up on the car seat, holding my knees. Rosemary made a series of turns. The streetlights slid in different patterns across the seat. Then we stopped. She turned off the engine, and the silence was a friend. Her cool hand touched my forehead.

"Wait right here and I'll send someone out for you," she said, then left, slamming the door behind her. A few moments later, a big Indian man opened the door and lifted me out, carried me effortlessly and silently up an old wooden stairway and through a door that Rosemary held open. The room smelled musty, old. It was a pleasant smell—dry and warm. He lay me on a sagging bed, then took cash from her and grunted as he left.

The bedspread beneath me had once been yellow chenille, but was now faded and stained. I shivered and rubbed my arms in semi-conscious misery, looking around at the peeling wallpaper, then looked at Rosemary as she locked the door and began to take off her coat. Her eyes shone like ball bearings.

"A little Christmas present, Angelina. Just a little Christmas present for an old lady, for an old, old lady." She sat on the edge of the bed and pulled wet strands of hair from my feverish, perspiring forehead. "An old lonesome lady wants a little Christmas cheer," she crooned. "Just a little Christmas cheer."

I was too exhausted, too sick, to protest. I saw the loneliness on her face, saw the desperation, saw the fear of rejection, I knew the feeling. I felt the dawn and turned my head toward the window. It was still dark, but I could feel it, it pulled the darkness from me and with the darkness went the last of my strength.

"Rose," I said.

She was unbuttoning my shirt. She stopped and ran her fingers across my cheek.

"What is it?"

"It's dawn."

"You go right ahead. I understand."

"Please . . . You'll be gentle?"

"Of course." And she bent over me and kissed me as tenderly as ever anyone could.

My consciousness faded, and soon I was in the cold land of dreamless, timeless inactivity. The lifeless place of the undead.

I awakened slowly to the ache, the ever-present ache

in my legs. I felt vague unpleasantry—something was not right. In fact, it seemed that something hurt, or my body didn't fit me right anymore, but the scalding ache in my legs overshadowed most other sensations. I was warm, there seemed to be pounds of blankets atop me, and I wasn't alone. Rosemary's tiny form was curled up, naked, at my back.

The moment I began to turn toward her, I made the second discovery—my bonds.

Shock silenced me for a long moment while I examined the leather thongs that bound my forearms together at the elbows and wrists. They were wide, of professional quality with polished silver studs and shackles. There were others that joined my legs together at the knees and ankles; the straps that held my knees were cinched tight to the straps that held my elbows, all of which fastened to a cord that connected with the bedframe. I was trussed up tightly, my knees held almost to my chest. Helpless.

My mind was always sluggish as I first awakened, and it took me a long while to puzzle out that I was being held against my will. But maybe Rosemary had just fallen asleep before she could end her game. Surely she wouldn't . . .

"Rosemary. Rosemary, wake up." I struggled to my back, knees in the air, tenting the covers.

An old, old face turned toward me. Devoid of makeup, Rosemary's wrinkled, puffy face merely acted as grotesque framework for those glittering brown eyes, those sharp pinpoints that captured each nuance of winter-evening light and bore deeply into me. "Hello," she said. "Sleep well?"

"I'm tied up."

"Oh, yes." Bony fingers caressed the leather straps, feeling the edges where they pressed into my skin. "Oh, yes," she repeated, breathlessly. My skin crawled. She yawned and stretched, then slid her scrawny body out of bed and walked naked through a door that I hadn't noticed the night before. I heard the sounds of running water and suddenly my bladder was full. The toilet flushed and she came out again, walking toward me, sagging breasts loosely moving.

"Please untie me."

"Oh, I can't do that yet."

"Rosemary!" I was astonished and beginning to be afraid.

"Don't be afraid." She sat on the edge of the bed, but I shrank away from her. "Rose doesn't want you to leave for a while, okay? Just a little while, and then we'll get into the car and Rosemary will drive you to Sarah's. That's what you want, right? Sarah's? We'll get to Sarah's, just . . . just a little more Christmas for Rose, okay?" Her hand stroked my arm, lulling me. I was still on my guard, but helpless, and wanting to trust her, wanting desperately to believe her. "Rosemary just wants some company right now, okay? Okay? Then she'll drive you to Sarah's." She crooned to me, and I felt almost sleepy as she did, until her clawlike nails dragged furrows in my arm and I shouted with the pain of it, shamed as my bladder let loose for a moment.

"Shhhh, Angelina, sweet Angelina. I'm sorry, did we hurt you? Poor sweet baby. Here, let Rosemary make it all better," and she grabbed the leather straps with a horrible strength and rolled me over so I lay curled on my side facing the edge of the bed. Blood seeped from my arm into the sheets. Then she walked around the bed and got under the covers behind me.

Oh, God, I thought. Oh, God. For a ride to Sarah's. For a ride to Sarah's. I can stand this; I can stand anything for a ride to Sarah's.

There was an alternative. I knew She would spare me this humiliation, this ultimate degradation. I knew I had only to call Her, and together She and I would put an end to Rosemary and her disgusting Christmas cheer.

I felt Rosemary's body heat, her skin could have been no more than a half inch from mine as she lay there, and my every fiber was alive with fear and expectation. I knew she would touch me, but I did not know where or when, or with what, and the terrible anticipation grew to immense proportions. Little vibrations moved the bed as she fiddled with something, I knew not what, but I knew that I was soon to discover the true extent of her deviation. I was again helpless in the face of life, in the literal claws of this horrible woman, and I had had enough of it.

The temptation to call upon Her was almost overwhelming.

And then it came. Something horribly wet and cold slipped between the cheeks of my buttocks, and everything that had built up in me over the past days threatened to burst forth. I felt the newness of the night, felt its strength. I felt Her within, and I grasped my hair with both hands and held on for dear life; I held on, trying not to give in in the face of this loathsome experience, trying to think only of Sarah, of Sarah and Samuel, and of her healing me, that which I truly wanted most in the world.

I knew that I could stand this. A ride to Sarah's was my reward. I could stand this. I would get to Sarah's.

My skin crawled and inadvertent moans of disgust rose from the bottom of my soul as Rosemary kept me tethered to the bed all night, her imagination growing ever more disgusting. I was powerless to stop her, powerless to save myself, my crippled legs giving me the only peace I could find. I dove into the excruciating ache as Rosemary whiled away the hours, snickering and giggling with her perverted talk and laughter, and I lived for the pain of my legs and tried to ignore her for hours on end as she fiddled with me and her suitcase full of specialty items.

After what seemed like lifetimes had passed, I felt the tug of the dawn, and blessed unconsciousness slipped over me like a shroud.

"One of the things my daddy stressed to me when he was first teaching me about hunting—in fact, he mentioned it before each trip we went on—was: 'Be sure you know what you're going after,

son, and why. And don't be comin' back with anything else. Come
back with nothin' if you need to, but don't be comin' back with just
any old thing to make the trip worthwhile.'

"The more I had to sit there in that Colorado bar and wait for
Angelina to surface, the more I had to sit and think about why I
was after her to begin with. Hell, I'd had a good job, had my pa and
my brother Bill back in Westwater. I could be construction-project
foreman by now, or I could have been going back to school, or doing
something with my life, instead of sitting in a stupid Seven Slopes
bar all the time, drinking coffee in the morning and beer at night,
trying to figure out how to catch that slippery little girl.

"What for, Boyd, I kept asking myself. You kill a deer, or a pig,
or a rabbit for meat. For food. For life. Why are you after Angelina
with such a desperation?

"Because I didn't want school. And I didn't want work. I didn't
want the same old friends and the same old place to live, right near
my old man and Bill, anymore. I was hunting something new in
my life. Angelina was just the symbol of that. I was ready for a
change from Westwater and all it had to offer, which wasn't much.

"No, this hunt had become something more to me. I was pursuing the bizarre, the strange, the threatening, the exciting. I was
pursuing a quarry that was smart, through an element that was
uncertain. It was the most exciting thing of my life.

"And I wasn't about to 'come back with nothin'.' The next time
I saw Westwater, I would be a different man."

26

I awoke again at sundown. The bed was soaked with my
bodily excretions; my skin was chapped and sore where the
leather straps had held the acidic moisture to my skin. The
room smelled of the things I imagined a well-used prison
cell to hold—urine, sweat, pain, and disgust.

I was alone.

Slowly, each minor movement a major difficulty, I slipped

out of bed onto the floor. The gray-brown carpet was worn through to its string weave in a path from the door to the bed, and from the bed around to the bathroom. Using the bed as support for my aching legs, I pulled myself to my feet and shakily walked to the bathroom, my entire being feeling violated and desecrated.

I showered until I felt dizzy, scrubbing every inch of my body, trying to scour away the feeling of the old woman's probing fingers, but the memories clung too deeply. I scrubbed, opening the scabs on my arm, and blood mixed with soap and shampoo and water and swirled down the drain in the stained shower floor.

The tears came when I knew I couldn't scrub deep enough, and I leaned against the cold shower stall, sliding soapily down as my poor knees gave way under the weight of my sobs. I sat in the bottom, hard spray pelting the top of my head and shoulders, and I cried with all the strength I had left. I knew I was paying for my sins, I knew that I had deserved everything Rosemary dished out, and probably more. I wailed and sobbed and shook my feeble fist at God, and finally I just cried.

Eventually, my strength for self-pity was exhausted, and so was the hot water. I reached up and turned it off, then pulled the curtain aside and used it to help balance me as I straightened out my deteriorating legs. A fresh towel was on the sink, and next to it stood all the necessary toiletries as well as some light makeup, lipstick, eyeshadow, mascara. I dried the shivers from my skin with the towel and wrapped it around me.

Back in the main room, I threw the sheets and blankets over the cesspool of a bed, and found my pack on a torn imitation-velvet chair. The clothes I had worn—two nights ago? two years ago?—had been cleaned, pressed, and folded neatly. On top of the clothes was a sealed envelope with "Angelina" penned on it with a flourish, and leaning next to the chair was a beautiful new cherrywood cane.

I picked up the cane to admire it. The handle was fashioned as a brass lizard, intricately carved, with its tail winding almost halfway down the wood, ending in a little lizardlike curl. It fit my small hand perfectly, my fingers closing around its cold throat. The cane was short, exactly right for my size. I loved it and hated it, needed it and resented it. Bless her, curse her. I sat on the edge of the chair, cane between my knees, and fingered the envelope. I lay it down again, unopened, and dressed.

She was gone. My ride to Sarah's gone. I had endured all—*that,* and now . . . nothing.

I was so disappointed I could have raged, except I had no energy for it. All my energy had flowed out in tears and swirled down the shower drain.

Once dressed, feeling tidy and clean, comfortable and warm, I again sat in the chair, cane across my lap, and opened the envelope.

Inside were three sheets of lavender notepaper, each one covered with a fine writing.

My dearest Angelina:

I am always filled with remorse after I succumb to my baser passions. Regaining my senses is always a shock, yet I maintain this flat for just such emergencies. I prefer to be prepared for my perversities than to fall victim to them in more terrible ways.

I am writing this as you sleep the deep slumber of one who's no stranger to baser passions, the ancient ones, if my instincts are correct. This is what makes me feel that you will understand, as few do, the depth of remorse of which I speak.

My remorse is such at this moment that I dare not face you this evening. I am afraid. I am afraid of your reaction when I loose you in the darkness, and I am afraid that my own guilt and self-loathing will drive me to succumb to you. And I cannot do that, for I have those who depend upon me.

And so I leave you here, augmenting my guilt and remorse. But it, too, will pass. I sincerely hope you find your way to your friend Sarah, and to assist you with your journey, please accept the gift of this cane.

I don't know if this will in any way repay you for the ordeal you endured here, but let me add this: Never before have I been so thoroughly entertained by one as soft and tender as you. The experience of the past two nights has been one of sublime ecstasy for my departed morals, and for that I am much indebted.

May peace be with you.

Rosemary.

Tears ran down my cheeks. I knew exactly what she meant. I could easily end up like her, old, alone, picking up crippled kids in out-of-town truck stops on Christmas Eve in order to satisfy that . . . that . . . what? *God!* I crumpled the letter in my hand and gave myself up to a half-dozen solid sobs.

I was different from her. I would never end up like her. Never. I could beat this thing. I would beat it. I *was* beating it. I just needed to get to Sarah's.

I tried out the cane, practiced with it, began to learn how to walk with less pain. When my insides had calmed down a bit, I washed my face again, blew my nose, and combed my hair. Then I hefted my pack and limped, cane in hand, through the door, leaving it open behind me.

I hobbled down the stairs and into the early nighttime traffic. It was cold, but there was no biting wind. I looked around for a few moments, trying to get my bearings, but then I had no bearings. I didn't even know what city I was in.

I still had the ten dollars the salesman had left me, so I walked to a little coffee shop on the corner. It was warm inside, one whole corner filled with policemen drinking coffee and talking quietly among themselves. I took a seat at the counter and ordered hot cocoa and a sandwich. The folded newspaper on the counter said I was in Santa Fe. I was close. Probably less than one hundred miles stood between us. I knew Sarah would take me in. She had taken me in when I was sick before, she would take me in again. She would help me, and this would be the last time I would ever need anyone's help. The very last time.

I drank the cocoa and ate a few bites of tuna, paid my bill, and walked over to the table of blue uniforms.

"Excuse me," I said, and immediately had their attention—all six of them. I leaned a little heavier on my cane. "Is there a bus station, or . . . some way for me to get . . ." I stopped and looked for a moment at the worn toe of my boot. I didn't know what to ask. "I'm trying to get to Red Creek. No. I'm going to Red Creek, but I don't have a ride. I mean I *had* a ride, but she . . ." I stopped again. They must have thought I'd been drugged. I felt as though I'd been drugged.

Then the worst happened. The tears that have pushed against the backs of my eyes since—since when, since I was twelve?—began to fall and splash in the dirt on the black-and-white linoleum floor.

"I need to get to Red Creek, and I don't know how." I hiccuped loudly, then took a deep breath, ashamed of my display. The silence at the table grew dark. After I had collected myself, taken a couple of good breaths, swiped at my eyes and my nose, I looked up at them.

All six of them were looking at each other, thinking, apparently, about my plight, then one said, "Have you got money?"

I felt in my pocket and drew out the four ones and change left over from my meal. I looked at it stupidly. I felt as if my senses had left me.

"That won't get you too far," said another. "Where are you from?"

"But I have more," I said. "I have a bank account in

Pennsylvania." Again they all looked at each other; this time they each seemed to be uncomfortable—embarrassed, almost—in my presence.

One of the policemen stood up, pulled a smooth five-dollar bill from his wallet. He held it out to me. "Here," he said. "There's a little motel a couple of miles down this road. It's called 'Fivers.' The lady who runs it is named Molly, and she charges five dollars a night. You get there and stay the night, and in the morning you call your bank in Pennsylvania and have them send you some money here, okay?"

I stood there, looking at the money in his hand, thinking about calling the bank in Pennsylvania in the morning. I wouldn't be awake in the morning. Banking hours were daylight hours, and I couldn't call them unless I was awake. And how on earth could I get miles down the road with these legs?

He shook the money at me. "Here. Take it. Don't hang around the streets here at night. It's dangerous." He looked at his friends. They avoided his gaze. "Here. *Take it!*" Reluctantly I accepted his gift. "Now get down to Molly's or one of us'll arrest you." His companions grinned, the tension broken.

I mumbled a thanks and turned around, went back to the counter and asked for another cup of cocoa. I couldn't believe what I had just done. Was I totally insane? Where had all my intelligence gone? My resourcefulness? My sense of adventure, my invincibility? To beg a policeman for money! Angelina!

I was so ashamed, I wished I hadn't approached them, told them my stupid story. I wished I hadn't taken the money, and now I'd ordered more hot chocolate and had to sit here in front of them and drink it, instead of running away, and worse than that, I had to pay for it. He didn't give me money for hot chocolate. Oh, God, I was miserable.

I picked up the Santa Fe newspaper and opened it up

to distract myself from self-destructive thoughts, and my mind gagged on what it saw.

Boyd's picture was on the front page. The headline read: "Colorado Slaughter Linked with Nevada Murders."

Seven Slopes, Colo. (UPI)—The murder of a crippled newsstand proprietor in Seven Slopes may be connected with three murders committed two years ago in Westwater, Nevada, according to a Westwater man in town to assist police with the investigation. Boyd Turner is in Seven Slopes to see if the murders have certain elements in common. "If they do, then I think we can piece some clues together. We may come up with the identity of a prime suspect," he said. The police chief declined comment.

The grisly murder of Vietnam vet Joshua A. Bartholtz has terrified the local population of Seven Slopes. Deadbolts have sold out of the local hardware stores. The town has emptied of tourists, and in addition to the prospect of a homicidal maniac loose in town, business people are faced with economic disaster. This is all very similar to a situation in Westwater two years ago when three people were murdered in one bizarre holiday weekend. Those murders remain unsolved.

I couldn't read on. I could only look at the photo of Boyd, captured with mouth open as he talked to reporters. His Stetson was riding high on his forehead, pushed back, no doubt, in a reflexive show of frustration. He wore his corduroy jacket with sheepskin lining, and he stood in front of the Snowson Hotel in Seven Slopes. A little tug of homesickness tweaked me in the midst of my horror.

Now Boyd was hunting me. He'd given up on small animals and birds. Now he had a quarry worthy of his tracking skill.

My senses seemed to snap back into place. I quietly folded the newspaper, finished the cocoa, hefted my pack, and picked up my cane. I walked back to the policemen and lay the five-dollar bill down in front of the officer who had given it to me.

"Thank you," I said. "I have no need for this. I'm really quite all right, and I do have a place to stay tonight. I just sometimes . . . lose track. Please pardon me." And I walked out with as much dignity as my ineptitude at being crippled would allow.

I will go to Sarah's, and I will get well. And then I will call Boyd and we will talk it over. I will let him take me in if he needs to, but not like this. Dear God, not like this.

I put my thumb out as soon as I was out of sight of the coffee shop, and got a ride right away.

"It doesn't seem to matter much what I do. It's all the same—life's all the same. I could be a Madison Avenue type, and it would be the same, dealing with the same types of people, doing the same things, handling the same disappointments, the same tests of character, and I'd perform just the same at any of those jobs. I'd just do it the way I'd do it.

"My old man worked construction until he couldn't anymore. His muscles and spirit wore out about the same time. He tried a desk job, but he was just too far gone. Life had worn him down. I keep thinking that maybe if he'd started out at a desk, he'd have turned out different. But he wouldn't have. That was his choice in life. He didn't have to wear down. He didn't have to work construction. But knowing Pa, he would have worn down doing anything. He just chose construction to do it to him.

"This attitude has given me a lot of freedom in life, but freedom is its own disappointment sometimes. I've never really settled down, never really committed to anything—until Angelina, that is. And when she came into my life, I said, Boyd, this is the vehicle for your energies, this is the thing for you to do.

"Selling shoes, ranching, being a cop—it's all the same stuff. So, I figure, if it doesn't matter what you do, then how do you choose what to do?

"The choice is the message. All the time I was hunting alone in the mountains, I'd pray for a real hunt. When I'd bring down a deer, I'd be grateful for it, but disappointed, too. Deer were no longer a hunt for me, but I didn't know what was. I'd just pray for a real hunt.

"So you see, I'd asked for this hunt. The choice of career, or hobby, or both, is your only shot at making a statement in life. To me, it's the hunt.

"The hunt is the message."

27

The car that stopped was a Volkswagen bug. The driver was a thirtyish woman, wearing an imitation fur coat and garish sparkles on her hideously long fingernails. Her name was Winnie, she said, and she flattened me to the seat with acceleration before I had an opportunity to settle in and buckle my seat belt.

"What the hellya doing out on a night like this?"

"Traveling to Red Creek," I replied. I was grateful for the ride, and I knew if I could endure Rosemary for as long as I had, I could endure Winnie for a couple of hours. I could do anything as long as it led to Sarah.

"What happened to your leg?"

"Legs," I said, realizing too late that it was the wrong response to discourage conversation.

"Legs, then. What happened?"

"They froze."

"Ooooh, Gawd, you froze your legs? How awful. How didya manage to do that?"

I sighed. Winnie was going to extract her fee from me. "I was outside in the snow, and my legs froze."

"Gawd, I can't imagine *anything* worse than freezing. I hate it when it's cold. Hawaii. I oughtta live in Hawaii, ya know? I mean I'm just not built for this kind of weather.

Brrr." She pulled her coat closer around her and stepped on the accelerator, as if that would help. Then she reached between the seats and pulled up a lever with a red plastic knob. Heat flooded the little interior. It smelled faintly of exhaust, and it blew bits of debris around the inside of the car, but it was warm.

"I just love the heaters in these V-Dubs. That's why I've got one, you know? They're great, these cars. Don't worry. You'll be gasping for breath soon. These heaters are great. So why're ya going to Red Creek?"

"To see a friend. I have a friend there."

"Good. Good." She snapped on the radio and rudely ran the knob back and forth, looking for some music to suit her mood. When she found none, she snapped it off again, looked down at my cane, and scratched around in her orangey-ratted hair.

"Nice cane. How is it to walk with a cane? I mean, do lots of people stare at you?"

"No."

"I think of old people with canes, you know? I always think of young people with crutches, or wheelchairs, but never a cane. Actually, a cane has class. Especially one like that. Wow. Look at that lizard." She reached a hand over and touched it, then lifted it closer to her eyes. With brief flicks of attention paid to the road before us, she examined the brass end of my cane, then handed it back to me with a searching look at my face. "Wow," she said. "That's quite a cane."

I settled my cane between my knees, feeling more and more proud of it, more protective of it by the minute. The cane had become a symbol of my commitment. I had been to the gates of Hell for this cane. No. I had endured Rosemary as my price to get well. I had paid my price, and received the cane as a bonus. The cane would help me reach my destination.

Of course I had a cane. Of course. One such as I ought

to have a symbol of achievement, and having come from where I did, what could possibly be more fitting? ... I rubbed my fingers lightly over the cast-brass scales ...

"I've got a job waitin' down at Carlsbad. My brother works down there, and he said they needed a little help, so he called me up. Pretty good, eh? I don't even know what kind of job it is, but I trust him. My brother's all right. He and I kind of look out for each other, know what I mean? At least it will be warmer than Colorado, I mean, Gawd, I wish he'd get me a job in Hawaii."

I settled back, listening with a small slice of my consciousness while Winnie entertained herself talking of Hawaii, and I concentrated on the ache in my legs. The blowing heat felt like it was searing right into the meat of my calves. I felt the heat with my hand; it wasn't very hot, or blowing very strong, so I knew it could be doing no damage. I closed my eyes and relaxed, then delved into the feeling of the pain to try to separate the different sensations.

The pain was almost like a musical chord, strumming in a universal key. The ache, which ebbed and flowed with each breath, strummed the same chord over and over. I could define each string, see the vibration of each separate sensation; I could see, in my mind's eye, the strumming of the chord, but I could not see the hand that stroked the strings. I wondered if, by the very use of my will, I could snip the strings and thus be rid of the pain. Actually, the pain wasn't really pain anymore—it was more like intense pressure. I had dissected the pain until it no longer hurt; much like saying the word "darkness" over and over and over again until it loses its meaning and becomes merely an absurd sound.

So. Pain could be controlled by the mind. Sarah would know about that, about yoga and mind control and all that. I would be her disciple.

Winnie droned on, obviously not caring whether I responded or not—as I never did—and the two of us in the little Volkswagen drove through the cold New Mexican night toward Red Creek. Eventually, in the heat and the sound of her voice, I slept.

I awakened with a start at the first chug of the engine. My legs fired to life with a blast of agony, and I rubbed them, hard, and tried to bring myself into focus again in the situation. We slowed down.

The Volkswagen chugged again, stalled, then started, as Winnie cussed it and ground the gears, popped the clutch, and finally coasted off to the side of the road. The lights dimmed as she ground the starter, until there was just a terrible clicking as the battery died.

She punched the light button in with a slap of her hand and a curse, and we sat in the darkness, in the quiet, for a long moment.

Finally a long sigh escaped her lips and she yanked on the door handle, threw the door open, jumped out, and slammed it so hard my ears popped. I saw her stomp up and down the shoulder of the road behind the car, her coat flapping around her legs in the backwash of the cars that whizzed past without slowing down. I huddled down into my coat, feeling the slight rocking of the Volkswagen with each passing car. I tried to think, to figure what to do. I had no knowledge of cars; I could do nothing to help this situation.

I could only begin a new situation.

The cold was beginning to seep in, riding the darkness, riding the wind.

Winnie got back in the car, bringing with her a rush of frozen darkness, popping my ears once again as she slammed us all inside together.

"Fuck," she said.

"What is it?"

"How the hell do I know? Do I look like a mechanic to you?"

"I'm sorry."

"Yeah, well, we're all sorry here. But what do we do now, shoot ourselves?"

"I've got to get—"

"To Red Creek. Yeah, I know. And I've got to get to Carlsbad. Any great ideas?" She turned and looked at me, her shiny eye shadow glowing in the harsh illumination of the oncoming traffic. Her lined face was thickly made up, cracking around the edges, her crooked teeth suddenly menacing behind the curve of her snarling orange-colored lips.

I shook my head, my eyes unable to meet hers. They fell, instead, on the lovely expanse of her neck, softly wrinkled, powdered. I saw a faint thrumming under the skin as her heart beat in agitated double time, and it brought such feelings up from the depths . . .

She pulled back from me and flipped up the collar on her coat, bringing me harshly back to the present. I noticed with embarrassment that saliva had slipped out the corners of my mouth. I swiped it with my coat sleeve, but the damage had been done.

Winnie's eyes were round and wide, her orange lips stretched over her teeth as she clutched the door handle in fear.

"I'll get us a ride," I said, and I opened the door and swung my legs out. Leaning heavily on my cane, I tried to stomp a little life back into the ache that had replaced my bones. Winnie reached over and slammed the door. I heard the lock click.

I walked away from the front of the car; far enough so oncoming traffic could see me, and within minutes, a car had stopped. It was a young couple, huddled together on the front seat. I opened the back door and threw in my pack, my cane, then followed, painfully.

"Car trouble, huh?" the boy asked.

I looked back at the Volkswagen, could barely make out the puffed outline of Winnie's hair in the dark.

"Yes," I said, almost blind with the ache. I shut the door

behind me. "I'll send someone for it in the morning."

"We're going to Texas," the girl said, then disengaged herself from under her boyfriend's arm and turned around on the seat to face me. Her wispy blonde hair seemed to float about her head; her features blurred in the pulsing, reddening madness of my pain. I had moved too fast—too far too fast. For a moment, I looked at her through the veil of the pain and thought ... thought ... "Where are you going?" she asked, and it reverberated in my mind: *Where* are you going? Where *are* you going? Where are *you* going? Where are you *going*? And then it was Her face, and it was Her voice, and the car was speeding away and I was trapped—trapped in the car with the woman who would do anything to have me, the woman who would never leave me alone—not as long as I refused Her advances.

I closed my eyes and sank to the car seat, resting my head awkwardly on my pack. In a few moments, the fire that raced through my legs died down and my head no longer spun. I opened my eyes and the girl still looked at me over the back of the seat.

"Are you sick?"

I breathed deeply. Was this the woman? Was this Her? I could no longer tell. I wasn't safe, not anywhere. Not with the power this woman had. I had to be very careful. "Just my legs. The cold ..."

"Oh," she said, and nodded with understanding. "Where are you going?"

"Red Creek," I breathed.

"Why'd you leave your friend in the car?" Our eyes met for a brief moment. I could feel her judgment, her disapproval. "Didn't she want to come with you?"

How could I explain that Winnie's fears had locked me out of her car? How could I explain the compulsion that overtook me, the escape route I was following? How could I explain that I had some terrible disease, or so it seemed, and my salvation lay in a little cottage in Red Creek?

I was too tired to explain.

Instead, I remembered my talent, long dormant, for charging the air in a room, and I closed my eyes and brought romance and mystery into the car, and a sense of adventure for the two young lovers.

"Leave her alone, Marsh," the boy said. "Let her rest."

The girl gave me a weak smile and turned around again, facing forward, snuggling under his arm, and again I was on the way to Sarah. Safe, for the time being.

"I'd prepared all my life for Angelina. I didn't know it, of course, but I had done my homework, and done it well. I learned how to track, how to sniff the air, how to learn habits and predict movements, how to develop my intuition.

"The police in Seven Slopes wanted to publish a picture of Angelina, so I gave her description to the police artist. It was very strange, seeing her face again as it came to life on his sketch pad. He added just the right touches, too, a little feral look, thin and desperate, wild and cagey, sort of like her apartment smelled.

"I took a copy of that drawing to the bar with me and just sat and stared at it. It was a face I've known all my life.

"I got off track there for a while in Seven Slopes, I was so bloody disappointed, but as soon as I got word that she'd been spotted in Santa Fe, all my senses returned. This was no crank call, either. This was an accurate sighting, by six policemen, for Christ's sake, and I flew.

"She was one step ahead of me.

"But one step behind was a lot closer than I'd gotten before."

28

We passed the time in silence, my mind growing sharper as we neared Red Creek. Eventually we entered the little town and drove straight through—through to the restaurant/bar that served as a bus stop. I had them let me out in the parking lot and they drove off without so much as a good-bye.

I turned slowly to look at the building. Three cars and a pickup truck sat in the bar side of the parking lot; the brick walls gave no indication of what was inside, only the neon signs advertising it for what it was.

I had been here two years before. I had been a child then; I had just left Lewis, I was afraid, uncertain, and I went about attacking life, wearing my naivete like armor. I remembered the bus ride from Westwater to here; I remembered getting off the bus and telling the driver that I wouldn't be continuing with him; I remembered walking down the road that cold night, hearing my boot heels tap a particular rhythm that spelled freedom.

And freedom was what I found. Freedom from all ties, all possessions, everything personal. Personalities, I had come to believe, function only with respect to each other, never in a vacuum. And so here I was again, free, vacuous, seeking, miserable.

I had not grown.

I turned away from the building. The end of my journey lay only a few miles up the road. With my pack slung over my left shoulder and my cane supporting my weaker right side, I began to walk the final leg.

I heard my boot heels on the pavement, and they tapped out a different tune this time, one hesitant—syncopated almost—in its unevenness, in its pain and misery. I listened carefully though, and heard hope, and heard more hope with each footfall, with each tap of the cane. I was close to Sarah's. I was so close I could smell her.

But the dawn was closer yet.

I don't know how far I walked; only three cars had passed me when my feet first began to drag pebbles beneath them. I knew the sign, I felt the dawn, but I resisted it, tried to pick up my feet, but my body was just too heavy. I began to stumble. I knew, then, that I dare not act the fool; I had to prepare for the coming day and find a place to sleep. Someplace quiet, private, away from the sunlight.

On my right I noticed machinery, piles of sand and scrap lumber. A construction site. Farther on, a single light bulb burned in the eave of a new metal building, recently erected, with no sign of tenants. I left the main road and very carefully picked my way amid the carelessly strewn rubbish, looking for a way into the building. The steel doors were locked. I kept looking, my steps weaker, my cane indispensable, yet awkward as it slipped off unsteady pieces of debris and sank deeply into sand.

At the rear of the building sat a large square trash dumpster, dark blue, with a sheet-metal lid. I looked both right and left, could see no reasonable alternative—could see no alternative at all—so as the actual rose color appeared at the horizon, I quickly found a bit of broken ladder, set it sturdily next to the dumpster, climbed it and propped open the lid. The interior was dark and smelled of paint. There were pieces of wood, chunks of concrete, old rags and papers, dozens of squashed soda cans, an emptied ashtray. A drop cloth was bundled in the corner.

I threw in my cane, my pack, then gingerly, one leg over at a time, lowered myself inside, being careful of where I stepped. The drop cloth was stiff with dried paint, but pliable to a degree, and I maneuvered it into an appropriate position, then reached up and brought down the heavy lid.

Quiet. Peace. Darkness.

I was on my own, making my own way again. I was away from Her, on my way to see Sarah, to get healed, to become whole—normal again.

I set my jaw against any invasion of my mind, and consciousness was sucked away.

Low moaning sounds awakened me. Sounds close, reverberating metallically from the thin steel walls around me, muffled by the stiff cloth that was my bed. The moans were all about me, emanating from every corner of the bin, bouncing off the weird conglomeration of sharp angles and soft corners, back again to my ears with their subtle tonal differences. Moans of distress, of discomfort, of the tortures of Hades. Moans from the soul, from the source of pain too deep to define.

The sounds were mine.

The air was close, and thick with hot fumes of paint. My head reeled and I grappled for my cane, but it had fallen away from me somehow and I couldn't seem to grasp it. The fumes rose about me in great jagged technicolor waves, poisoning my brain cells as I lurched, reeling like a praying mantis, trying to escape from my toxic prison. I seemed to move in slow motion, one movement forward and then a long rest while a million bees encircled my head. I scrambled up a mountain of concrete shards on my hands and knees until I could stand and push up the lid. It was hot to the touch; the sun had just settled below the horizon, and it had left its impression, left me to bake in a tin oven filled with poisons.

Fresh air flooded in, and I gasped at it, growing weaker and sicker instead of stronger and more alert. I sank back to my knees under the weight of the lid, but the stench below, the smell of the drop cloth on which I had slept all day, was overpowering, sickening, and I scrambled frantically for my cane, found it, and worked slowly but desperately to get out of the bin. I pushed on the lid and it rose, higher and higher until it fell over backward and clanged against the back of the dumpster with a sound that sent great purple jags through my vision. They repercussed for a long while as I grasped the edge of the bin, breathing deeply. When they faded, I dropped my cane over the edge, then hitched one deadening leg over, rolled my shoulders, and fell to the ground with an "oof!" as my lungs took the shock. I lay there for a long time, trying to clear my head of the bizarre visions, trying to clear my ears of their audio hallucinations.

A new pattern of red blips crossed my vision; I thought I heard something, something outside of the ravages of hallucination, but I willed it away; I wanted to be left alone, to be ill, violently ill, anything, anything to end this terrible sickness, when suddenly my skin seized up all over.

Someone had just touched my arm.

I saw him through peaks and swirls of color; his sounds echoed in my head for days. I struggled to sit, to stand, but flopped on the ground instead, my muscles no longer connected to my nerves or my brain. There was one thing, I remembered, that would calm the raging storm inside my head.

I moaned, long and loud; it smoothed the waves of color into sedate pools of light. It evened out the rampaging echoes and calmed my fibers. I took a deep breath and calmly unleashed a mantra that relaxed me and brought a sense of my being back into focus.

The boy lifted me and carried me to the back of his pickup truck. There were two boys, as I now recognized; one was unrolling a sleeping bag while the other held me. I mustered all my strength and will and concentrated on forming my words carefully. "My cane," I said. My symbol.

The boy who held me smiled down at me. "We got your cane, don't worry. We're going to take you to the doctor, so just don't worry."

I concentrated again. "Sarah," I said. "Sarah's house."

The boy lay me on top of the sleeping bag, the other put my cane by my side. I listened to them talk between themselves. "Do you suppose she means Sarah Monroe?"

"Sarah'll probably be able to help her."

"They must know each other."

"Sarah'll at least know whether we should take her to the hospital, you know?"

"Won't hurt. She's at least making sense. Jesus, what do you think she was doing in that dumpster?"

"Sniffing paint."

"Jesus."

"C'mon, let's go."

The doors slammed red slashes across my vision and the truck pulled out, each movement dragging some nauseating color across my eyes. Again, I was at the mercy of strangers. Again. But they were taking me to Sarah's, I would be there in a matter of minutes. This would be the last time I would be at someone's mercy.

The last time.

"I know that the police have a lot of things going on at the same time, and even though they were doing their best, their best wasn't very good. The police in different counties don't even communicate with each other, much less the police in different states. The Federal system finally pulled it all together, but holy smokes, it took a long time.

"I might have been a little more patient, too, if I either had something else to do but sit around and think about Angelina, or if I could have served in some official capacity with a little authority. As it was, I was just a hanger-on, and I'm not used to that.

"But a murder is a priority for only so long, and then the police get bogged down with other matters, and it gets put on the back burner. If I hadn't been on their backs all the time, Angelina might have . . . might still . . . well, it's hard to say."

29

I kept my eyes on the stars and my concentration on breathing deeply. Each turn the truck made clicked with the road map in my memory, and a small smile began to form at the corners of my lips. I felt free already, but the freedom wasn't from casting away everything that was real, it was embracing that which had value. Sarah had substance—the real feelings of a woman, a complete woman, a warm woman.

She would touch me and then I too would find those terribly elusive feelings that had kept me separate all this time.

The truck stopped, shuddered, kicked, and was still. Two doors slammed, and two young faces looked over the tailgate at me.

"You all right?"

I nodded.

"Stay put. Looks like Sarah's at home, all right. We'll get her."

I nodded again, tears of relief hot and hard inside my face, and I lay there, waiting with desperation.

Soon there were footsteps along the gravel path and low talking sounds. I heard Sarah's voice. It had been sounding in my mind for two years, but in the continuous replaying, my mind had laid down tracks of grit, scratches, and static, so my memory of the sound had lost the most beautiful of its tones. Sarah's voice was deep and pleasant.

"I can't imagine who it could be," she said, and then she looked over the edge of the truck bed.

My legs began to twitch. I propped myself up on my elbows, lightning flashes crashing across my vision. "Sarah," I said.

"I don't . . . I don't know who you are," she said. "Are you a student?"

"No, no. Angelina Watson. Two years ago . . . sick by the road . . ."

"Oh, yes, Angelina. I remember. Well, what do you want?"

"Please," I said. "I need your help."

She sighed and my heart lurched. "I can't help you, Angelina. I can give you a bed until you recover, but I can't help you."

"Yes," I whispered. "You can. You're the only one who can." I lay back down as the edges of their faces began to vibrate in shades of blue and gray and expand and contract with my breathing. I was near the end of my endurance. "Please." I closed my eyes. "Please understand."

"We thought maybe she needed the hospital, Sarah," one of the boys said. "We found her when she'd just climbed out of a dumpster filled with paint cans."

"Okay. Can you boys bring her in?"

"Sure."

The tailgate grated down among blue flashes and I held on to the sleeping bag as they pulled it out the back of the truck. Then I was in someone's arms, with my cane in my hand, and we followed Sarah, the world biliously bouncing with each step.

She held the door open, and her scent floated moon-globes across my vision as we passed her.

Inside, the cottage remained just as I remembered it. The colors were perhaps a bit faded, there were piles of clothes about, but basically it was the same. A mass of twinkling lights in the corner hurt my eyes. I squinted in pain, and realized it was what I had hoped to find at Sarah's. A Christmas tree.

"Here. Put her on the bed."

The bedspread radiated with orange and red and I felt its design tattooing itself on my back. My legs still twitched. I was cold and beginning to shiver. Sarah covered me with a yellow blanket and left the room. I heard her talking with the boys, then doors slammed and the truck roared off down the road. When she returned, she held two steaming mugs of hot tea.

With a gentle hand behind my head, she lifted me up for a sip, then settled me back down with a pillow. She sat on the edge of the mattress and regarded me with cool brown eyes while she blew the steam across her own mug.

I couldn't meet her gaze.

"Angelina," she finally said. "What are you doing?"

"I had to come here," I managed to say. "I need your help."

"With what?"

"With . . . I can't—I need—I don't— Oh, God!" I was

incapable of explaining through the paint, through the frustration, the years, the lifetimes of bizarre experiences.

"I think you need some sleep. We'll talk in the morning."

"No, no, now, please now."

"No, it's getting late. I have work to do yet tonight and I have to dance tomorrow. I have to sleep. You stay here and I'll sleep in Samuel's bed."

"Samuel. Where is he?"

"With his father," she said with a touch of something red that I could not identify but could plainly see in the tonal difference of her speech. "Good night."

"It's good to see you again, Sarah."

"That's nice," she said, then turned out the light.

I lay awake, watching the patterns of my visual hallucinations dance across the ceiling, feeling the cold, empty numbness in my entire body, feeling the ache in my legs. I was glad to be in Sarah's little house, and even though she wasn't pleased to have me here, she soon would be. We would be good together. Very good together.

As the night deepened I slept, and dreamed of the dawn, then dreamed no more. When I next awoke, it was the following evening, and Sarah was frantic.

Before my eyes were completely open, she had jumped on the bed and was shaking my shoulders. "Angelina! Angelina! Wake up." I tried to push her off of me with my hands, but they were awakening slowly. I did little but brush at her.

"God, I thought you were dead. The doctor said you were in a coma, because of the paint fumes, and you might never wake up."

It took a moment to understand what she was telling me. "Doctor?" I asked, a queer taste on my tongue.

"He's calling an ambu— Wait!" She jumped up and went into the other room. I heard her talking excitedly, then they both came back into the bedroom and stood looking down at me. I blinked up at them, willing myself to wake up, to be alert, to say something—if not significant, then at least intelligent. My body ached anew.

"Well, young lady, you gave us quite a scare." The doctor wore thick black glasses, a plaid shirt rolled up at the cuffs, and blue jeans. His dark hair was beginning to gray at the temples.

"I'm sorry," I said, then scraped my tongue on my teeth, trying to dislodge the taste.

"I'll get you something to drink." Sarah looked to the doctor for his nod of approval, then disappeared.

"Not everyone recovers from a poisoning as toxic as the one you suffered. Hardly anyone recovers without some brain damage. I took the liberty of examining you, and I must say, I'm quite surprised you survived." He settled down on the edge of the bed, taking on a confidential demeanor. My awareness was growing; I was naked beneath the sheets. I localized the pain in my arm, and rubbed it.

"I gave you a shot there to counteract the toxins. Now, Angelina, I'm going to ask you a question, and I want you to answer me with the truth, okay?"

I shrank away from this man. I owed him nothing. I wanted nothing from him and only wanted him away from Sarah and me so we could talk.

"What kind of drugs have you been taking?"

"I don't take drugs."

"Oh. I see." He backed off, thinking I lied. "Well, I think we'll check you into the hospital for a while, just to make sure you're okay. Sometimes toxins can have a delayed effect."

"No hospital. I'm all right."

"I disagree."

"I don't care. I have no need of a hospital or you. Please leave." I was wide awake now, and the thought of this man examining me while I slept was revolting, although I believe Sarah acted in a manner consistent with her beliefs.

"Young lady—"

"Angelina."

"Angelina, you have been in a coma for the past—at *least* twelve hours—"

"Asleep."

"I beg your pardon?"

"Asleep. I was asleep."

"Angelina. I'm a doctor. I know the difference."

"Then come back tomorrow. I sleep every day, all day, just like that."

He was silent. We looked into each other's eyes for a long moment. Then there was the briefest flicker of—something that caused him to jerk. There was some base recognition that passed between our souls, and he reached down to his black case, closed it, snapped the brass catch, and stood. He looked down at me for a moment, then turned and left the room. He and Sarah spoke briefly in her kitchen, then the door closed and a car started.

At last. Sarah and I were alone. And the night was young.

She brought hot tea to me, and a plate of fresh fruit and crackers. I drank the tea straightaway and she left to refill the mug while I smelled an apple slice and a berry. They were unappetizing.

"The doctor said you were uncooperative and there was nothing more he could do."

"There isn't," I said as I sipped the second cup.

"What do you expect me to do?"

"I'm not sure. I need to learn your ways. I need to become healthy, in mind and body, and I know you can help me do that."

"Oh, Angelina," she said, and set down her mug of tea. "I can't even help myself these days. I don't have anything left to give."

As my senses came into focus, I could see that Sarah had gained weight. Her hair was lusterless and dirty, a pasty pallor had replaced the fresh-faced glow of her complexion. Little wiry gray hairs ringed her hairline and a network of lines surrounded her eyes. "What is it, Sarah? What has happened?"

"A lot. Too much." She looked at her hands and began to pick at her fingernails.

"Tell me."

"Samuel's father came to visit, saw that Samuel was obviously his child, did a little arithmetic to make sure, then he took Samuel away. We're battling in court. I spent so much money on lawyers that I had to work two jobs, and I didn't do either of them very well, I was so worried about Samuel. I got fired from both. Now I can't pay the attorneys, and they won't work for me anymore. Samuel is in San Francisco, and Victor says if I want him, I have to move there. He said I had no right to keep knowledge of his son from him. Christ, I hardly even knew Victor. He was just a one-night stand." Tears flooded Sarah's eyes and overflowed down her cheeks. She silently continued to pick at her cuticles.

I was dumbfounded.

Sarah jumped up and went into the bathroom. I heard her blow her nose, then she turned the water on in the sink. When she returned, her face was pink from the splashing and she was rubbing hand cream into her cuticles.

"So," she said. "Enough of my sad story. Back to you. The first thing you have to do is get straight with the doctor. He knows more than you do, Angelina."

"He knows nothing, Sarah. I was not in a coma. I sleep all day, and am awake at night. That's one of the things I need to change."

"That's easy to change. You just change."

She didn't understand. She couldn't understand. I looked at her, saw how she'd changed, and felt reluctant to talk to her. This was not the Sarah of my memory. Rosemary's words came to mind. "A life raft. Someone to save you. You will find that it won't work." I began to be afraid. Sarah *had* to help me. I had to at least try. "No," I said. "You don't understand. I'm afraid."

"Of?"

"The light." I rubbed the sparse flesh of my arm where the shot had been administered.

"What do you think might happen?"

"Well, the voice tells me that I can no longer live in the light, and She seems to be right. I can't stay awake toward dawn, and as you can see, I can't be awakened until night."

"The voice?"

"I think it's the devil. A she-devil. But I'm not sure. She makes me do terrible things. Terrible things."

"You hear voices?"

"Oh, Sarah, it's not what you think. I know it sounds a little crazy, but it's not like when insane people hear voices that tell them to do things ... My voice—there's only one—She more like *invites* me to do things, and when I please Her ... when I please Her ..." Soft strains of the music played through my ears and the soft pain in my arm vanished. I listened for a moment, entranced. I'd forgotten how beautiful ...

"Yes?" Sarah's voice was a harsh interruption. The music stopped. The pain returned, doubled.

"What?"

"Do you see her?"

"Oh, yes. She comes to me in two ways. One way She's like mist, floating and wispy, but with substance. The other way I see only Her mouth, Her lips and tongue. Teeth." Sarah's face faded into the dusk of the room and I closed my eyes for a moment. They were there, the lips, moist and perfect, quivering ever so delicately, a question poised there so eloquently I could have plucked it like a flower. Open, I thought. Show me the deft edge of tooth, the wet pink tip of perfect tongue. Show me. Show me.

"What does she say to you?" Sarah's voice rasped through me like a rusty handsaw.

"What?" I said, irritated with her questions that brought back the light, the pain, the hopelessness.

"What does she say to you?"

And then I remembered, Sarah was to save me. I could not succumb to Her seduction. I had to stay with Sarah, stay conscious.

"What?" I asked again. "I'm sorry. What?" Sarah sighed with exasperation. "I'm *trying* to help you, Angelina. But I can't do anything without your cooperation. Now concentrate. What does this voice say to you?"

I tried to remember some of the things She had said to me. There wasn't anything I could repeat; we had shared feelings, experiences, excitement, peace. We had loved each other and said and done all those things that lovers do in their private world, and there was nothing really that I could share . . .

And the lips parted and She spoke to me, loudly and clearly in the voice that was melodic and familiar to each cell in my body, each spark of my soul. The voice said, "I speak to you of love," and my whole being thrilled.

"She speaks to me of love," I said.

"And together we serve."

" 'And together we serve.' "

"Together we embody the highest aspirations of mankind's search for justice . . ."

Was this our wedding vow? " 'Together we embody the highest aspirations of mankind's search for justice . . .' "

"And together we shall be . . ."

I caught my breath. " 'And together we shall be . . .' "

"United in love and duty. Forever."

She had never spoken like this to me before, and I cried with the beauty of it. I echoed the final phrase of my vow in barely a whisper, and as soon as I had done so, the pain was gone; I felt strong again, powerful, wonderful, invincible.

I sat up on the bed and looked at Sarah, poor pitiful Sarah, so nice, so noble, so misdirected. Great dark circles sagged from her eyes halfway to her cheeks.

"Sarah," I said. "Perhaps Samuel belongs with his father;

perhaps I belong with the one who loves me; perhaps you belong with someone, too."

"Angelina, I don't think—"

But I had her wrist, and my strength was a thing of beauty. The powers of the universe flowed through me. I tightened my grip until I saw mystery, fascination, pain, anger, hurt, and fear cross her vision. They filled me, and I relaxed, basking in the sensations, in the aura that She was putting forth in the room. It was heavenly; it was whole-some; it was nourishing.

And then Sarah began to fight in earnest. I laughed. She was so sincere in her endeavors. Before she had finished, both wrists and one collarbone were broken, and I mounted her and teased her, running my fingers through her greasy hair and letting it fall back onto her face, creating sliding moire patterns as the hair swirled across her features.

Eventually she tired. I knew the taste. Prey must be played with for only so long, and then the hormones of exhaustion add acid to the blood. The climactic moment was at hand.

"Sarah," I said, and her weak eyes squinted up at me. "I knew you would help me find the way." She squeezed her eyes shut in pain and misery, took a deep breath, and began a new attempt to dislodge me from my perch on her chest. "Thank you, Sarah," I whispered, my lips brushing her small ear, and then I nuzzled the softness of her neck, feeling the tiny hairs tickle my face, tasting the salt of her exertions, smelling the odor of her fear. I nibbled on her groans and chewed to her screams, right through, so the sounds bub-bled out with the nectar, watching the thick blood froth and flow for a moment before burying my face in the sweet fragrance and drinking my fill.

And when I was finished, I heard the music, it swelled into great clouds about me; the lips spoke with pride into my ear, and I knew I had come home, at last, that whatever else I had thought had been in error—this was my destiny;

this was the thing that made me the happiest; this was life, and it was life everlasting.

She welcomed me back with kisses and floods of ecstasy, wave after wave of orgasmic pleasure, each cresting with the music and falling, only to rise again and resume.

I lay in rapture all night, my body held tightly against Sarah's, my face buried in her hair. When the music turned to the call of dawn, I pulled her from the bed and into the closet, bringing with us the soiled bedding. I dug the shoes from the corner and leaned her coquettishly against the wall, then I wrapped her, swathed her in all the beautiful fabrics I could find.

As morning encroached upon my strength, I hollowed out a nest among the fabrics, then curled up in Sarah's lap and closed the closet door behind us.

COLIN W. SHERWOOD, M.D.: "I came back the next day to check on the girl, but no one answered the door. I really wanted to do some tests on her. She had no right to be alive, I mean it. I peeked in through the bedroom window, and the bed was stripped, so I figured Sarah was off doing laundry, or at work or something, and the girl had gone on her own way.

"Jesus, you don't think they were both . . . in the . . . while I was . . .

"Jesus."

30

I cannot believe that any mortal man or woman could ever experience the likes of the honeymoon that She and I had that night. I opened myself to Her so completely, so totally, that I felt filleted, exposed, with no secrets, nothing with-held. She touched portions of me that no man ever could, vulnerable spots no other person could ever even know that I had. Her intimate touches were probing but tender, letting me understand that my vow to Her was all-encompassing.

Eternal life included stark honesty, and I held still for Her examination, and I enjoyed Her pleasure as She found me acceptable.

We rode the music together as I bared my soul to Her. She tested, tasted, approved, and returned it to me, altered, marked, stamped with Her authority as judge. And when She was finished, I was joyous at Her final acceptance, and we flew to the heights, sweeping the stars with our love and our laughter, until I realized that I had given everything and She had given nothing.

The music turned sour the very moment that sad thought entered my mind. She tickled me, cajoled me, tried to take my mind from it, but I insisted. The marriage was not equal unless She opened as willingly as had I.

A minor chord strummed through the ether. What right have you to demand equality in this marriage, She asked.

Dark clouds of deep notes echoed in the well that surrounded us. The stars closed the lid on my prison. She was not willing, and I was bereft.

"Angelina," She teased me, whispering across my ear, but I pulled away, the match unequal, unfair. The fun was lost, the joy had fled. Sadness flushed through me, the granite disappointment a huge, looming monolith.

"Please," She said. "You don't know what you ask."

"I do know."

"You don't."

"It is over," I said.

"Angelina, please, no."

"Show me."

"I dare not."

"Show me."

"Angelina, please."

"Show me," I demanded, "or we are dead. I have given you my life, my soul, and you have given me nothing. Show me the whole of you now, and we shall remake our vows. Together. Forever. Now. Before it is too late."

She retracted from me, hesitant. I could feel Her hold Her breath, tentative, fearful, as She waited. I remembered, when younger, on my odyssey across the country, jumping from a high waterfall into the river below, knowing for extended moment after moment that eventually I would jump, yet not jumping and not jumping. Fear kept me back, but it was pointless fear, for I knew that eventually I would proceed. She knew me so well that She called up that memory for me; She stood on the brink of self-revelation, and I held my breath to calm Her fear.

She stood apart, and once again I heard the voice, the words crystal-clear, saw the lips as they spoke into my ear. I saw my body twitch in its unearthly sleep, in its physical recognition of pleasure, even as it lay entwined within the gaudy shroud of the cold corpse. Once again She implored me to let things remain as they were. "It is perfect as it is, Angelina. Let us be so."

I shook my head. "If you be Satan himself, I must know it."

The music paused. The silence roared in the darkness. She drew Herself up to a thin line of ephemeral mist and waited. One beat, two beats—and then She disappeared. Slipped silently through.

The breath I held released in a sigh. I had chased Her away—

But my reaction was premature, for the next moment the universe opened, and as horror after horror assaulted all of my senses, I understood Her reluctance to show me the vileness of Her nature.

Each of my fears was openly acknowledged; the things that I held most disgusting were presented in all their lurid detail; insecurities and faults were pried open and stuffed with insult; the soft spots of my being were punctured, the crusty worldliness of my experiences merely a scab to be picked and left to bleed.

The horror of the assault left me too astonished to

retreat, to defend myself, to ward off being pelted by these insidious table scraps of Hell. My newly probed and freshly peeled being was a ripe victim for the salty lashes that all but destroyed me.

It lasted but a moment, stretched to eternity, and when the last clash of cymbals died down and the holocaust had passed, I had been sliced to thin ribbons and laid to waste at the feet of She who had attacked me.

The darkness settled down, quieter than ever, no music, no sounds, all had been expended in the extravagance of the moment, there was nothing left. Anywhere.

And then the light touch of Her wispy fingers gently felt the bruises on my psyche and I moaned for Her to leave me be.

"Look at me, Angelina."

What else could She do—there could be no greater condemnation than that which She had opened to me.

But wait. Those were *my* terrors, *my* horrors. Where were Hers? Where was Her revelation?

I turned my eyes toward Her, and at last I saw Her for who She really was. I thought She had pulled from me all the terror I owned, but upon seeing Her face, again terror ripped through me. And then amazement. And then hope.

Finally, *finally,* I understood. Of course I could never escape Her affections. How foolish I had been to ever try.

A younger, freer Angelina hooted with extravagant enthusiasm somewhere within my heart. And then I understood love, and freedom, and satisfaction—a satisfaction so deep, so adult, so solid and substantial, that the joy of our evening just past paled in comparison.

My joints were stiff when awareness sloshed through my body. I disengaged myself from Sarah's cold embrace and opened the closet door, listening. Heightened senses were suddenly mine, as was the ability to mask pain through the use of internal music.

I showered, noticing a new posture of my body. My skin seemed to have a translucence about it; blue veins showed plainly. I no longer looked scrawny and unhealthy; I was lean and statuesque. Overnight, I had changed into a person worthy of worship.

I dried myself and combed my hair straight back, using Sarah's comb. My face had gained years, wisdom, confidence, character features that were ever so handsome. I viewed my face for a long moment in the harsh light of the bathroom mirror, then turned out the light. In the dim glow cast by the moon and captured by the mirror, my cheeks and eyes hollowed in the shadow of prominent bones and ridges. The skin of my face was clear and unlined, pale and fragile. Yet it was strangely incomplete. Something was missing.

I returned to the bedroom closet. Sarah's jaw was stiffening with the rigor, and it took all my strength and the high heel of one of her displaced shoes to open her mouth. With my forefinger, I swiped the back of her tongue, bringing forth a thickening scoop of the elixir of life for which Sarah had no further use. Returning to the bathroom, I applied it slowly and carefully to my lips, evenly coating each curve, each nuance. Then I licked my white teeth and spoke softly to the new face, the starkly chiseled features that looked back to me, and I said, "Angelina," watching the tip of my tongue show for the briefest of moments as the L came alive. Yes. It was Her. In my mirror reflection. These were the lips, the teeth, the tongue. Dark, wet, and seductive, the lips now had a total face to bring them true life.

She and I had become one—or was it always so?

"I almost gave up. In Santa Fe. We'd missed her and I tasted the disappointment of the waiting game, searching the newspapers, putting out bulletins to uninterested policemen, and knowing she'd probably slip us up at her next stop anyway. I knew someone else would carry on; I knew someone else would continue the search, I didn't have to; I could go home.

"To what? To a stupid job in a boring town with my punk brother and my worn-out father?

"As much as I hated to admit it, Angelina had given me something to live for, something to look forward to, other than just living, growing old, and dying in Westwater.

"And I guess I was kind of afraid of catching her.

"But then that cop finally, finally *fucking* remembered that she said she needed to get to Red Creek, and it was right then that I knew Angelina'd changed. She'd turned, somehow, and she was looking for a place to rest, lick her wounds. A den. A hole.

"I smelled a wounded animal when I read that cop's statement. A wounded animal is unpredictable. Angelina must have been delirious to talk to a policeman at all, much less tell him where she was going. Yep, I smelled a wounded animal, and when an animal's wounded, you've got no choice but to track it until you find it. A wounded animal must be brought down.

"A wounded animal changes the whole hunt. It's changed, insane, dangerous. Everything changes when you're looking for a hurt one. There's no time to lose, and no longer a choice. I was in for the duration, because I had chosen the hunt.

"Extinction is unnatural. Everything escalates. If an animal is not too far gone, it'll go into heat, to try to breed before it dies."

31

I found myself requiring time alone, time to become accustomed to my new properties, my new gifts. I also needed cash.

I rummaged in Sarah's dresser and found the envelope marked "Rent." It had one hundred dollars in it. There was another ten in her purse, which I took without remorse. Money was a mundane thing; Sarah had no further need. I borrowed her car and drove to a small motel several miles from Red Creek and checked in, requesting a room at the back.

I posted a letter of explanation to the bank in Wilton,

giving the motel as my current address. By return mail, they sent me, per my request, a cashier's check.

The week I spent waiting for my money, I also spent adjusting. I had acquired some wild talents, the most dramatic of which was the use of the music. Yet the tremendous gift of music was nothing next to the immense confusion it brought. Questions and answers, mismatched and abstract, tumbled about in my head like laundry in a dryer. I would hook up one question to an answer as it fled by, creating a composite question, leaving me to chase down another answer that refuted the first, masking the question and turning the whole of my conscious mind into a vast bowl of noodles, questions and answers all wrapped around each other, with no beginning and no ending.

Was I odd at birth or did I acquire oddities? Were there others like me? Were my oddities perversions of the personality, or was an outside influence controlling me as I once thought She had done? And if and when I discovered *that* influence, would it wash over me in a moment of extreme hostility and become part of me, leaving me to discover that there was still yet another influence, higher, more covert, more ominous? Was I at the center of a hideous puppetry plot that would reveal layers of self as I matured? Had I a disease or a gift? Was the music universal? Could others hear it? Could others control it the way I could?

How I longed for the simple questions of adolescence, the questions of "Why me?" Now it seemed that a sense of eternity hindered my thinking, expanding the simplest of ideas into a complex march of countermoves and strategies.

Could I change the future? Could I change the past?

For five nights I sat in the motel room and pondered the questions. For five nights I listened to my internal music, turned it up, down, on, off, changed the tempo, and studied the effects. It erased the pain in my legs. The cane was still a necessity, as my legs were not healed—they were weak and inconvenient—but they no longer ached.

I worked with the music, fine-tuning its minute varia-
tions and reveling in the dramatic changes I could make in
the room with the slightest alterations of tone or substance.
As I worked, I began to find a confidence in myself, a
confidence that I had always associated with wisdom. I felt
confident that I could begin to deal with the more delicate
of life's situations—could issue the appropriate music at the
crucial time.

Altering the mood of a room filled with people had
always been a talent, but I'd gone about it blindly, instinctively. Now I had tools, insight, and a scientific approach.
The knowledge calmed me.

When the envelope from the bank came, I merely wafted
a delicate mist of melody under the clerk's ear and he gladly
cashed the check.

I paid my motel bill, bought some clothes, as my pack
had been lost in the paint-container episode, and filled the
gas tank of Sarah's car.

The following evening I left New Mexico forever, heed-
ing the call to the north. I drove back toward Pennsylvania—back to Wilton, back to my roots, back to the frozen
soil of my birth.

Freedom was a different thing behind the wheel of a car.
I was independent, and independence felt like responsibility.

The headlights gleamed along the desert highway ahead
of me, and I soon became accustomed to the brightness of
the consistent, oncoming traffic. The tires on the road made
their own music, monotonous, low-key, depressing.

Then a flicker of something at the side of the road
ahead caught my eye. A hitchhiker. Company. My attention
perked as the tires slowed.

He opened the back door and got in. A boy—dirty, odor-
ous, offensive from the first moment. This was not what I
had in mind for company, but perhaps . . . I lashed at him
with a sharp run of command notes and he opened the
door again and got right out. Then I sent forth a seductive

little tune and he spun around, then opened the front door. He was so simple to manipulate. So simple. He was not to my liking, but there would be others. I made him shut the door, then open it and shut it again, without getting in, then I had him whirl around, touch his toes, then whirl again and again, and I watched him dance to my music. I jerked the puppet on my strings until I began to giggle, then I drove off, alert, watchful for more possibilities on my journey to Wilton.

I drove, minding the speed limit, into Texas before I saw the next hitchhiker, but I couldn't stop. The morning was approaching, and I had to find a place to bed down.

I exited the freeway, drove slowly past dark service stations and awakening bakeries. Just inside the little town was a boulevard lined with supermarkets, their parking-lot lights shining down on acres of deserted asphalt, criss-crossed with territorial parking-space lines. I parked in an unobtrusive corner.

The early morning traffic noise grew even as I sat there for a few moments. Soon deliveries would be made to the markets, then the shoppers would come, and the parking lot would be abuzz with activity. I smiled. Some fat shopper would be leaving her children, clean, healthy, succulent little babies untended in the car, parked innocently next to mine. I would be asleep. The thought was distinctly pleasurable. Comforting.

I opened the roomy trunk of Sarah's car and pulled out papers, toys, and Samuel's boy-sized tennis shoes. A large car has many conveniences. I spread out the blanket I had taken from the motel, covering up the little accumulations of debris, then unstrung a shoestring from one of Samuel's little shoes, and climbed in. I tied one end of the shoestring through two holes in the trunk lid and knotted the other end around the jack handle, then lowered it on its weight, not heavy enough to latch, just enough to look latched.

I stretched out, corner to corner, my head and one

shoulder on the short rise to the back. This was heavenly. Roomier than the closet, more intimate than the motel room. It was close, warm, secure. It smelled like rubber, highway, road grit, and axle grease. I relaxed my muscles, settled in, and began to make music. I played the music to surround the car, to keep thieving hands from stealing it, curious hands from touching it, helpful hands from latching the trunk. I played the music until the car fairly hummed with the vibrations, and then the darkness receded and my consciousness went with it.

When I awakened, I awakened suddenly. My eyes opened with a snap and my senses were fully alert, primed, ready. I listened to the activity around me. Shopping carts rattled on their bad wheels, car doors slammed, children cried, a bottle broke.

I felt for my cane, held it on my chest, fingered the cold brass lizard, fingered each of its carved scales, its long graceful sweep of tail, its smooth throat, its little brass eyes. I ran my fingers over the smooth, highly polished shaft of wood, and I heard it sing, as the rim of a wine glass will when stroked with a wet finger. I heard chords in the grain of the wood. So. The things around me had their own music. I had a lot to learn. It would be a long time indeed before I could realize what I had gained in the blending of my personality with Hers.

Slowly, with difficulty and little grace, I exited the trunk and slammed the lid down. I turned to find three ladies watching me, and I serenaded them each in turn and their eyes glazed over, their faces softened, and they went about their business.

I started the car and pulled out into the early evening traffic snarl, remembering with remarkable clarity the map I had studied at the motel. I felt a great need for Pennsylvania. I sensed also that Boyd was already with Sarah, and he would waste no time in his pursuit.

I had no sooner brought the car up to speed than my headlights reflected the patterned clothing of a couple, a man and a woman, standing by the side of the road. I sped past them, making decisions, then pulled off onto the shoulder. They both ran toward me, illuminated from behind by the string of approaching headlights. The man opened the door and looked in. As he did, a terrible noise erupted, blanketing all the freeway traffic sounds, and the woman began to dance around, shrieking. Automatically I sent music to calm, but the noise continued, heightened, and a little yellow cat, its fur horripilated, fell out of the woman's coat and danced, stiff-legged, around the blacktop on its toes.

"God!" the woman said. "He ripped my chest to shreds!" She brought a bloody hand out from inside her coat. The cat continued to hiss and spit, fuzzed up and frenzied, and I tried to calm it with music, but to no avail. I tried to bring some semblance of reason to the agitated scene outside my open door, but the woman was crying and the man torn between his loyalties to the cat, to the woman, to this rare ride that would take him where he could be finished traveling with woman and cat. My messages were confused and I could do nothing in the situation. The sight of her blood made my skin tingle and I was rendered impotent by the variety of emotions that swirled just outside the car door.

I stomped on the accelerator, the door slamming on its own, leaving them to stand there in the cold, dealing with their own problems. My emotions reeled from the confusion, my legs ached, my heart pounded, my hands stiffened on the steering wheel in the freezing cold.

Limitations. There were limitations.

I took deep breaths and recreated my environment. I eased the pain, erased the cold, settled my stomach. I could ill afford to allow another situation to distract me so.

But the blood on her hand . . . The blood on her hand . . .

The night was new and I was a lover.

Thoughts of Pennsylvania fled as I slowed the car and kept my eyes open for the lone person on the highway.

There. Just ahead. Confidence and certainty flushed through me with the intensity of relief. It was a young man. A college student, holding a sign that read "Princeton," and he was clean-shaven with white teeth. I could not believe my good fortune. I loved him instantly.

He threw his sign, one suitcase, and a shoulder bag into the back seat of Sarah's car, then climbed in the front. He smelled of soap, he smelled warm, he smelled of life. I surrounded him with friendliness and welcome. He responded with enthusiasm.

"Hi! I'm Jack. Gee, I'm glad you stopped. It's colder'n hell out there."

"Yes," I said. "It is, isn't it?"

"Jeez, it's cold in here, too. Can you turn up the heat a little?" He rubbed his hands together and blew on them.

I immediately turned up the music, warming him from the inside, rather than the outside.

"That's better. Thanks. Say, where are you headed? I'm going back to school. Christmas break is over, time for the new semester to start. I'm studying anthropology. Hey, nice car. You from Texas?"

His vibrancy caught me quite off guard. It had been a long time since I'd been so close to someone so vibrant. His young, virile, animal scent brought all my senses to their highest attunement. I had to be careful here. I could mesmerize him into blind obedience, like the ladies at the supermarket, but that would be a waste of his youth and vitality, and therefore a shame. Better to find the balance between desire and fear on one side, enthusiasm and greed on the other side. It would be a delicate task, requiring precise concentration. I hoped my skills were up to it

"No," I said. "I'm from Pennsylvania." He smiled at me, and nodded, anticipating a long ride in a pleasant atmosphere, and I trilled inwardly, for the pleasure of us both.

"I got really sick when I saw what she'd done to that lady in the closet. I'd never actually been on the scene with one of Angelina's victims before.

"She slipped us up again, so I had a lot of time to dwell on it, too. A lot of time to think about her.

"How could she do it? Why didn't she stop? I sensed that she didn't think she could, but we always have a choice, don't we? I mean we always have a choice, don't we? Don't we?

"Unless maybe there comes a time when our choices are taken away from us. When we no longer have a choice.

"My choice disappeared when I sensed Angelina as a wounded animal, one which must be caught before ... before ... I don't know what. I had a moral obligation to restrain her, because those are the rules of the game I play.

"What rules did she go by? And when did she lose her choice?"

32

My options overwhelmed me. I drove, gripping the steering wheel too tightly, listening to Jack's chatter while trying to make sense of my new feelings. This new set of tools went with a new set of emotions, not necessarily conflicting, but confusing. I didn't know where to take him, or how to approach him. My nostrils were filled with the pulse of him and my appetite was primed and ready, but I couldn't seem to make a decision.

Finally, frustration got the better of me, so I drugged him with the music—had him fall asleep so I could think as we sped through the night. She had always given me the answers before. Shouldn't I now have Her imagination?

I looked over at Jack, his head bobbing gently, his eyes closed, a smile gracing the corners of his mouth. He was so easily manipulated, so fragile. He was so beautiful, so available, and I was so alone.

My passions told me to stop the car where we were and

have my way with him, love him and be nourished, give in to the necessary violence, grasp viciously with pleasure; my reason told me to wait, anticipate, stretch the moment, learn restraint. Without practice, my methods would always be coarse and vulgar.

I needed to stop, I needed a place to take my lover, and then a thought landed gently on my mind, and the idea brought a smile as I realized I had the power to do the impossible—I could create a place in his mind.

I pulled off into a darkened rest stop and parked the car at the far end. In the middle of the parking lot was a building with restroom facilities, phones, and drinking fountains. Behind it was nothing but flat, empty field for as far as the headlights shone. I turned them off, and the moon echoed my impression.

"Jack." I touched his arm, noticing with disgust the high artificial-fiber content of his clothes, desperately willing my fingers to merely touch, not clutch, and I altered the music until he stirred and awakened.

He turned sleepy eyes on me, then blinked a couple of times and rubbed his face. "Where are we? Hey, I must have dozed off. Didn't even know how tired I was. Terrific company, huh? I'm sorry. Say, where are we?"

"We're at my summer home, Jack. I thought we could both use some sleep. Then tomorrow we'll get back on the road. I'll even take you all the way to your school."

He looked deep into my eyes and for a moment I was afraid that he'd found me out, that he could read the lie written there upon my soul. Afraid he could see Rosemary's face in my seduction technique. In defense, I turned the music up and his probing look shallowed.

"Great," he said, then reached in the back for his things.

"Leave them," I said. "I'll send a man for them."

"Okay." He and I got out of the car at the same time, and I began a symphony for him. The music was a new sense to me, a new ability; I could compose and perform without any more concentration than seeing, walking, and talking at the same time. Jack turned to the empty field, and his eyes roamed over the imaginary mansion I had built there, and he said, "Wow."

"Come," I said. "Let us go inside." And I led him into the field.

I opened for us an ornate wooden door, and guided him through an exquisite foyer. The furnishings were heavy, dark. Massive carved furniture, ancient tapestries, velvet curtains, and huge portraits absorbed the dim light from crystal chandeliers. I wondered at my own imagination, and involved him more deeply into the music so he would never notice that the portraits had no features. The carpeting was plush and blood-red, and we mounted the stairs together, I preceding him, both of us trailing our fingers across the smooth, highly polished banister. Jack was speechless, and when I turned to look at him, his wide-eyed wonder at the opulence filled me with gladness.

Building upon my success, I created my bedroom with even more lavish touches. The bed was small, intimate, covered with deep velvet. Shelves filled with thick tomes lined the walls; antique lamps shed soft light throughout. Burnished red-leather chairs surrounded a marble coffee table, and a bar stocked with liquids in crystal waited conveniently in the corner.

"This is your bedroom?" he asked, and I saw admiration fire up in his eyes, admiration that fueled desire, the desire that the powerful, the wealthy, always draw.

"Yes," I said, and he pulled me close and took me in his arms. The scent of him sent a dollop of saliva to land in a spot of white foam on the carpeting.

"Come." I pulled back from him and led him by the hands to the bed, turning off lamps on the way, our eyes never breaking from each other, the moment truly romantic and magic.

"I can't believe this," he said. "It's like a dream."

I dwelt on increasing the music, or decreasing it; worried, suddenly, that I was not experienced enough to sustain such a lavish illusion, and for a moment, the whole structure wavered under my doubt. I felt the bed tremble under my indecision. Then, as my confidence returned, the bed regained solidity and Jack was bending over me, transfixed by my eyes, my power. His teeth gleamed in the moonlight as a smile of passion drew back his lips.

"You're beautiful," he said, and I knew I had not overly sedated him.

He licked my neck and trailed his tongue around down between my breasts as he unbuttoned my blouse, and the smell of his excitement was overpowering, maddening. His pulse beat loudly in the room; I knew I had to have him or lose control, and that would mean losing everything.

I pushed him back and unbuttoned his shirt. He kept looking at me.

"Look at these breasts. I've never seen breasts like these before. They're so . . . they're so cool, and white. Look how *white* your skin is." He took a nipple between his fingers and began to roll it. "Even your nipples are almost white." He looked at my face. "And your lips. Your lips . . ."

I gently turned him on his back and shed my pants. I straddled his bare chest, feeling his body heat soak endlessly into my warmth-starved legs.

I gripped his hair with both hands and brought the music up to orgasmic pitch, watching his face, loving him so severely that I thought to keep the music there for him forever, and when he closed his eyes, I sank my teeth into his neck, bit through the artery, and suckled.

As his warm blood pumped into my stomach, I knew him. As his blood became mine, I began to own his experiences, his thoughts, desires, aspirations. Pictures ran through my mind as Jack's life ebbed, and I knew him, from the day of his birth, I knew him, completely.

When the final shudder came and death rattled its cage

deep in his chest, I stopped, and kissed his face, his forehead, his nose, his lips. I sat up on his chest and buttoned my blouse, then shook the weeds from my pants and put them back on.

Back at the car, I put his sign and two bags into the garbage bin and then sat in the driver's seat, digesting my experience. It was incredible. Who would ever have thought that love could have feelings like that, such desperate passions slaked so thoroughly.

I waited, pondering, entertaining myself, enjoying the afterglow, and then I drove off, sated, comfortable, heading again for Wilton. And as I drove, thoughts and memories that had been Jack's began to tickle my consciousness. Before long, I was barraged by his thoughts, his impressions, his ambitions, his own passions. Even his thoughts of me were now mine to examine. I had no idea that this would happen, that I would know my victims so well that I knew their families, and would grieve with them as they discovered their loss.

Except that I had given him eternal life within me.

The night was at its deepest, and I drove fast, faster than was safe, but there were few other cars on the road. Jack's face loomed ever larger in my mind's eye, snatches of conversations he'd had with his father—about medical school, about obtaining his degree, and going to Africa and Southeast Asia to help. His girlfriend, they had made love to each other for the first time this past Christmas Eve ... the Christmas Eve I had spent murdering Joshua in his shop window. Jack's sports triumphs, his cleanliness, his idealism, they were all reminders of the poisonous beast I had become and I had to be rid of these reminders of it, rid of all of them, rid of them before I went mad.

There must be a way to keep from dwelling on him, I thought, and no sooner had I the thought than I had the answer.

Kill again.

I took the next freeway exit and slowed down, driving automatically as if by directional finder, toward the seedier side of town.

There I found a wino, a single wino, sitting next to a lamp pole, feet in the gutter, brown paper bag clutched in a greasy glove. Here was a person with no aspirations; here was a person who would give me nary a moment of guilt. Here was a waste of humanity that the world would be better off without.

I opened the car door and began to play for him. He left his bottle in the gutter, and unsteadily made his way to the car. The stench of him was sickening, but I knew I had to do this or go blind with internal rage. He sat next to me, entranced, and I leaned across his disgusting lap to close the door, then I drove to the warehouse district, sure to be deserted at this time.

I parked behind a bulldozer and, anxious beyond caution, ran around the car and opened the drunk's door. I dumped him onto the ground and fixed myself onto his neck, sucking furiously, ripping when the blood would not come fast enough to erase the echoing memories of Jack. The blood was poisoned, the bum was sick to his death with something in addition to drink, and I knew I would be sick from it later, but for now it was still blood, and I chewed and chewed, feeling his spirit weaken and his body give up the ghost.

I sat up, panting from the exertion, smelling his fouled clothes mixed with the oily heat of the engine and the tar of the construction site, and in one gigantic heave, all that I had drunk spewed forth in a gush that splattered the car door and lay in a puddle next to the dead man.

I stood, dizzy and feverish, and leaned against the car. I had been wrong. The wasted flesh that rotted at my feet had once been C. Wakefield Caldwell, a corporate executive, a millionaire, a philanthropist, a father, husband, and son to a proud, proud family—until the disease of drink captured his soul, long before I captured his body. His aspirations were of a different sort than Jack's, but no less filled with conviction and altruism. His suffering pained me; he was unable to stop drinking; he was addicted to it, even though it destroyed the very fiber of his being. He watched his family lose respect, and leave; he watched his empire collapse; he had seen the last scrap of rug pulled out from under him when his mother had the locks on her apartment changed. He knew what he had been when he scavenged in the free-clothes barrel at the Salvation Army and sold the rags for wine.

Jack's voice slipped back to join that of Joshua and Sarah and the others. Background music.

I now had C. Wakefield Caldwell for company.

"The waiting was the hardest part. Jesus, she slipped by us at every turn. It seemed like she was a pro. She seemed to know all the right dodges, all the right things to do that would leave absolutely no trace of her whereabouts, or clue to her direction. I couldn't believe she was that crafty, although maybe she was. I rather think she was lucky.

"Whatever. It gave me time to dwell on her. And myself. I didn't like thinking about myself too much, but I fantasized a lot about Angelina. I was always trying to put her in a situation in my mind and have some flash of intuition or something that would be strong enough for me to actually proceed in some direction with the investigation. As a result, my imagination took me into some pretty bizarre realms. This territory was darker than any forest I'd been in; this bounty was scarier, more perverse, more dangerous, than any I could ever imagine.

"But trying to get inside her mind was the worst. You always try to second-guess the animal—will it go to high ground, or to water, or underground?—and to do that with any accuracy, you must know a little about the species.

"I knew nothing about Angelina—only what I made up in my head. Sometimes I was accurate, most times I wasn't. But the

worst part was when I had to admit that I was enjoying the dark
meditations I began to have, where I tried to think like her, tried to
be her, to imagine how she thought, where she would go, how her
sickness would progress.

"I gave up everything for her. Everything. Family, friends, job,
everything. For her. Her, and those dark meditations."

33

Six nights later, Sarah's car died a noisy and inconvenient
death just outside of Wilton. The night was at its strongest,
so I left the automobile carcass where it lay and began to
walk.

The night was moonless and still; there was no traffic
on the little two-lane road into town. I had become quite
adept at depending on my cane for stability; the rhythm of
my footsteps was regular and pleasing, slow and deliberate,
thoughtful and restrained. It was good to walk the highway
again.

I watched the night deepen, felt the cold crinkle of the
stars in the clear sky, listened to the sounds of the night
animals in the fields.

I walked past the little green sign with its pebbly, light-
reflecting letters that said, "Wilton, Pa., Pop. 4780," and I held
my head a little higher, my back a little more erect. Home.
The place to which I vowed I would never return, for it held
ties—emotional ties—and I cared little for all the burdens of
human life.

Yet here I was, and it wasn't an emotional cord that
tugged me back into this place; it was something else, something stronger, darker, more substantial than the petty stuff
of human emotions, yet its nature eluded me. I knew only
that this was where I was meant to be.

The night was on the wane as I walked past the first
service station, then the barn-sized tavern that exuded

country western music of a weekend night. I walked on into town, beyond the feed store, past the laundromat, the bank, and the real estate office. I stood on the corner by the one theater, which played only family features, and I looked to the north.

The neighborhood was up there, on the knoll. The house where Rolf took Alice and me to live, the place where Alice eventually died, was there somewhere, dark, filled with sleeping strangers. An occasional light showing through a square pane was all that signified that a neighborhood was there, and not just an empty field full of Pennsylvania January.

I turned and looked south. The train tracks ran along the back side of the main street, and it was four blocks beyond this that Alice and I had lived before Rolf. The house I was born in, the house that my father laughed in, died in, the house that held memories of childhood ostracism—the house I swore I would never see again—stood just four blocks away.

Like a magnet, it drew me.

There was a third of the night left, at the very most, when I viewed the house from the outside. It seemed unchanged. It remained untended, unpainted—unkempt. The tree in the front was winter-bare and spindly. Dirty mounds of snow built up in the corners and under the bare hedges, while patches of yellow grass showed through, looking forlorn and spooky in the dark. The memories of this house were clear to me but oddly devoid of emotion.

The emotions of too many others swirled about inside of me; I had no room for my own.

The lock on the cellar door was probably still broken. My footsteps crunched delicately on the snow of the drive-way as I walked to the side of the house, then around the rear. The steps down to the cellar door were covered with undisturbed snow; I stepped through it without hesitation, descended the steps, and lay my hand on the frigid, tarnished knob. The sound it made as it turned was as familiar to my ears as the sound of my own heartbeat. It was never locked; it was always stuck, but I knew the right combination of movements: Push on the top corner, pull on the knob, jiggle once, and lift up.

The door opened inward, scraping softly on the concrete floor. I slipped in and closed it gently behind me.

The smell was the same—sweet and moldy, as if centuries of drying apples had permeated the damp concrete and wood with their scent. This was my favorite smell of all time. I breathed deeply, closing my eyes, tuning my senses, feeling—home. Relieved. Tired. Back—after a long, long journey.

I would sleep later. First, I had to discover the occupants.

Carefully, I discerned the litter in the cellar: bicycles, boxes marked "Xmas," fishing equipment, a basketball hoop, a huge, ripped archery target. One corner of the cellar had been built up with shelves, and the shelves were filled with home-preserved fruit, vegetables, jellies, and sauces; the lower shelves were stacked deep and high with canned goods.

A spiderweb caught across my eyelashes as I walked under the stairs where the old round washing machine was still stored. This was the pink, metal washing machine I remembered from my childhood. It had an electric wringer on the top. I trailed my finger in its dust. An old red hobby-horse sat in the other corner, along with a dismantled crib and a child's white play kitchen that had been left mid-tea party, with dolls still in their seats.

Two children in this family, I thought, and went to the stairs. I remembered which creaked and which did not, and with the help of my cane slowly mounted them, and at the top opened the door to the kitchen.

Four humans slept in the house. I could smell them.

The kitchen was the same as the last time I'd seen it—the black-and-white linoleum tile, the chipped countertop, the stained sink; the rude yellow walls were maybe a little dirtier, a little sicklier.

The living room was completely different. The furniture here was cheaper, shabbier, than any we had ever had. Evidence of rowdy children was everywhere: marks on the walls, toys left to be stepped on and tripped over, broken vases poorly glued together, teeth marks on all the chair legs. There were burn marks in the tables, in the upholstery; the whole house was worn, too worn, depressing.

But on the mantel, above the fireplace, the woman here had arranged two candles and pictures of the children, one little ceramic frog, and a dried flower. I knew this to be sentiment, and for a moment wished that I had a mantelpiece of my own to set things of sentiment on. I gently blew the dust from them and as I did, I felt someone stir. My heart pounded in reaction. Someone's depth of sleep had altered. The boy. I walked quickly and silently to the hallway to wait, to watch.

Within moments, the vibrations of sleep were resumed. I walked quietly down the hallway and pushed open the first bedroom door.

Blonde strands of hair, curled at the ends, scattered over a pillow. A girl child of four, maybe five, years, slept with mouth open, her lips like little moist pink petals, her breath sweet on the pillow. I touched her silken cheek with my finger. It was so warm. She was so soft and secure, worryless and safe, happy and oblivious, and suddenly my knees went weak. I was exhausted. I longed to sleep the restful sleep of the child. I leaned closer to her, to fill my nostrils with the scent of youth, just to smell her purity, and she moved her little doll-sized legs under the covers, rubbed her face with one hand, and opened her eyes.

She reacted in surprise at my face so close to hers, then she smiled, the smile of an angel, sleep still clouding her brain. I sent to her a lullaby—a sweeter one I've never heard—and watched as her eyelids drooped and finally sank, and the smile faded and her breathing resumed the deep regularity of child sleep. I fingered her hair for a moment, fine golden threads, then turned away. I had more to explore and little time.

The next room had been my bedroom; the door was closed tightly. I turned the knob gently and pushed it open. The floor was littered with toys and clothes; bookshelves lined all the walls. A set of iron bunkbeds lay directly ahead, the bottom bunk covered with debris, the top bunk holding a boy.

I picked my way among the scatterings toward the child. He was much older than his sister: twelve, maybe thirteen. His dingy, stained sheets were pulled down to his waist, the smooth winter-white skin of his back exposed, waiting to be touched, stroked. A lock of light-brown hair fell rakishly across his forehead, his thick eyelashes lay quietly on cheeks just making the transition from childhood chubby to adolescent soft.

I played the music softly for him. No sooner had I started than he relaxed, sinking deeper into his mattress. He had been on the verge of awakening. I ran a finger down his back, ever so softly, tickling, feeling the cool smooth skin. I brushed the hair from his face and traced an eyebrow, a cheekbone. He reminded me of someone. I touched the bridge of his nose, ran my finger across his lips, back again, parting them, feeling his front teeth with the tip of my finger. I increased the music. Who does he remind me of? I opened the lips and looked at the teeth. The front two crossed, just barely, and I took in the curve of the cheek and the fullness of the lips and then I knew. I pulled back, the music changed, and I regained control quickly before I woke him up; before I woke everyone up. He reminded me of Boyd—reminded me so severely of Boyd that I almost knew for sure that if this boy opened his eyes right now, there would be a dark-brown spot over the pupil of one eye.

Silliness, Angelina, I scolded myself, and gentling the boy again with my music, I stepped up on the lower bunk, cringing as it squeaked, and I kissed his neck and smelled his maturing manhood. It was a delicious smell, and I kept my nose in the hollow between shoulder and neck for a long while, not quite daring to taste.

I felt the night wane. I would survive the night without feeding; I would not survive without shelter from the day. Reluctantly I left the boy, deeply pleased that two perfect children slept in my new home.

I closed his door and stepped across the hall. The master bedroom. The parents' room. I stooped to examine the wallpaper. My blood spot was still there, faded to no more than a little dirty smear, but there it was. I remembered that night as clearly as if it had been this very evening. Had that smear of blood called me back to this house?

Their door was closed. Slowly I opened it and stepped in.

The woman slept naked, the sheet and blanket wrapped tightly around her husband, leaving her barely enough to cover one leg and one arm. Her body was slim and conditioned, the hair on her head an auburn shade, much lighter than the semen-encrusted hair between her legs. The stench of sex hung thickly in the air. The husband, with dark greasy hair curled around his head and black beard stubble gracing his ample jowls, slept noisily in striped pajamas.

She was beautiful, the woman, just as beautiful as her children. I walked to her side of the bed and played the music for her as I gently touched her, touched the portions of a woman that I had never touched before, never even seen before. I saw her through the eyes of eternity; I stroked her flesh, absorbing the warmth, as I watched her body mature and grow old right before my eyes. I gently tickled, pinched, and probed, and in spite of myself, the music changed and she began to respond.

I knew I was treading dangerous ground, but I felt I

had teased my nature beyond any reasonable amount of restraint this night, and I urged her responses, and swallowed as saliva threatened to overflow.

And then I heard the voice. It was my own voice this time, clear and sweet. "Angelina, the dawn is upon us," and it was true, I could see my own shadow over her as the sky began to lighten.

Reluctantly I pulled back, kissed her lightly on the breast, and vowed to return. I made my way with weakening steps back downstairs, consciousness falling away, willing myself one more minute and one more, cursing myself for being so foolish, and I crawled under the stairs with the dirt and dust and crispy insect carcasses, and I stretched out and slept.

SONJA HARDESTY: "It's all my fault. Oh God, I knew it was down there in the basement, I knew it. I felt it. I—I almost saw it.

"Okay. From the beginning. Right about when all those murders started happening, I started having these erotic dreams. So did my husband, but not quite as much as I.

"I thought it was some kind of sexual-identity stage I was going through. At least I hoped it was . . . and yet I thought maybe it was something else too, something real, a physical force that was doing something to me late at night while I slept. I was so scared . . . I would sit at Amy's bedside for hours and wonder if it was real enough to affect her and Will, and still I hoped it was just me, a stage I was going through, a mid-life crisis or something.

"But all the while, I was kidding myself because I knew about that—that feeling in the basement.

"And I wasn't surprised when those sexual things kept going on with me, night after night, and all the time those terrible things were happening in Wilton, all the doors were locked and everybody was so afraid . . . I began to wonder about myself I thought maybe I was just discovering that I was, you know, one of those kinds of people who get turned on by grisly neighborhood murders . . .

"Anyway, I was so scared that I pretended it wasn't true. I wanted to believe I imagined it—I would rather believe I was per-

verted than to really think that the murderer was in my basement, so I never said anything to anybody.

"Some mother, huh?

"Oh God, the worst is that I thought if I said something to somebody, it would be over, and somewhere deep inside myself, I didn't want it to stop. I thought, being middle-aged and having two kids, that sex was kind of over, well, not really over, but not what it used to be, and this was so . . . tender, almost. Loving. I was afraid and reassured at the same time. Sounds weird when I say it.

"So you see, I barely gave a thought to what could possibly happen to Will, or . . . or Amy . . . God, I can't believe I'm saying this."

34

When my eyes opened and consciousness wavered for the briefest of moments, then slid into focus, clear and serene, I had the answer to my difficulties.

Children. Sweet, innocent children. They smelled so fresh; they would taste tender, rich, soft, unspoiled. Children had not poisoned their bodies with drugs and chemicals; they had not hardened their hearts against the travesties of life; their lives had been brief, their aspirations limited. I could live with the knowledge and consciousness of children—I could live with the optimism of children—far better than I could live with the bitter draught of adult memories.

And two perfect children lived right up the stairs. My nest egg, my reserve.

The house above was full of activity. The floorboards over my head squeaked as footsteps traversed them, and I tuned in and recognized the vibrations of voice. The evening was young—dinner preparations were in the making. Someone could hear me, or see me as I left the cellar. Must I wait until they bed down? I looked around the dismal cellar. I could not.

I arose and pulled cobwebs from my hair, brushed dirt from my clothes. It seemed from my experience with the two hitchhikers and the cat that there were limits to my mind-clouding; I could not mesmerize more than one person at a time. Maybe, though, I could surround myself with the music as I had surrounded the car when I slept therein. Maybe I could cloak myself, become as a shadow to their eyes for the briefest of moments—that's all I would need, a moment—and then I would be on my way and they need never know another thing.

I walked to the outside door, feeling the cold through the cracks. I turned the knob, and as I did so, the kitchen door at the top of the stairs opened, throwing noise down; a bare bulb that hung over the stairs flashed to life, illuminating everything that wasn't in the shadow of the stairs. Feet encased in soft shoes trotted lightly down the wooden risers.

I crouched, feeling the hair at the back of my neck prickle. A feral growl waited at the back of my throat. The woman came into view, tall, slender, wearing jeans and a white T-shirt, her long auburn hair brushed and dazzling. She stopped before the stacks of canned goods, her back to me. She began to sway as she considered the array, making a mealtime decision.

If she turned around, she would see me.

She picked up one can, and then another, replaced the first, and still she scanned the assortment. I began the music, not directed toward her, but to raise the level of my own vibrations, to render my flesh safe from prying eyes or dangerous discovery.

The woman stopped swaying. She slowly turned toward me, and her eyes flicked across the expanse of cellar, resting for a long moment on the cellar door. She did not see me, but she sensed me. Her slim fingers rubbed her arms, and I could smell the acrid scent of fear. She looked quickly at the can in her hand, grabbed another almost without looking, and ran up the stairs, flicked off the light, and slammed the door behind her.

Relief weakened me. It had worked, but only to a degree. She knew I was there—she may not have known the nature of my being, but her instincts had found mine, and so my time must be short here, short and cunning.

The cellar door opened with little noise, and I was again standing in snow.

I walked through the backyard, alongside the neighbor to the rear. I turned north on the next street and headed for town, beyond town, for the nicer neighborhood, for the upper class of Wilton, where they fed their children butter and sweet cream, where the children were plump and tender, pinchable and delicious.

I moved quickly through the early evening, keeping to the shadows and along the walls. I wanted no one to stop me and inquire about my business—maybe even recognize me from my childhood. With the cane, I could walk lightly, and so I did, across Main Street and up into the brightly lit neighborhood on the knoll.

This neighborhood, for all its costliness and prestige, had very small front yards and virtually no space between the houses. I knew there were large yards to the rear; many of the homes here had swimming pools. But the homes all stood shoulder to shoulder at the street, as if guarding their privacy to the rear.

I walked slowly along, letting memories slide across my mind. I had schoolmates who had lived in these houses. Where were they now? What were they doing? Who was living and who was not? Who was successful? Who had babies? Who was alcoholic and who was adulterer? Who embezzled and who abused themselves? Such a nice neighborhood must mask a multitude of perversities.

The winter evening was earlier than I thought. Boys, dressed in snowsuits and armed with snowballs, played with each other in the streets. They all stopped and watched me as I passed, and I listened to their whisperings. They wondered at my lack of winter clothes; they speculated about my cane; they dared each other to throw a snowball at me, but none did. I kept my head down, assuming the posture of a crone, and kept on, slowly on. I no longer felt the cold. I only felt the children's warmth as I passed.

The homes were lit with warm colors; yellow light poured out of their windows into the black-and-gray evening. I walked the length of the first street, then turned up a block and walked the length of the next. Through open draperies, I watched the neighborhood as dinners were served, then kitchens cleaned and televisions turned on. I walked and watched, hearing my boot heels on the icy sidewalks.

And then I saw her. Standing at the picture window of her living room, hands cupped to look past the reflection of the fire, out at the night. Out at me. I stopped and watched her, thrilled by her tiny beauty. Miniature black pigtails held up by lengths of bright red yarn stood out from the sides of her head. She wore a little white dress with red hearts on it; I felt as though she'd just come back from a trip to Grandma's, or somewhere equally as special and important, and was up late because she was too excited to go to sleep.

She couldn't have been more than four, and little baby teeth grinned at me as I watched her. She waved at me and then turned and ran, and a moment later an older sister pulled the draperies closed.

I walked around to the side of the house, afraid that the next light to go on would be on the second floor, but I was wrong. The child had a ground-floor bedroom.

I watched her change into red pajamas, her round little tummy smooth as a drum above the little red-and-white underpants. I saw her mother come in and together they knelt by the side of the bed and said prayers, then the little one crawled into bed while the mother read a story.

I stood outside, feet firmly planted in the snow, fingers

gripping the outside edge of the windowsill, and watched. I watched the love and joy transpire between them, knew the child was well nourished, and my impatience grew.

At last the mother kissed the child, turned out the light, and left the room. I began to examine the framework of the windows.

The outside was a storm window, held on by little screw-in catches. I thumbed them down and lifted the window to the ground. The inside window was locked, so I began the music, quietly, gently.

Within a few moments, the child opened her eyes, and I spun for her the music of a circus, of Mommy's approval, of excitement and fun, a special treat for being such a marvelous little girl. She came right out of bed and over to the window, then had to go back for a little chair to stand on in order to reach the catch. She wrestled with it. Her little cherub face grimaced with the strain, then she smiled as the half moon slid around.

I opened the window, and she looked at me with huge brown eyes. "Is it true?" she whispered with a tiny lisp, and when I nodded, she got off her chair and toddled back to her bed. She pulled the dark green blanket from the bed and held it up to her face—thumb securely in her mouth—and padded again to the window. She regarded me for a solemn moment, then released her thumb and held her hands up to me. I lifted her out the window and closed it.

This was the warmth that my body required. I sat with my back to her house and hugged her tinyness to me, wrapping her dark blanket around us both. I continued the music for her, weaving a magic spell, taking her to the circus, the carnival, safe and happy, and she, with thumb in mouth, giggled gently against my chest.

I nuzzled my face down next to her neck, plump and moist in that crease, and it was so perfect I couldn't bear to destroy it, as famished as I was. The thought of biting, tearing, ripping, seemed inconsistent with my feelings, with my purpose, and as I tasted her, taking little licks, tasting her salty excitement, I thought maybe I could, carefully, suck up a large fold of skin and take one bite, piercing through, catching the artery just at the right point.

I mouthed her neck, listening to little moans of pleasure from deep in her throat as she experienced the clowns and rides and delights of the ultimate childhood dream, and when I felt the pulse the strongest, I pulled a great amount of flesh up, then bit swiftly and carefully through with front teeth, and the blood began to gush.

Oh, sweet melody. I hugged that child to my chest, she was so small I could hold all of her—I needed not to sit on her chest or wrestle with her, she came to me willingly and filled with trust. I put both arms around her in a passionate embrace as her living fluid drained into my warmth-starved body, and I knew her joys, her games, her childhood worries and cares. She was wonderful.

When she was empty, I continued to hold her, I rocked her as her essence flowed through me, and I knew I had the answer to my life: innocence.

Innocence. The feeling wrapped around my throat like a scratchy woolen muffler. Innocence. I had never had this. I had never experienced the blind trust that this child had evidenced in climbing out the window to me. I had taken her trust and sucked her dry, and only because she was innocent.

Innocence was her crime. Innocence was her crime and my salvation. Could I better live with the innocence of my victims than with the warped and shattered dreams of the adults they would eventually become?

Yes.

I lifted the child, now a shell, a pathetic, limp rag doll, and tossed her to the side, seeing as I did, two precise slits in the side of her neck—my neatest work to date—and then her face was buried in the snow where she landed and I could see it no more.

I wrapped the dark green blanket around my shoulders, hoping to hold in some of the warmth the small meal afforded, noticing that, with minor alterations, it would serve as a new cape. I brushed the snow from my back, found my cane, and was once again on my way.

"I think Wilton kept it to themselves pretty well. They didn't want to start any kind of a panic or anything, but if they'd only have been a little less private, if I'd known, I could have maybe prevented . . . well, I don't know. A lot of kids died, though. Angelina was ruthless.

"A monster is what she was, a monster. The stolen-car report didn't connect from Pennsylvania to New Mexico until spring. And by that time . . .

"Well, by that time, Angelina was warped beyond recognition. But I knew her.

"I knew her."

35

I made a fine home for myself in the cellar. I rearranged things under the stairs and in the dead of night I brought scraps of wood and things in to make a private space, a close, comfortable, personal place. I built a place where I could escape from the worries of light, of discovery—where the gleaming ivory flesh of my face would not attract attention as I slept in the shadows. I built a box.

My wardrobe improved as I scavenged here and there—I found great pleasure in roaming the halls of the homes I infiltrated. I enjoyed the closets, the cellars, and the children of the occupants, rearranging the furnishings a little bit until they were more to my liking, resting and enjoying a book, sometimes, in the den, after breakfasting.

None was so fascinating to me, however, as the family that lived upstairs. I dared not harm them, they were too close, too precious. My nightly visits to them became routine. I enjoyed the woman with a touch of perverse jealousy. She was so beautiful, so warm and complete, and she enjoyed an active and satisfying life with her mate in the sunshine. I enjoyed toying with her, and sometimes with him, learning about men and women, learning about what made them run. Particularly intriguing to me were their sexual responses, for this is what drives humans to reproduce.

I would sit by the side of the girl child and smooth her hair back from her gently rounded forehead and give her nice dreams as I watched her breathe, watched the flickering of her eyes under the thin lids. In my mind, I gave her the name of Diana, Moon Goddess, goddess of the hunt, of all that is sacred.

The boy I called Daniel, for he seemed fearless to me. Always he was on his guard, sleeping lightly, his consciousness sinking only when I played the music for him. I examined Daniel, as I did all the occupants in the houses I visited—except Diana, of course. Diana was purity inviolate. Daniel, I examined every night, touching, probing, watching his reactions, his responses. The music changed automatically, anticipating the necessities of his dreams, keeping his consciousness in a deep trance.

I enjoyed this music nightly as I toyed with his flesh, and his sleeping smiles and soft moans of pleasure were counterpointed melody to my ears. Such symphonies we created together! I learned to play Daniel's body like a musical instrument, and through his unconsciousness, we grew very close. I knew that he knew me; I had invaded his dreams and he knew me.

Eventually, his trance deepened even as I entered his room. Automatically, his body responded to my presence, which was a delightful turn of events.

And I thought that if he knew me, he loved me.

Night after night I resisted the temptation to waken him;

I longed to sit and talk with him, to just be together, in the darkest of night, our secret society of two, just discovering each other and being together.

I should never have succumbed, but the loneliness became too great, this lifestyle of utter isolation. Ultimate control over my victims left me without companionship of any kind. A new feeling was growing in me, a different kind of hunger, a starvation for someone who was like me, or could be like me. I wanted someone I could share with, for even though I was a creature of the night—one whose will had turned toward the dark—I still felt, aspired, wanted.

There were others of the night. I had seen them—moving shadows. Whether there were others like me, I have no idea, for I shunned them all. I wanted nothing of what they had. I wanted only the warmth, and the living ones, the ones with the succulent flesh, were the only ones who could give me the warmth. I doubt companionship with any of the myriad night compulsives would have sated my appetite for conversation.

I knew that the time would come when I would meet someone I could teach, someone who saw in me something of his own aspirations, and I looked at this boy child and wanted it to be him; I wanted so badly to roam the streets with him, to teach him all I had learned, sharing my life. One night, the temptation, the desire for companionship, overturned all my sensibilities, and I wakened him.

I did it slowly. My control was absolute. I could, with a run of a scale, put him back to sleep; I wanted him to become accustomed, perhaps gradually, over several nights, to my being there, with him, in the flesh.

I felt his consciousness rise; my heart pounded in excitement. I was to awaken my lover, I was to actually be with him, converse with him, truly, in real life as I had so often in my fantasies.

I sat next to him, my legs dangling off the edge of his top bunk, and I trailed a finger through the familiar light hairs that grew in a line downward from his navel while I brought his consciousness up, slowly, level by level.

He would be so surprised to see me at last; the girl of his dreams, his nocturnal partner, the one who had spent such erotic moments with him. He would be so pleased. I could hardly wait. The anticipation jittered my internal organs until I thought I would have a seizure. This was him, this was the one, this was my life partner. Surely this child would choose me.

His eyelids fluttered, and then opened, unfocused. They closed again, as I swirled the music at a semi-conscious state. The bedroom was dark; the moon was new, there was little for him to see in the dimness.

He opened his eyes again, and saw me. I relaxed my vigil, waiting for the first sleepy smile, the recognition of a loved one, but his reaction held none of the intimacy I expected. His mouth opened in horror as he saw me; he filled his lungs, ready for a shout; his brown eyes grew huge in terrified madness. In my surprise, I hesitated for a moment, not knowing what to do; my first impulse was to smother the brat with his own pillow, but his bouncing would throw me right off onto the floor.

The music. I brought it up, loud, powerful, and he lost consciousness immediately.

Sweat poured from me and my limbs shook. He would remember this; I could not erase my simple-minded act. What a fool I was.

There were no others like me.

I stayed there, next to him, until I felt the tug of dawn. I stroked his back and played deep, dark tones of restful sleep for him, hoping he would awaken sleep-drugged and mistake my blunder for a simple night terror.

Or I could kill him.

No. This house must be kept sacred, no one must search the cellar for clues in this house.

The dawn drew near and I patted my Daniel on the

cheek, then jumped lightly from the bed. I pulled my dark green cloak around me and slunk, feeling lonelier than ever, to the cellar, to crawl into my dirty, makeshift box beneath the stairs and lie, quietly, waiting for the next evening.

When I next awoke, a crucifix hung from the stairs directly over my box.

I had felt the change coming over Wilton. Interesting, a town under siege. First I smelled the paranoia that lay like thick fog over the streets and around the homes. No one walked the streets after nightfall; no children played in the pleasant spring evenings; doors were locked and curtains drawn. The whole town retreated into a private sort of mourning.

Then the police came out, and the vigilantes. I walked the streets without fear of them at first, for they noted my silhouette and deemed me ineffectual. But as my nightly raids continued, as the pitiable victims continued to open their locked doors to their doom, the men began to gather their fear into groups, and some ancient memory in me awakened and began to fear them. I would see them, standing in groups or roaming the streets, silently, unobtrusively armed. Their black silhouettes backlighted by streetlight or starlight reminded me of villagers in torchlight. Through a growing sense of eternity, mixing past with present with future, my eyes saw frantic fathers, brothers, and grandfathers, grief-stricken and worried, but my mind's eyes saw witch hunters, lynch mobs, and angry, outraged gatherings turning monstrous themselves.

I danced around them, darting behind trees, bushes, around the corners of houses. I danced around their impotency, knowing that my time in Wilton was shortening, yet drawing it out past all limits of good sense. I should have left Wilton a month ago, but I hadn't. I couldn't bear to leave my Diana, my Daniel. My home, my soil. I would be more careful.

And then I awakened Daniel, like a fool, and the next evening I found a crucifix dangling over where I slept.

It had been Daniel's work, I knew it in an instant. He loved me too much to give me away to the mobs who would rip me apart; he knew too much lore. No, it was clear he hoped to immobilize me with his puny effort, so as to talk to me, to control me—his very own succubus that lived in his cellar. His secret. The one secret among many that my Daniel and I shared.

I unhooked the crucifix and examined it while listening to the sounds overhead. It had, no doubt, belonged to his mother. I considered waiting for him, but then I knew that he would never come down while his family was awake; he would wait until they were all asleep. We would rendezvous in the darkest of the night. I had time to leave and return.

I slipped out the door and felt the light misty rain falling around me. The land had turned green in the past few weeks, and the fresh smell of damp earth and the rotting spoils of winter decomposing floated lazily on the air between the raindrops. The town's paranoia swirled about my feet like a hungry cat, and I smiled to myself, knowing that adrenaline adds spice.

There was a new scent on the air this night, though, and it was fear. One single, sharp, acrid note of fear wafted clearly though the obstacle course of the mist. Someone was outside and afraid. Someone close.

I swung my cloak over my shoulder to keep the rain out and started off.

"At last Angelina and I were in the same town at the same time. She was in Wilton, all right. Murdering children. Murdering defenseless children. God!

"I knew she was in Wilton, but I didn't know where. We worked with a silent desperation, the mayor and I. I tried to stay in the background until I'd assessed all the information—I couldn't stand having her slip away again.

"The town was a panic-stricken mess, but at last I felt that my net was closing in on her. I tried to take things methodically, the way one does on a hunt. They were impatient. I had no authority, though, so while I collated information, they set a trap for her."

36

I followed the fear scent for two blocks. The smell sharpened and focused and I became suspicious. No one was out of doors after nightfall in Wilton anymore. No one. Everyone was inside, locked in with their stale air and their fear, breathing the fumes of their own desperation.

Why, then, could I smell the hysterical silence of a young girl—outside?

I slid into the shadow of a house and thought. The pull of the child's humanity was powerful: The scent pulsed in my nostrils, saliva began to flow. But there was something wrong here.

I opened the rest of my senses, I tried to puzzle out my reluctance to this free and easy meal—like a radio antenna, I trained my point of focus around the whole area, and came up with the only conclusion I could make. It was a trap.

Indignation arose in me. How dare they consider me to be such a fool! Let their little bit of bait meat suffer the night through and be tortured by nightmares for the rest of her life—I would not touch her, I would not fall for their pathetic ruse.

I lay my hand on the house whose shadow I enjoyed and felt the vibrations of family within. This house, I thought. This is the house I will claim tonight. And I shall enjoy each of its inhabitants.

I listened more with my hand, and waited until the house quieted. Then with the use of the music, I persuaded the husband to open the door. He, I took in the foyer. The wife went to her damned reward in her marriage bed, and the twins I greedily disposed of and threw on top of her. All the time my indignation rose and fell; I was seriously wounded that the fathers of this community would be such insensitive dolts. Well, this would give them something new to discuss among themselves.

When I finished, I sat quietly in the living room, knowing that I had overreacted, overindulged. My body was terribly uncomfortable. I sat gently, hoping I would not lose it all to the carpeting in front of me. So I stayed there, waiting for the overstuffed feeling to go away, waiting for the peace to come, waiting for the warmth, waiting.

But instead of the peace came sadness, a sadness for this family, a sadness that my only associates were music-drugged victims. A sadness that there was nothing else for me in life, and there was no one to share it with. This was not a new feeling, but the depth of it was frightening. The despair immobilized me as I thought through my life, my weird sense of eternity giving it a continuity beyond any previous bouts with nostalgia. I saw the uncanny inevitability of my station—I saw that even the things I read, dreamed, thought, and did as a child were brought forward to their natural conclusion. The logical conclusion was me sitting, gently, sick again, on the sofa of a family of dead strangers.

My eternal vision of the future was warped; it was like looking through layers and layers of glass, each giving the scene its own particular distortion, the accumulation of each partition becoming almost opaque in the distant future, and I knew that my actions tonight, and each moment of my life, determined the direction my life would take in that bizarre funhouse of the future. Nothing was planned out, nothing was predetermined. Tendencies, habits, and preferences were programmed into the life scenario, but the final decisions lay with me.

This was the saddest cut of all, for I no longer had a choice. I could never go back. I could never again adopt the life of a normal human—not even of a crippled human. I had gone over the edge with Sarah months ago, and now even my physical self had altered. I had been given gifts, powers—

No. I had chosen my path, and I would continue.

My stomach settled a bit as I thought again of the four people whose spirits were reunited in eternity within me. I held their knowledge, their cunning. With each new kill, the previous voices receded, but were still heard in my mind— in the chorus of Hades. This kill had been automatic, there was no sport in it whatsoever. I had done it as retaliation to the trap laid for me by the incompetent vigilantes, one of whom was willing to sacrifice a daughter. How offensive.

Offensive, Angelina? Shooting fish in a barrel is offensive to the sportsman as well.

But I am no sportsman. I kill to survive.

Overkill is wasteful. You wasted this night, wasted.

I got up from the couch and began to wander about the room. I went into the woman's bedroom, saw the children scattered over her like broken puppets. Something drew me to her bathroom, and I went in, cautiously.

I was drawn to the scent of lavender soap. The woman bathed with lavender soap. I had smelled it on her skin; maybe that was the reason for this unconscionable melancholy. Lavender soap. Alice had used lavender soap; so had I, but I had left my last bar of it at Lewis's, and had not smelled it since.

Slowly I untied my cape and let it fall to the floor. I took off my boots and socks and pants and shirt. My body, lean and white, gleamed in the dimness. I turned on the shower and stepped in, feeling the water wash over me, but gaining no warmth from its heat.

The soap would not lather. It rubbed about my cold skin in a greasy way and would not leave its scent. I scrubbed, with growing desperation, but to no avail. I sank another level into dark depression.

I turned off the water and stepped out, drying off without feeling that I had ever gotten wet. I went through her closet and found fresh black underwear that looked bizarre next to my pure white skin. She also had a black sweater and pair of black silk pants.

I was admiring myself in the mirror when I heard the noise in the kitchen. Automatically I fell to a crouch, the music went up, cloaking me from attention, from view, and as I concentrated on the music, on the pounding of my heart, on scanning the house for intruders, for the cause of the noise, I saw my reflection in the mirror fade.

I was not real.

My subconscious judged the noise to be a natural settling of something, nothing of threat, and I stood in front of the mirror and brought the music up and down and watched my reflection fade in and out. I was no longer a thing of substance. I was no longer real. At some point I had passed over the physical line from life into shadow . . . It was others *like me* who passed me in the shadows of the night. I must appear to them the very same.

But Daniel—Daniel saw me, didn't he?

What did Daniel see when he looked at me?

I looked again at the three bodies on the bed.

They were nothing. They were pathetic. Even Daniel was nothing, just a lad, a boy, mortal and afraid. Out there somewhere was my ideal victim. Out there somewhere was the person for whom I would put my existence on the line. Sometime in my future, a contest of wills would take place, and to the winner would go the spoils. *That* is what life is about now, Angelina, I thought. Survival. Perpetuating the species. Somewhere exists the perfect victim who will, when taken, fight me to the death and that fight will mean his life. Life in eternity. Yes. A companion in eternity.

Hope lightened my attitude for a moment. I was capable now. Ready. Fertile.

Still heavy with my excesses, I wrapped my cape around me and went outside, listening to the sounds of the neighborhood. The rain had stopped, leaving the streets glistening. The scent of fear was still clear on the air, but it was no longer sharp, acrid.

The child in the trap knew, somehow, that the danger was less likely this late.

I longed to go home, to slide quietly into my coffin, yet a curiosity held me, guided me toward the accumulation of men. I believe I had to test my superiority. And the limits of my unreality.

I knew exactly where they were. Their auras redly illuminated the porch of a house down the block. I wrapped my cloak tighter about me and raised the music, feeling solid and competent, and walked down the center of the street toward them. I heard my cane tap and my boot heels scrape. I lifted my head and dared them to see me.

The child, like a lure, was cast out on the edge of the lawn. She was wrapped in a sleeping bag, with only the top of her head showing. She slept, but her sleep was troubled; the knowledge of her father and his large friends watching her was never far from her mind.

I sauntered down the center of the street, stopping in front of the child. I twirled around, scraping my feet on the gritty wet pavement, kicking my cape up around me.

The color of the aura around the porch changed. They sensed me.

"Listen," I heard one man say.

"I don't hear nothing."

"Shut up."

"What did you hear?"

"Shut the fuck up!"

"I saw a shadow."

"Where?"

"Out there."

"Will you guys shut up?"

I enjoyed them almost too much; I raised the music and danced in the street. I twirled faster and faster, knowing I was no longer real, knowing and hating the fact that I would never be warm again, knowing that my frigid, bloodless nostrils would never again smell a stew, that my icy fingers would never again feel the texture of anything but living flesh—I had traded the senses of life for the new sensual experiences of the eternal wasteland, and I danced with it, danced with the frenzy of the damned.

Then I stopped, and while they could not see me or hear me or really even know I was there, they *knew* I was there— and I stopped and thrust my cold finger into the bait-child's ear.

She rose up screaming hysterically, screaming and screaming, and the men came streaming from the porch, shotguns and flashlights waving in wanton disarray. I looked upon them sadly, gathered my cloak about me and walked softly back home.

I slid quietly into my coffin, completely forgetting Daniel—and his crucifix. I lay awake for many hours, replaying the scene in my mind, fretful and restless, trying to capture an essence that flitted through, something that I had missed, an important element of the evening that was eluding me, had eluded me in my excesses and overindulgences.

I lay on the cold concrete floor, not unhappy, yet not pleased with the revelation of my new nature—just cold and alone, and I waited for the sleep to come and erase my thoughts.

And when I awoke, I smelled Boyd.

"The next day there were funerals. Children's funerals. There were six children's caskets lined up at the cemetery, all draped with identical blankets of flowers.

"Odd, that funeral. I saw no emotion, not even from the parents of the children we buried. I looked around at the faces of the people in the crowd as the minister gave the service, and they all had deep lines etched in them, as if slashed there by razor blades. There was

no conversation, no talk, no tears, no nothing. This town had been sucked dry over the months. Sucked dry.

"After the funeral, we held another meeting. That's when the emotion emerged, and it came out as rage. She'd killed another four people the night before. She knew about the trap—the guys who set it even thought they'd seen her, but they didn't know . . . They didn't have any idea of what we were dealing with. Neither did I, really.

"Anyway, it was on a Thursday, or a Friday—I can't really remember, except that it was a school day, and we held the meeting at the fairgrounds just outside of Wilton. Everybody in town must have been there—all the factions were divided up. It was an angry crowd, and they had no one to vent their anger at, so they took it out on each other.

"One group wanted to call the National Guard. Another group wanted to call the Pope. One guy gave us a deadline. He said he would be going to the national press to sell his story and the story of Wilton's bloodsucking monster on Monday. If we wanted it kept quiet, we would have until Monday. The people who would benefit from a town full of gawkers wanted to tell the press anyway; the police and the mayor only wanted to tell people who could help.

"It was a mess. An entire town united only in fear.

"I just wanted to find Angelina's hiding place before she moved on.

"And then I saw him. A kid, hanging out on the fringes of the crowd. He had a look on his face, a cockiness, a standoffishness in his attitude. He knew where she was, I was sure of it.

"But by the time I'd been introduced and told them what I knew about her, told all the townsfolk about my years of tracking her and what we'd found in her wake, there were too many questions and explanations. I couldn't keep my eyes on him.

"He was a kid, though, and the only one there. No kid was staying home from school those days in Wilton. Escorted to and from and no one was left alone or at home. Except this kid. He knew something, he had to."

The fear I felt upon awakening was a painless pressure—clearly recognizable as fear, only it held no physical reaction as it does for mortals with normal responses. Like the ache in my legs, which had become a physical heaviness, so too the fear was a sensation of weight, of pressure.

I felt cool and clear, calm and knowledgeable. I had tarried too long in Wilton, and now I was being tracked—hunted by the best. My senses came to life, sharpened by this fear.

Boyd had come for me.

Boyd. The thought of him brought back memories—strange memories that seemed steeped in confusion, but then they were from a different time, a different age; they were experienced by a different Angelina.

Boyd. What would it be like to see him again, to talk with him, to be close?

Could we hunt together, Boyd and I?

Yes, Angelina, I told myself. He is hunting. He is hunting you.

I backed up from my—romantic?—notions and began to plan. It was time to move on. Maybe I had made mistakes in Wilton that I would not make elsewhere. Maybe I would change my habits. The time had come to put away my childish fantasies. The time had come to indulge only enough to ensure my survival and put my energies instead into discovering a companion, a friend, a confidant, a comrade.

A lover of the night.

I moved to slide from my sleeping cell, but something was different. I felt the walls around me—they were different, they were solid. I pushed up on the top with all my strength, but it didn't budge. Fear hugged me close and I stopped struggling and began to think.

Daniel. Of course. He knew I was there and he had told me that he knew; he had hung the crucifix to alert me, and I had foolishly done nothing about it. And now, while I slept, he had imprisoned me, nailed me securely inside a freshly built coffin.

To knock my way out would alert the whole household. Furthermore, it was questionable whether I would be able to free myself. The construction seemed competent. The box was solid. Then again, if I made enough noise, surely the parents would come and release me. No. Daniel would convince them otherwise, and then I would have more to deal with than just Daniel. I could deal with Daniel if he was alone.

I tried the music, but the box yielded neither to the strains of melody nor to my lack of substance. I was still entirely solid, just vague in appearance when the music soared.

I tried to locate Daniel and force him, by way of the music, to come to me, to release me, but there was no one home. I searched throughout the house; there was not a heartbeat, not a breath, not a living cell in the building.

Daniel had outsmarted me. He had taken advantage of my weakness and gained the upper hand. He would pay. He would pay.

I gave the wood one solid kick in frustration and winced at the loud noise reverberating in the closed space. It would be impossible to escape. Reluctantly I settled back to wait, bringing my hands to my chest in the most comfortable resting position. The crucifix lay there, cold on my chest. I toyed with it, feeling the little golden chain, running my thumbnail over the cross-hatching on the front.

Fury felt the same.

The boy would pay.

"The kid disappeared before I could get to him. No one else seemed to have seen him—at least no one else could tell me who he was. After the meeting at the fairgrounds, everybody seemed pretty heated up; we told them to all go home and check their fruit cellars and garages and the trunks of old rusted-out cars. She had to be hiding somewhere. That helped to diffuse their mob-style

agitation. It gave them something active to do instead of dwelling on their impotency. I went back to the mayor's house, where we'd set up a kind of temporary headquarters.

"Just before sundown, as the streetlights of the town were beginning to come on, families started to congregate together for safety. We set up shelters in the schools and churches. Nobody was to stay at home. The children laughed and played, thinking this mass slumber party was a celebration, while the adults clung together in fear so physical it had scent.

"I was having a cup of coffee on the mayor's porch, nodding and waving to the folks as they passed by with blankets and food and children, when that same boy came tearing down the street and ran right up to the porch, slamming the screen door behind him. He stood there, his face red, panting for breath, and he had to breathe hard for a minute or two before he could speak. He had the wild look of a scared rabbit in his eye.

"Mrs. Haskill, the mayor's wife, came out, saw who it was, and said, 'William!' She looked at him with mild concern on her face. 'Sit down here, Will, and I'll get you a glass of juice.'

" 'No thanks, ma'am,' Will said, then took some deep breaths. 'I just need to talk to . . .' He indicated me with a shake of his head.

" 'Boyd,' I said.

" 'Mr. Boyd. Please, Mrs. Haskill?' He was desperate for privacy.

" 'All right, of course,' and she closed the door behind her.

" 'Sit down here, Will.'

" 'No thank you, sir. I caught her, sir. I caught her. I caught the killer. I put her in a box in my basement.'

" 'You did what?'

" 'She killed all those people. She killed our neighbors, and I could have stopped her, but I didn't. I knew she was down there, she woke me up the other night, and I put Mom's crucifix over her, but she got up that night and killed that family. I didn't know about it until the meeting at the fairgrounds, but then I left there and went to Dad's shop and built a big strong box; she'll never get out of it, sir, and I put her in it and now I'm scared. I'm so scared.

She'll wake up at sundown, right? And she'll know I did it. She woke me up one night, she was sitting on my bed . . .' He began to cry. 'Oh, God, it was awful.'

"I patted the boy's shoulder and let him be alone for a moment while I went in for Kleenex and some of that juice Mrs. Haskill had. When I came back, he was hiccuping lightly, his face was still red and his eyes huge.

" 'Okay now, Will,' I said, after he'd gulped some juice and blown his nose. 'Tell me what she looked like.'

" 'Tiny,' he said. 'Little and blonde. Skinny. Real light, I had to pick her up to put her in the box. Real small, bony and cold. Cold like damp concrete. But light.' He shivered. 'She was sleeping in a little fortlike thing she'd made under the stairs in our house. I had to dismantle that and pull her out of it, then lift her into the box, and she never even twitched. I'd have thought she was dead, except that she was so . . .' He moved his arms around.

" 'Limber?'

" 'Yeah.' He went back to his juice. 'I was afraid she'd wake up. I almost couldn't do it I was so scared.' He rubbed the goose bumps from his arms. 'She was almost pretty, you know, I mean, I could see where . . .'

" 'Yeah,' I said. 'I know.'

" 'So we wait until morning and then put a stake through her heart, right?'

"It wasn't until that moment that I realized the insanity that had taken over this town. Here's a young kid, probably fourteen, talking about putting a stake through Angelina's heart. He probably wanted to cut off her head and stuff her mouth with garlic, too. God. But then, I shouldn't have been surprised. The whole town was on a witch-hunt. Superstition abounded, there were hexes and charms hung over every doorway and around every person's neck. There were people who predicted—for money, of course—who would be next; I even heard that some were ripping open chickens to read their futures in the entrails. I tried to ignore it all, but when Will said that, it hit home. I knew we had to proceed very, very carefully to avoid a catastrophe.

" 'No, Will, things aren't done that way. She's a person, just like you and me.'

" 'No, she ain't.'

" 'She's just sick, that's all.'

"He looked at the floor and shuffled his feet. 'So what're we going to do?'

" 'She's locked up tight, you say?'

"He nodded.

" 'Well, then we'll wait until tomorrow and unlock her. And then tomorrow night, when she wakes up, we'll talk to her.'

" 'You're nuts.'

" 'I know her, Will. You saw for yourself how small she is. You don't think you and I can handle her?'

"He looked at me with big eyes, and I saw a little of myself in him. 'I don't think anyone can handle her,' he said."

38

The night wore on. I lay in a foreign box, immobilized and furious—helpless and hopeless, and I waited. I waited. My fingers became intimately familiar with the little gold cross as I lay there, waiting.

I waited through the night. No one entered the house, no one drew near. I fanned my consciousness out, roaming the house, the neighborhood, searching for Boyd, for surely he was behind this degradation. The mounting swirl of fear maddened me in my impotent state.

Can't you face me, Boyd? Must you send a child to do your work in the daytime, to chain me as I sleep? You follow me, hunt me, dog my trail for years, Boyd, with your self-serving attitude, and when the final moment comes, you care not to see for yourself?

I have little interest in your piddling ways, Boyd. Better men than you have died under my loving touch, and were grateful for it. Release me and let us meet.

If you dare.

"Will and I talked into the middle of the night, then we got some blankets from Mrs. Haskill and slept on the daybeds out on the porch. I listened to the boy breathe for a long time before he fell asleep. I stayed awake a lot longer than that. Knowing that Angelina was crated up and helpless was somehow of no comfort. I knew the town was safe from her for the night, but I felt her presence, felt her awful, almost-inhuman wrath, and I knew that when we released her, she would be very difficult to deal with. We just had to do it right—carefully, and without causing a panic in the town.

"When we can show them that it's just Angelina, just a warped little girl and not some legendary monster from Transylvania, then they'll settle down. But if they mobbed Will's basement, we'd have a big problem.

"I could see her, almost, locked inside that dark box. Every time I closed my eyes I could see her face—eyes wide open and glittering with a luminescence of their own, skin thin and glossy, stretched too tightly, too whitely, over sharp bones. I saw her and saw her lips—bloodless they were—saw those terrible white lips curl up in a smile as her eyes flashed in recognition and she said my name. 'Boyd.'

"I sat up quickly, feeling bile rise, the perspiration running down my face. I must have gone to sleep, although I couldn't remember nodding off. The voice of my dream kept bouncing around inside my head, but it had been just a bad dream. Angelina didn't look anything at all like that . . . that . . . grotesque living skull I imagined in my sleep.

"I wrapped the blanket around me a little closer and lay back down. Tomorrow would come soon enough to settle this whole thing.

"The next day the townspeople were frantic with relief. For the first time in over four months, a night had gone by with no killings. I tried to enjoy their pleasure without letting on the reason. I begged with them to not relax their vigil, but it was to no avail.

Like oppressed citizens who never lose their hope, their optimism, they were all convinced that the plague had ended, the bad dream was over, and they came up joviously for air, anxious to return to their previous way of life. I tried to convince them that caution was advised here, but they weren't hearing me and I couldn't exactly tell them what I knew. Not, at least, until after Will and I had taken care of Angelina."

39

I awakened with all faculties absolutely alert. My position remained the same; the security of the box, I could tell, was unchanged. The difference was in the house. My family had come home.

The parents were watching television, my precious Diana was playing softly in her room, and my Daniel . . . I scoured the house, seeking a whisper of his scent. He was not home.

The house felt pleasant, the air relaxed.

The neighborhood had lost its fear.

I could see my lovely Diana, goddess, angel, and I sent her favorite lullaby to her—the one I had played for her night after night, the melody of which she never grew tired, the one that had given her pleasure every night for months.

She heard it, and I had her.

I followed her progress as she silently emerged from her room, walked past her parents, through the kitchen. I saw her hesitate at the door to the cellar, but I urged her, bringing the music up, and then down, threatening to pull it away; just come, little darling, just come a little closer and I shall play for you a symphony, one to enfold you in pleasure and keep you suspended . . .

She opened the door. The darkness of the cellar rose to meet her.

I called to her with the music—don't turn on the lights.

This is a symphony of the night, and it is beautiful only in the dark. Do not be afraid, there is only the music, there is nothing to be afraid of, the music is beautiful, and loving, and so are you. Come to me, come to the music, just down one step.

She came down one step.

I trilled in pleasure and she came down another to please me, and another, baby hand gliding along the handrail, then another, and soon she lowered herself onto the next as fast as she could, giggling.

She reached the bottom. The darkness surrounded her and sucked the giggle from her throat. Her bottom lip trembled, and she almost turned around to go back up. Or, worse, call out.

"Diana," I spoke, my voice muffled, soft. She knew this pet name, and she adored it. The threatening tear receded as the music once again calmed her. She took little steps to me, tentative, yet unafraid.

"Diana," I said. "Can you get into the big box? Can you figure out how to open it?"

And I could see my prison through her eyes and the latches were simple. Three large hasps lined the box lid, and each had a small dowel pushed through for surety.

I watched with increasing anxiety as baby fingers fumbled at the adult metal locks.

"Pull the sticks." She understood, and tried, but frustrated easily. My agitation mounted as she wiggled one loose, then went on to the next one. The second was harder, but the last came free easily. Then she had to turn the metal ring to line up with the hasp slot. This was harder for her, her hands hurt, and she was beginning to be afraid in the dark. I was losing patience. My freedom was so close—I could foil whatever plans Boyd and the boy had for me if only this little wimp of a child could free me.

Settle down, Angelina, I had to remind myself. The child is doing her best.

I began the music again, softly stroking her golden hair with it, easing us both through this tense moment. The burred edges of the metal bit into her soft little fingers and the smell of blood was so loud that I almost screamed inside my prison. The first lock twisted and she lifted the hasp off.

Good girl, good girl. Now the next one. I could barely stay conscious, I was starving; the tension of the moment had me wanting to explode. She began to whine with the second one. The box was off square, and the hasp didn't line up right. It was hard to turn.

I increased the music, hoping to give her extra strength. She worked hard at it, her little pink tongue poking out one side of her mouth. She grunted and groaned, began to cry a little bit and whimper as her blood flowed across the hasp, but I just increased the music; I wouldn't, I *couldn't,* let her stop. I was almost out.

It worked. The second was free.

The third was easier to do, and she turned it, then very slowly lifted the hasp off, took two steps back, and put her bleeding fingers into her mouth.

I quieted my heart for a moment, not believing my luck. Then I reached up and pushed on the lid. It swung open on silent hinges, and there she stood, like an angel.

I climbed out and knelt before her, promising her a child-delight journey into the land of her heart's desire later this evening. I played a light melody for her as I watched blood-tinged saliva, golden green in the darkness, appear at the corners of her mouth. Very gently, I removed her fingers and examined the cuts, then put her fingers in my mouth, tasted the delectable fruit, the plump little knuckles weeping delicately onto my tongue, whetting my appetite.

I looked into her eyes, the eyes of my rescuer, and I wanted to sweep her up and dance her around the floor, sinking my teeth deeply into her neck and enjoying the golden flow of this most glorious child. But I dared not. Slowly, reluctantly, resisting temptation, I pulled her tender fingers from my tongue and patted her gently on the head.

"Go to bed now, my sweet, and I will be along later to tuck you in." She turned and ran toward the stairs. I halted her with a clashing of cymbals, a storm warning only she could hear. "Tell no one of this." She looked at me, innocent eyes questioning. "Our secret," I said. She nodded solemnly and went quietly to the world above.

I smiled to myself, then resealed the box and sat in the corner.

Boyd and the boy would be along presently.

I would meet them on equal terms.

"Even though I believed Will's story, I didn't let the mayor or the police know. I had several reasons. First, because they might go and blow her to pieces, or worse, let her escape in the confusion. Second, it might not be her at all, or she might have already gotten out and left. And third, which is probably the only real reason I kept it to myself, is that I wanted her all to myself. I didn't want to share the confrontation with anyone else—especially not with a crowd. This had been my hunt all along, and it was only fair that I bring her down myself.

"I probably should have gone with Will the moment he told me she was in his basement. But I couldn't. I couldn't. It felt as though the appointment had been made, and I needed to sit and think, prepare for the moment. The moment I had been rushing toward in impotent frustration for years was suddenly here and I needed to consider it for a while. I needed to think of what to say to her, how to act, how to feel.

"Anyway, I was busy in meetings all day, talking to the people who were trying to control the town. Everybody had gone back home, like I said, but a handful of us knew the danger wasn't over, so we were trying out new strategies for search as well as for keeping the townspeople from being killed and the media from turning Wilton into a carnival.

"All day long, through all the meetings, I knew where Angelina was, and I didn't tell anyone.

"I finally met Will at the mayor's house just before ten that night, and we walked over to his place. There was not a doubt in my mind that Angelina was in that house. I knew it when we were more than three blocks away. I could feel her.

"Will's parents were watching the news. He introduced us and told them he was going to show me his collection of books on the occult. They were quite preoccupied and didn't pay much attention. We went into Will's room to wait for his folks to go to bed before we went downstairs.

"He had all kinds of books on the occult and witches and things, and he was all fired up about showing them to me. I tried to talk to him, tried to tell him that what we were dealing with here was a very sick young woman. Compulsive, obsessive, self-destructive, and homicidal, true, but sick nevertheless. There was no supernatural here. It was just Angelina. Just Angelina. A misdirected, sad, psychopathic case.

"But he would have none of it. He just looked at me with eyes that had somehow seen beyond my experience, and he patiently told me again about stakes through the heart and rituals that were ghastly to say the least.

"I heard the television go off, and his parents called a soft good night to us, then their bedroom door closed.

"Will got very quiet, and so did I, and we just sat there on the lower bunk, with only one lamp on, and we listened to the sounds of the house around us.

"The time seemed to pass without our awareness. I looked at the clock at ten-forty-five and a minute later it was eleven-thirty. Neither of us had spoken or moved for forty-five minutes. We were listening, I believe, to the evil in the walls.

"I noticed that going into the cellar was the last thing in the world I wanted to do. Fear was collecting in my bowels, and I knew if I stood up to take one step toward her, it would squeeze out, along with everything else. My hands had lost their strength; I couldn't even make a tight fist. Fear had reduced my nerves to jelly, and with a glance at Will, I knew the same had happened to him.

"With wide eyes and sweat-slicked forehead, he whispered to

254

me, 'Just before dawn. We'll release her just before dawn. It'll be safer then.'

"That would have given us a good five hours to sit there, steeped in our acids.

"But at midnight, we heard his sister's bedroom door open."

40

I sat on a dusty box of books, waiting, my mind twisting around itself. The taste of Diana's blood upon my lips was feeding my obsession, endangering my life. I felt myself growing weak and cold in the wake of too much anticipation and too little nourishment. I had wasted too much energy during my imprisonment, and then I had to wait for Boyd and the boy, and as I waited, I grew fainter.

I would rather hunt. And feed. And be warmed.

Diana. I tasted her still, I ached for more. Yet I had to wait.

They came home; I heard their footsteps loud on the boards above my head. I listened to the murmur of their voices, and I knew they fancied themselves superior, believing I lay locked and helpless beneath them.

Boyd. The years I had spent thinking about him, wondering about him and me, and what could have been. What had he thought of me over the years?

I knew. I knew what he thought. He had hunted me, tracked me, and had come to leisurely enjoy his kill. He thought I was locked up.

Well. Our confrontation would occur, but no doubt a little differently than Boyd imagined. I would never become but another trophy in his collection.

Suddenly it became very clear to me why She had fostered this queer relationship with Boyd. She had left nothing to chance in my development, and this night I would pass my final exam.

I needed to be clear-headed, swift of reaction, in case he

had tricks of his own. Hunger weighed heavily on my mind, the weakness devastating to my faculties.

Diana. I tasted again her sweetness on my tongue.

I searched the house with my consciousness. The adults had gone to bed, I lowered their eyelids and put them to sleep with a brief wave of conducive music. My Diana was sleeping, too—lightly. Boyd and the boy were in the boy's room, both sitting on the bottom bunk. Books rested on their laps, and they talked. They talked of destroying me while in the very room that used to be my own. That room used to be my bedroom, where once I had childhood dreams, thoughts, childish motives and emotions. My room. My place, my sanctuary, my boundaries of life, from birth through age twelve.

They were arguing about me.

I sent some music to keep them occupied, and I enjoyed monitoring their reactions to my fine-tuned talent. I wove nets for them, nets of danger, of injury, of pain, and I drew them tighter and tighter about the two, reveling in the stench of fear that fell through the floorboards and into my lap. I wound the nooses tighter around their necks, wrapped them securely with bonds of insecurity, ineptitude, ineffectiveness, and futility.

I had them secured in their own emotional excretions far tighter than Rosemary ever bound me with her leather and shackles.

And then I concentrated on Diana.

Wake up, my darling. Remember my promise? Come to me and I will give you everything.

She remembered. She got up and with very little encouragement opened the door and walked through the house. She never hesitated to turn on a light; she remembered about the symphony of darkness. She was too good, too precious, too wonderful. My saliva glands ached in appreciation.

Come directly to me, through the kitchen. Open the cellar door. Take the steps, one at a time, oh, my child, oh, yes, come, come to Angelina, she will give you everything. Everything and more.

My body went limp with hunger as I saw her little pink pajamas pad down the dusty cellar stairs. The precious child, I would soon have her life, her experiences, to hold as my own; I would know her for who she really is; I would, for a short moment, be one with her, two personalities merging into one, and then her identity would flicker and vanish, but I would have her essence; I would have her unspoiled virgin expanse, and I would not squander it as her parents and society eventually would. I would keep it fresh, eternally youthful.

Or maybe she could become mine, I could introduce her to life as I had known it. My precious Diana could become my legacy to Wilton, Pennsylvania; I could leave behind a little piece of myself, another of my kind.

Or she could become my companion, and she would call me Mistress.

Come to me, Diana, my precious.

And then she was in my arms, soft and cuddly, smelling warm and sweet from sleep, and she rubbed her fists into her eye sockets as I danced her around the floor.

"*Amy!*" I heard her brother call, and I shot him with a harpoon of fear that cramped his stomach. She's mine now, you brat. You just leave her be.

We sat together at the tea-party table, she so prim and proper in her fuzzy pajamas, with sore little hands in her lap, and I drank in her smell as I smiled and lifted a tiny, empty plastic teacup in a mock toast to her health. She looked down at her hands.

"Diana, my darling, what is it? Oh, I know. I promised you a journey, and here we are in this ugly, scary cellar." I stood up and held out my hand to her. She looked up at me with those trusting, loving eyes, and I knew I had to give her that, just that; I had to give to her the child-pleasure dream of a lifetime. Then she put her little hand in mine, and I led her to my hiding place under the stairs and she crawled in with me. I held her warm body close to mine, so close that I could feel her pulse even in her little legs, and I began to gently remove her sleepsuit as I spun her final illusion.

"Suddenly I could breathe again. It felt like I'd been tied to the chair with thick ropes around my chest, and then suddenly they disappeared.

"Will was taking great gasps, too, holding his stomach, and I knew by the look on his face that his bowel control was not quite as good as mine.

"But something had changed; the air felt different. The fear was no longer oppressive. Will tested the strength of his limbs, then took clean clothes to the bathroom to change. On the way out, he looked at me and said, 'A psychopath did that?' and left me with a new type of fear and a thought or two about stakes.

"When he returned, he said, 'Amy's gone down there. C'mon. We've got to go now.'

" 'Wait a minute, Will,' I said. 'Amy can't get to her, nor she to Amy, right?'

" 'Well . . . Right. I guess . . .' His answer was not as confident as I would have liked.

" 'Don't you think we should wait until just before dawn, like we said? She's secure in the box, right?'

" 'I've got to get Amy.'

" 'Wait. Can Amy open the box?'

" 'No.'

" 'But you could.'

" 'Yes.'

" 'If Angelina can make you that afraid, maybe she can make you open the box.'

"Will came back in and sat down on his bunk. His face wore the pain of self-sacrifice in the name of guilt. 'Boyd,' he said, 'she's my baby sister.'

" 'I know.' I looked at my watch. 'It's just after midnight. Dawn is at five. Let's at least wait a couple of hours.'

"Will pulled at his hair. 'Oh, God,' he said, then buried his face in his hands, while we sat there, waiting.

"I believe I did the best I could do under the circumstances. My conscience is as clear as it can be about that night. I truly believed that Will's box was strong, and that his little sister couldn't open it. I guess maybe I was a little afraid to go down there—I mean, who wouldn't be?—but I really, honestly, believed that the little girl would be all right.

"But it was less than a half hour later that Will cried out, and I knew that I had underestimated everything."

41

Curious, it was, that my enjoyment of the child was heightened by the presence of the two upstairs. It was reminiscent of Joshua and his newspaper stand back in Colorado. Not the circumstances, certainly, but the publicness of it. There in the picture window of his store; here under the feet of the child's brother and Boyd—humanity's self-appointed savior.

I despised them.

The child was sweet and wonderful, warm and nourishing, and I enjoyed every drop of her, until the very end. At the very end, when life finally winked out and the torrential outpouring of memories and experiences flooded my mental vault, I felt the child cry out for her brother, and I felt his answer. I knew at that moment that I had sucked in a little of this Will person as well. The two of them were close, very close indeed.

Even so, the kill lacked adventure; it served its purpose, and merely confirmed my instinctive feeling that a greater conquest—an exercise of my supreme talents—yet waited.

But then the child was dead and I needed to remove the carcass from my presence.

The boy's hand-hewn coffin. A perfect repository. I crawled from my space, pulling the corpse with me. I quickly undid the catches and dropped the body in, then refastened them. I heard the restlessness above. While the child held my total concentration, I had let lapse the music for those above. And now they were aware—free and restless.

Come, then, and let this be over between us. I sat on the edge of the box, tapping the worn tip of my cane on the concrete floor, waiting. Come, boys. Come to Angelina.

They came. They walked through the kitchen; I could feel their hearts pounding. They hesitated at the door; then it opened, and a flashlight swung down over the stairs. I was bored with them already. The warmth of the child's blood flowing through me made me want to stop all this, made me want to rest, to sleep.

Then the bare bulb flashed to light, momentarily blinding me, but I recovered quickly, and when I could again see, the two were crashing down the stairs.

I stood, cane in hand, ready to face them both.

Boyd came toward me first, the boy in his shadow.

"Angelina?"

"Hello, Boyd."

"Angelina, what's happened to you?"

"I've grown up. Matured. And you?"

"Grown up? Look at you. You're a mess."

Insecurity flashed through me, and the music came up automatically to protect my vulnerability. I couldn't afford to dwell on it. In a moment, I was back in control. "I have what men have searched for throughout the ages."

"What's that?"

"Eternal life."

"Where's Amy?" The boy spoke from behind Boyd.

"In the coffin you built for her. Convenient disposal, thank you."

"Oh, Angelina, knock it off." Boyd's abruptness was inconsistent with the memories I had of him. "Do you like this lifestyle you've chosen?"

Like it? He didn't understand.

"You don't, do you?"

I looked at him, I watched the boy peer at me from around Boyd's side. He prodded Boyd, who gritted his teeth and elbowed back at the kid.

"Come with me, Angelina, and we'll take care of you. We'll give you everything you need—"

"No! Kill her!" The boy lunged at me.

I stabbed him with music and he dropped to his knees. Boyd bent to his aid, then looked back at me. I relaxed my stance, eased the boy's discomfort, readied myself against Boyd. We stood no more than six feet apart, glaring at each other, antagonism pouring forth, for a long moment. The boy held his stomach and moaned.

"You all right, Will?"

"He's all right," I answered for him.

Boyd stepped closer to me. I stood straighter, not flinching from his gaze. He looked softer than I remembered, more . . . human, mortal. Warm. He held his hands out in the gesture of peace, and his eyes, brilliant in their intensity, held me with the little brown spot on one iris. Such depth in that spot.

"Come with me, Angelina. Stop this."

I had always known that Boyd and I would meet again— there was a mysterious bond that held us. I had known it since we first met.

"Please, Angelina. It's not good, what you're doing here."

He took another step closer to me, and I was drawn to him, attracted to him by more than his scent; there was something more, something I had once known about Boyd but forgotten, forgotten in the drama of the scenes we had shared since meeting, forgotten in my fantasies, forgotten in the madness of my life . . . forgotten.

"Angelina, I—Angelina, you don't have to live like this anymore." He held his hand out, and I looked at it. Large and warm, open and inviting, soft and safe. I was so tired, so sleepy.

Then a scuffle from the floor, and *"No!"* and the boy leaped at me. In surprise, caught off guard, I took one step back and the coffin stopped me. My knees buckled and I sat down hard, bringing the music and my cane up at the same time. His eyes turned glassy in response to the music as I took careful aim for his temple, but as I swung the cane in a mighty arc, his sister, within me, betrayed my aim. She halted my arm midswing. I hesitated for the briefest of moments, just long enough for the music to falter, the boy to recover his trajectory, and my aim to waver. Then I was back in control and I brought the cane down with all my strength, cracking him hard. But I missed his head and broke my cane on his shoulder. The cane flew from my stinging hand, and then the boy was on me, crushing the breath from me against the box.

"Will, stop!" I heard Boyd cry, but then he, too, was holding me down atop the coffin and my music and I were powerless to stop them.

I struggled, but my legs were weak and of little use. They slid me from the coffin to the floor, where the boy sat on my legs as he worked with one hand on the hasps. The other arm dangled uselessly at his side. I had damaged him; I could see his pain, red and purple all about him, and still he was in a heat to avenge his sister. Such resilience. Such motivation. I was impressed.

Boyd held my wrists to my shoulders and looked down into my face. Again, in the midst of my fury, fear, and agony, I had that feeling about Boyd. I began to softly play the music for him while the boy cried and pounded, cursing, on the box. Boyd responded. He relaxed just the slightest bit, just enough.

The hasps came free and the boy threw open the lid.

"Don't look in, Will," Boyd said. But, of course, he did, and he began to moan. I lay quietly, panting from the exertion, just playing the music lightly for Boyd, keeping the touch feather-light, letting the boy immobilize himself with his own stupid emotions.

"Help me lift her in, Will."

Will looked back at Boyd with a flushed, perspiring, tear-stained face. "Amy," he said.

"Help me put Angelina in the box, Will," Boyd said, and I had to increase the music just a touch to counteract his emotional response to the boy.

Will reached his good arm into the box to pick up his sister, and I cast uncertainty into Boyd at just that time. He was torn between restraining Will and restraining me, and his balance shifted slightly.

I twisted violently and caught his forearm in my teeth. I clung to it with all my energy, feeling my teeth rip into the tendons and cords, sucking deeply, desperately, all his juices, blood flowing across my face, into my eyes, as I sucked his spirit, nursing his soul from the flesh.

I saw the blow coming, but heeded it not. I had tasted in Boyd something new, something so extraordinary that I needed every moment to ponder it. It brought me a new sound, a new music; it opened up new vistas, new arenas; I broke through to the next level in self-discovery. I clung with my life to his arm, drinking more, more; there could never be enough of this, it's all so new, and the mysteries of the universe began to unfold.

And then the boy hit me and I retreated into the void, to rest, to heal, to wonder.

"I recognized her by her eyes. I knew by the eyes. She had changed so much over these years; she'd grown to be a monster, but the monster was definitely Angelina.

"It was strange to finally confront her in that basement. I'd lived for that moment, and it was finally upon me, and soon it would be over and that made me kind of sad. It had been quite an adventure. She had given me a lot, Angelina had.

"I can't exactly say what happened down there, it all happened so fast. Parts seemed to be in slow motion, and parts seemed to be distorted, weird, as if I were drugged or something.

"Will was really upset over his sister, but his grief nearly got him killed. Angelina could have killed him with that cane, but she only got his shoulder.

"Anyway, we finally got her into that box; we just threw her in on top of poor Amy. I guess we didn't have to do that; Angelina was unconscious. Will knocked her out when she bit me, but God, even after she was unconscious, she wouldn't let go. She kept, like gnawing, and sucking, even though her eyes were rolled up into her head; she was, oh, Christ, I just wanted her off of me. We had to pry her jaws open with the brass end of her cane. Once the suction was broken, she went limp.

"When we got her in that box, cape and all, and that lid down and locked, and my arm wrapped in my shirt, I started to shake. I couldn't believe we really had her. I sat there, and Will and I hugged each other and we both cried. We cried because it was over, but it wasn't quite over yet. Will still had to deal with his sister's death and throwing Angelina on top of her poor little body, and I still had to deal with my torn-up arm, and . . . and . . . and the fact that when she was sucking on me, I thought for a moment my heart would explode, it hurt so bad and felt so good all at the same time. All I could think about was how I'd screwed up my life, how much I'd hated—my dad, my brother, myself—how life was the shits and it hurt all the time, life hurt, and how ashamed I was that it had turned out that way, but I really didn't care enough to change. And now, Angelina . . . God, it hurt, but it was good. I didn't want her to stop. She was punishing me because she loved me.

"And I deserved both—both the pain and her love."

42

A year has passed since I began this journal. My doctors will read it and we will discuss it, and the lawyers will try to corroborate the details, and everyone will wonder in horrified titillation just exactly how much of it is true.

It is all true.

But that concerns me not at all, for I have discovered the advantages of a cage; it may keep the imprisoned one away from society, but it also keeps society away from the prisoner.

I am most fortunate.

Society knows its strengths and its weaknesses, and this hospital has a civic duty to keep its reputation untarnished. This hospital will do everything in its power to keep the public from knowing that towels occasionally disappear from the linen rooms and show up around the necks of the dead. Society would rather lie and cheat and cover up its ineptitude than believe my story, rather than believe that I live safely, happily, here, as long as there is a solitary night guard who can be beguiled with a simple melody.

At last I have learned that it is not death that makes such a difference; it is life. My life. I kill to live. And it is a fair trade. I suckle the life from small animals, leaving their juiceless remains for the scavengers—three or four a night is plenty—and only twice have I been unable to resist the craving for a human.

I kill to live. I have grown through the passions of the larvae, through the dangerous excitement, the extravaganzas of killing. I have grown through the pupa withdrawal and emerged into adulthood. Now, as my view of eternity is gradually brought into focus, other priorities draw my attention.

For now I have a Student of my own. I have passed through solitude, and have entered into a partnership—an internal realm filled with peace and happiness. I teach, and my teachings are reminiscent of my teacher.

How well I remember Her, and how much She meant to me during those early times.

Will my Student turn out to be a different refraction of

my own soul? Or is this Student actually a separate, breathing, warm human being? I have no answers, but I am patient. The answers will come. I know only that my sharing with this One is the very essence of fulfillment.

I am no longer alone.

Tonight when I awoke, I found a little cake the other patients had placed by my bedside. The nurses will take notice in the morning whether I have eaten it or not. They have never seen me eat. But they will find it intact, its chocolate frosting unnibbled, the yellow 21 written in warped hand will be undisturbed.

I am fortunate to have found such peace at this young age.

The cane they gave me is metal tubing and distasteful, but it serves me. I pretend with it, as I pad along the halls, that I hear the grit of the roadway beneath my boots, and the stomp of a solid cherrywood cane with a brass lizard as a knob. I feel the cold wind biting through my cloak, and I talk and laugh with my Student, watching the growth, the progress, growing myself through our association, knowing that I am, *that we are,* immortal and eternal.

"They put her in an asylum somewhere out in the country. I went to visit her several times when she was in the hospital in Philadelphia, but she was always sleeping.

"I went back to Westwater, got my old construction job back, but after only a week, I quit. Being consumed—obsessed, I guess—by something for years and then having it be over, resolved, left quite a void. I'm not quite sure what I'll do now. Go back to school, maybe, or do a little traveling. Chasing Angelina all over the country wasn't exactly traveling, but I've kind of got the bug to go explore some.

"I don't know.

"My arm healed. It's all scarred, and I've lost some of the movement in my wrist, but it's not bad. I can still pull a trigger.

"Pull a trigger. God, what a dream I had last night. I'm not sure I can even talk about it.

"I dreamed I was hunting, all alone, up in the mountains. I was sitting on a rock, just waiting, my rifle cradled in the crook of my arm, and a big buck strolled right into the clearing. It was the same buck I'd tracked for weeks. Weeks. And there it was, right in front of me, bigger than life. Very slowly, I lifted the rifle, sighted, and pulled the trigger.

"The rifle kicked me in the shoulder, and the sound knocked snow off some of the trees. I remember bouncing on the bed, it kind of woke me up, but not really. The buck started, and took off for a dozen yards, then went down, and I ran over to him. I guess maybe I've never watched a deer die. At least I never saw it like this.

"I hit him right where I'd aimed, right through the throat. Hot blood pumped from the wound in his neck, and steamed into the snow. I watched it spurt. I just watched it, the deer kicked a little, then stopped, and soon the blood slowed, then the spurting stopped and it just ran out for a while, through his hair, melting the snow. It was so beautiful, that dark red against the white.

"I just watched it and I was so glad that this deer I'd hunted, this buck I'd come to know, come to love, could die such a beautiful death.

"When I woke up, my pillow was soaked with saliva, and a hunger rumbled deep within my soul."

PAPERBACKS from Hell

HUNGRY FOR MORE?

Learn about the Twisted History of '70s and '80s Horror Fiction

by Grady Hendrix

"Pure, demented delight."
—The New York Times Book Review

Take a tour through the horror paperback novels of two iconic decades . . . if you dare. Page through dozens and dozens of amazing book covers featuring well-dressed skeletons, evil dolls, and knife-wielding killer crabs! Read shocking plot summaries for beastly bestsellers about devil worship, satanic children, and haunted real estate! Horror author Grady Hendrix and vintage paperback book collector Will Errickson offer killer commentary and witty insight on these forgotten thrillers that filled the paperback racks with sin, Satan, and Nazi leprechauns.

- -

AVAILABLE WHEREVER BOOKS ARE SOLD.

Visit QuirkBooks.com for more information about
this book and other titles by Grady Hendrix.

QUIRK
BOOKS